"My grandfather wants to see me dance again."

"If that's all it takes to make him happy, Michael," Renata replied, "surely you could do it for him."

He shook his head and looked away. "I knew you wouldn't understand."

Renata flushed. "Don't shut me out, Michael," she begged him. "This Native stuff is all new to me, but that doesn't mean I'm not listening with all my heart. If I don't understand, don't put me down. Just explain it to me."

His eyes met hers for a long, tense moment. "A mechanical rendition of an old dance or two wouldn't do a thing for my grandfather. When he says he wants to see me dance, he means he wants to see me *dance*. He wants me to *feel* Winnebago."

Renata laced her fingers with his. "Michael, you can't be somebody you're not, just to please him."

Quietly he replied, "And I can't be somebody I'm not, just to please you."

7

Dear Reader,

Welcome to Harlequin's Tyler, a small Wisconsin town whose citizens we hope you'll come to know and love. Like many of the innovative publishing concepts Harlequin has launched over the years, the idea for the Tyler series originated in response to our readers' preferences. Your enthusiasm for sequels and continuing characters within many of the Harlequin lines has prompted us to create a twelve-book series of individual romances whose characters' lives inevitably intertwine.

Tyler faces many challenges typical of small towns, but the fabric of this fictional community will be torn by the revelation of a long-ago murder, the details of which will evolve right through the series. This intriguing crime will culminate in an emotional trial that profoundly affects the lives of the Ingallses, the Barons, the Forresters and the Wochecks.

Spring's arrived with a vengeance, and old Phil Wochek's broken hip is finally on the mend. Why not follow him down to the crafts fair Alyssa Baron has helped organize on the town square? The theme is original Native American artwork, and you'll also find classic hand-pieced quilts.

Edward, Phil's son, has promised to take time out from his duties at Timberlake Lodge and attend. Of course, Alyssa will probably do her best to avoid him. Still, you never know. She has a lot of questions plaguing her, especially after the gruesome discovery Brick Bauer makes in Phil's closet....

So join us in Tyler, once a month for the next six months, for a slice of small-town life that's not as innocent or as quiet as you might expect, and for a sense of community that will capture your mind and your heart.

Marsha Zinberg
Editorial Coordinator, Tyler

Arrowpoint

Suzanne Ellison

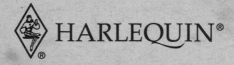

HARLEQUIN®

TORONTO • NEW YORK • LONDON
AMSTERDAM • PARIS • SYDNEY • HAMBURG
STOCKHOLM • ATHENS • TOKYO • MILAN • MADRID
PRAGUE • WARSAW • BUDAPEST • AUCKLAND

Special thanks and acknowledgment to Suzanne Ellison for her contribution to the Tyler series.

Special thanks and acknowledgment to Joanna Kosloff for her contribution to the concept for the Tyler series.

HARLEQUIN BOOKS
225 Duncan Mill Road, Don Mills,
Ontario, Canada M3B 3K9

Recycling programs
for this product may
not exist in your area.

ISBN-13: 978-0-373-36341-4

ARROWPOINT

Copyright © 1992 by Harlequin Books S.A.

www.eHarlequin.com

Printed in U.S.A.

CHAPTER ONE

IT HAD RAINED all night, but by the time Renata Meyer saw the sign that said Tyler, Three Miles the sky was only dripping, a misty remnant of the deluge she'd left an hour ago in Milwaukee. It wasn't quite summer yet, but for the past month it had already been so hot that this cooling thunderstorm was more a relief than a burden, especially considering where Renata was going to spend the weekend. Her Milwaukee apartment had a feisty air conditioner that kept her chilled most of the time, but the old family homestead north of Tyler had poor insulation, few windows and only one ancient oak tree for shade. The improvements made since her great-grandparents' time had been minimal. Air-conditioning was not one of them.

As a free-lance artist, Renata didn't have a lot of income, but she did have a lot of freedom as to where and how she spent her time. She lived on the periodic sales of her paintings and her more frequent free-lance commercial assignments, which embarrassed her artistic pride but kept a roof over her head. At this point she found that being in the city—where she could brush shoulders with gallery owners, better-established artists and sympathetic art-buying friends—was a tremendous help to her fledgling career. But living in the thunderous rattle of Milwaukee wore her down from time to time, and it was always a relief to know that there was somewhere to go to renew herself. When life got to be a bit much, she turned north and headed back to Tyler like a homing pigeon, even when she hadn't received a summons from an old friend.

Alyssa Ingalls Baron wasn't a friend in the intimate sense of the word; she was more a fixture of Renata's tiny hometown.

She was of Renata's mother's generation, though the two had not been particularly close. Everybody knew Alyssa, at least by name, and everybody liked her, even if they were a bit jealous of her family's wealth. Renata's family had been in the area just as long, but since for the past four generations they'd unpretentiously run a farm that barely broke even, nobody had ever paid much attention to the Meyers. The Ingalls clan, on the other hand, had the Midas touch. They owned land and a thriving business, and kept a guiding hand in local politics. Fortunately, Alyssa wasn't snooty about her wealth and power—she was a sweet and gentle person—but when she suggested, as she had to Renata, that a Tylerite ''volunteer'' to do something for the good of the town, it somehow felt like an order.

Renata had loved the warmth of her hometown as a child and hated it as a teenager. She hadn't been Tyler's wild child as a girl—Alyssa's younger daughter, Liza, had sewn up that title—but she had been a bit eccentric in the town's eyes.

Renata had always been more interested in painting than pom-poms. When the rest of her high school classmates were swimming in the summer or skating on winter ice, Renata was alone at her easel. Kicking local tradition in the teeth, she had skipped the junior prom, the senior homecoming game and one of the Ingallses' Christmas parties—by accident—when she'd started painting after dinner and forgotten about the world till after midnight. Tyler people still teased Renata about her early paintings and her dramatic choice of clothes. She couldn't wear her paintings, so she tried to make a statement with fabric and whenever she could. And when she couldn't do that, she usually found herself wearing a paint-spattered T-shirt and water-colored jeans.

There had been times when she'd found herself in such bad straights that she'd had to return to live in Tyler for several months—once it was a whole year—but Renata had never been poor enough to consider selling the old place. Regardless of the demands of her ambition and her art, she took deep comfort and joy from the knowledge that twelve acres of lush farmland had remained in her family's hands for nearly 150 years. Granted, the house was old and drafty—a two-story box with a pair of upstairs bedrooms, one bathroom with a hand-held shower, an old-fashioned parlor and a kitchen that hadn't been updated since World War II. Every time she came home, Renata vowed to start remodeling the old place, but she was never there long enough to justify the expense. Someday she knew she'd want to come home for good, but at the moment it would be too inconvenient to live in Tyler full-time.

And too lonely.

She pulled up at the mailbox and rolled down the window of her old red truck before she remembered that one of the Hansen kids picked up her mail once a week when he checked over her house, watered her roses and mowed the lawn. She couldn't really afford to pay him, but his mother, Britt, was so strapped since her husband's death that Renata hadn't been able to turn Matt down when he made the offer. Even knowing that the mailbox ought to be empty, Renata felt a twinge of sadness to find it that way. When her parents were still living, a mound of good tidings and junk mail had arrived every day.

Before she had time to get maudlin, Renata was startled by an eerie, distant sound. At first she thought it was merely the whisper of the storm, but it almost sounded like humming. No, it wasn't humming. Not exactly. But she couldn't exactly call it singing, either. It sounded human. Well, not human so much as not-animal. Sort of other-worldly.

Heyeh, heyeh, heyeh, hiyayayayayaya, heyeh, heyeh. It was a chant of some sort, a weird, eerie chant that made Renata's flesh crawl. It was soft, which either meant it was loud at the source and very far away, or else…or else it was coming from just up the road.

And the only house up this deserted gravel road was Renata's.

Maybe it's just the rain, she told herself stoutly. *Sometimes the trees creak in a high wind and sound like someone moaning.*

It was a reassuring notion, but Renata didn't really think the noise had anything to do with the weather. Someone—friend or foe—must be up at her place, expressing himself or herself in some kind of bizarre mantra. But the sound of one voice didn't mean that there was only one person. It could be one of those devil-worshiping cults! Renata hadn't been home in a long time, and everybody who lived in Tyler knew it. What better place for weird cult gatherings than an isolated spot like this?

But what kind of a cult gathers at nine a.m. in the rain? a more rational voice asked. Maybe it was just Matt Hansen, humming whatever was hip among the high school crowd these days.

In the end her curiosity overcame her apprehension. After all, Renata prided herself on her acceptance of new things. She'd always been a bit of a radical, moving through life at her own pace to a drumbeat of her own. She wasn't a rebel, in that she didn't fight society anymore; she just ignored it when it got in her way. Renata sought her own brand of happiness, and she pursued it with joyful glee every day of her life. She wanted no less for the people around her, but she never tried to force her ways on them.

As she drove on toward the house, she realized vaguely that it was starting to rain more heavily. But she didn't care. She was too consumed with curiosity to roll up her window. Curiosity tinged with a tiny bit of fear.

Concern and awe washed away the fear the instant she pulled into the gravel driveway and got a good look at her front lawn. Renata had to blink a couple of times. She couldn't believe what she saw.

Under the shaggy oak tree sat an old man—a very, *very* old man—hunched cross-legged on a tattered blanket that was drenched and saturated with watery mud. He was wearing buckskin leggings, moccasins and some kind of beaded deerskin shirt. He wore several strands of bones and shells—bears' teeth, maybe?—around his wrinkled, leathery neck. Feathers dangled from the two long braids that hung halfway down his chest.

Renata knew that Tyler had once been part of the hunting grounds of the local Indians—she couldn't recall which tribe—and she knew that her grandfather had loved to tell stories about running into them now and again as a child. He even had a collection of old Indian artifacts he'd found on the property; it was still somewhere down in the basement along with the beading loom kit Renata had fussed with as a child. But in Renata's lifetime, Tyler had been virtually devoid of Indians. She knew some native people in Milwaukee, of course—had taken art classes with more than one—but they were, for all practical purposes, assimilated. She couldn't imagine any of them sitting on a blanket in buckskin in the rain, chanting to…well, to whatever deity this leathery-skinned Methuselah was probably directing some sort of tribal prayer.

Renata did not particularly care that the old man was trespassing. She wasn't even dying to know what he thought he was doing or why he'd chosen her place. At the moment her thoughts were more practical and pressing. This old fellow looked as frail as parchment and he was obviously soaked to the bone. There was no telling how long he'd been here, but it took no genius to realize that he was in danger of getting pneumonia. She had to get him dried off and warmed up at once. And that meant she had to get him inside.

His eyes were open and he was more or less facing her way, but he showed no sign of seeing Renata. She wondered if he might be blind. She wondered if he might be crazy. She wondered how on earth he'd gotten here without a car. Surely nobody would have left this old man out here all alone!

She took a few steps forward, then crouched before him. The lawn was saturated now and the rain was lashing the ground again. She knew that if she didn't move him soon, she'd end up drenched as well.

"Excuse me, sir," Renata said quietly, afraid to startle the spooky old fellow. "I'm Renata Meyer. I live here. I've got warm blankets inside and I can have some hot coffee going in no time. Wouldn't you like to come in and dry off?"

The chanting continued. His eyes showed no sign that he

knew another person had joined him. Could he be deaf and blind? she wondered. Or was he in some sort of trance?

Uneasily, she moved closer and risked laying one hand on his arm. It was a thin arm, devoid of muscle, but it didn't even twitch.

"Please, sir. Maybe you don't care about the rain, but I do. I'm getting cold. Can't we go inside and talk?"

The chanting changed pitch then—higher, more eerie. It occurred to Renata that maybe the old man didn't speak English. She had heard that there were old Indians who still spoke their native tongue. And this one looked old enough to have ridden against Custer...or maybe Columbus.

Renata bit her lower lip and tried to decide what to do. She felt absolutely helpless. She still remembered her own dear grandfather, who'd died at the age of ninety-six but hadn't recognized any of them at the end. If somebody had found him wandering around, befuddled and confused, she would have wanted them to take care of him.

She knelt in the mud right before the old fellow, put both hands on his shoulders and tried one more time. "Please, sir. I know this is important to you. But getting you warm and dry is important to me. Can't we go inside now? Later, when the rain stops, you can come back and finish. Or you can even chant in my living room."

This time his eyes flickered over her in what almost looked like sympathy. He brushed one hand in her direction, as if to say, "You go inside. Don't worry about me." But he did not stop chanting. And he did not rise.

It was pouring by now. Renata couldn't see herself forcibly dragging the old man into the house even if she'd had the physical strength to do it. There was a dignity about him that made her feel awkward about calling some authority to take him away. But she'd rather have him mad at her than have him die of exposure right here on her lawn.

"Is there anybody I can call?" she asked. "Do you have family or friends near here?"

It occurred to Renata that Timberlake Lodge was a stone's

throw from the back of her property, and it was feasible that he'd hiked here from there. When the lodge had belonged to the Ingallses, Liza and Amanda had sometimes walked over to her place to visit, and since Edward Wocheck had turned it into a resort, she'd encountered a few tourists nosing around on their morning meanderings. But Edward's resort catered to a ritzy crowd. Renata couldn't see this wilted old guy as a typical guest or morning jogger. He seemed more like a candidate for Worthington House, the convalescent center in town.

Relieved that she'd finally thought of a few leads to check out, Renata said, "I'm going to try to find out where you belong, sir. If you change your mind while I'm gone, just come on in and I'll fix you some breakfast. I'm going to put on some coffee."

He kept on chanting as she turned and headed for the house, oblivious to the thunderous new cloudburst that nipped at her heels.

"COME IN, BRICK," squawked the radio in the police car. "I've got a message from the captain."

Under other circumstances, Michael Youngthunder would have grinned. He remembered when he'd first met Lieutenant Brick Bauer, a kind, decent man struggling to pretend he wasn't madly in love with his female precinct captain. Beautiful Karen Keppler—they called her "Captain Killer" now—had ruled the station house with an iron hand, but she'd been kind to Michael and his elderly grandfather. Now she was married to Brick, publicly admitted she adored him and actually allowed her dispatcher to convey messages to her husband when he was on duty without using the complex county police code that was more trouble than it was worth in such a small town. Everybody knew everybody else's business anyway.

Michael had no interest in Tyler's business, and he would never have come to Tyler at all if his grandfather had not begged him. Last winter Grand Feather, as he'd affectionately called the old one since childhood, had heard about the proposed expansion of Timberlake Lodge near Tyler around the same time he'd heard that some Native Americans in other parts of the country were reclaiming sacred bones from white museums and preventing development on traditional burial grounds. Tyler, the old one insisted, had been built near the site where his ancestors were buried…on land "stolen" by white people 150 years ago.

Michael, the manager of a busy Katayama Computers retail outlet, had better things to do with his time than root through the countryside searching for nonexistent Indian bones. But the suit and tie he wore to work each day could not totally obliterate the part of him that was still Winnebago, and the nice paycheck he earned could never compete with his love for the old man who had raised him. So six months ago he'd come to Tyler, talked with Captain Keppler and Lieutenant Bauer, who'd been kind enough to spend a day driving Grand Feather to all possible sites for the burial ground, which allegedly could be identified by a horseshoe of oak trees. They hadn't found anything and that had been the end of it.

Until last night. Until news of the scheduled ground breaking of the new wing of Timberlake Lodge Resort had been broadcast on the only Madison station that his grandfather's puny television picked up in Wisconsin Dells. An hour later Michael had received a call from his uncle, who now owned a tiny remaining piece of allotment land near the old shack where Grand Feather still lived and where Michael himself had grown up. It broke Michael's heart to see the old man live in such squalor, but Grand Feather would not be moved. He said he'd lived as a true Winnebago on that patch of land back when the old ones still taught ancient rituals that they'd learned from their foreparents before the arrival of the whites. He was born a Winnebago, he had lived a Winnebago, and he would be buried as a Winnebago when the time came. More than once he'd claimed that he was ready to die and could not rest until he knew he would not be buried among white strangers.

Although Michael lived in Sugar Creek, a good hour and a half from Wisconsin Dells, the family always called him when there was a problem with Grand Feather, partly because they knew that nobody loved the old one more and partly because Michael was the best equipped of all of them to deal with white people in the outside world. He was the only one with a college degree and a VCR, the only one who stood out like a sore thumb whenever he went home to visit. His cousins called him a half-breed, even though he wasn't, and treated him like a white, even though his heart was still Winnebago. At least he thought it was; he knew he wanted it to be. Most of the time he was too busy to think about it, a condition that was easier to handle than was grappling with his tangled cultural roots.

This morning he was too tired to think, but he had never felt his Indian status more keenly. For twelve solid hours he had been trapped in this police car, searching for Grand Feather in the storm-soaked farmland surrounding Tyler. It was an all night walk here from the Dells, and a long hike even if the old one had caught a bus or hitchhiked to Tyler proper. And it had been raining all night long. Michael's fear was a living thing, a serpentine rope of nausea that threatened to choke him. He knew he'd disappointed his grandfather terribly by choosing to follow the white man's road, but he worshiped the old one and would have done anything, anything at all, to protect him.

"Go ahead, Hedda," Brick Bauer said into the radio.

"Captain K says she got a call from CeCe Scanlon at Worthington House that might relate to your search for the old Indian. Apparently Renata Meyer is in town for the weekend and called over there to ask if they were missing anyone. They're not, but later CeCe heard your grandma talking to your aunt about how you'd been up all night looking for somebody, and it occurred to her that there might be a connection." Brick's eyes met Michael's as the dispatcher continued, "It occurred to the captain that one of the places you took the Youngthunders before was out to the Meyers' old place. Renata's line is busy, but Captain K thought you might want to swing by there."

Michael took a deep breath, relief and fear twisting his innards into tiny knots. "It's my grandfather, Lieutenant," he told Brick Bauer. "I know it."

To the radio, Brick said quickly, "We're on our way."

RENATA HAD ALREADY MADE a dozen futile calls by the time she heard a car pull into the gravel driveway behind her own. A quick glance outside told her the police had arrived, but she wasn't sure if that was good or bad. She'd deliberately avoided calling the Tyler substation because she didn't want to get the old man in trouble. Somebody else must have, or else their arrival here was just coincidental. Either way, she was at her wit's end, and she was grateful that there was some authority she could turn to.

As Renata hurried outside, wet and shivering, she felt a flash of relief as she recognized the policeman getting out of the black-and-white cruiser. Brick Bauer wasn't a close friend, but she was on good terms with him—or had been the last time they talked, a few years ago—and she knew she could count on him to be gentle with the old man.

"Hi, Brick!" she called out, pulling on a jacket to fight off the worst of the rain. "I heard you got married!"

Brick smiled back, both dimples deepening, looking a little bit embarrassed and terribly pleased. "It's true, Renata. Married my boss. Finally found a woman who could keep me in line."

It was during this brief exchange that Renata realized somebody else was bolting out of the car, somebody in a rumpled suit and loosened tie who was sprinting toward her so fast it was frightening. She only got a glimpse of him—young, dark, good-looking—before his gaze fell on the old Indian. He slammed to a stop, clutching the side-view mirror of her truck for support. The sight of his painful swallow filled Renata with a great ache for him. Love for the old man was written all over his face.

It was a magnificent face, the kind any artist would love to use as a centerpiece of a painting. But Renata knew at once that it wasn't the artist in her that responded so keenly to this man's barely veiled virility and passion. He was tall and lean, with dark brown eyes and thick lashes and a strong jaw. His bronze skin and handsome, angular features hinted strongly at some sort of Indian ancestry.

But Renata only had time to register his compelling good looks and his panic before Brick said softly, "Renata, this is Michael Youngthunder. We've spent the whole night looking for his grandfather."

Brick was wasting his breath. Michael Youngthunder didn't even see Renata; he certainly didn't hear Brick or respond to his courteous introduction. Every nuance of his attention was directed toward the old man.

Under other circumstances, Renata would have resented being so totally ignored. But she had loved her own grandfather, and she understood the anguish in Michael's bloodshot eyes. Even without Brick's explanation, she could have guessed by his haggard demeanor that he'd been searching for the old man all night.

Instinctively, Renata stepped toward him and laid one hand on his arm. "He's all right," she said quickly, even though she knew Michael could see it for himself. "I found him about half an hour ago and begged him to come in. He won't budge, but his voice isn't getting any weaker."

Michael's well muscled arm was tensely knotted beneath Renata's fingers, but a mighty sigh of relief escaped his invitingly full lips. For the first time he glanced at Renata, but even now she didn't think he really saw her. Habit more than conscious thought seemed to prompt him to murmur, "I'm sorry for the intrusion. It may take me a few minutes to persuade him to come away."

"Don't worry about that," she assured him. "Just let me know what I can do to help. I draped a rain slicker around his shoulders—" she gestured toward the yellow vinyl garment sprawled across the grass "—but he just let it fall to the ground."

Again Michael's beautiful mahogany eyes met hers. "Thank you," he repeated in a choked voice.

When she felt the ripple of tension in his biceps, Renata realized belatedly that she was still holding on to him. Abruptly she let go. But Michael wasn't paying any attention to Renata. His gaze was once again on the old man, who was still chanting. Not once had his eyes even flickered toward his grandson.

"I tried everything I could to make him come in and dry off," Renata explained apologetically. "He acts as though he doesn't see me. Doesn't hear. I think he's in some kind of a trance."

"Trance?" Michael repeated, as though the single word alarmed him.

"Well, I don't know what else to call it. It's as though he's gone somewhere that I can't reach."

Michael closed his eyes, shook his head, then whispered, "I'm not sure I can reach him, either."

At that point Brick joined them, laid a hand on Michael's shoulder and said, "This is like talking down a jumper, Michael. I'll speak to him if you want me to. I would if you weren't here."

Quietly Michael said, "Thanks, Lieutenant, but this is something I have to do myself. If he doesn't finish, he'll find a way to come back here later. The best thing for me to do is to hurry him along a little."

"Finish?" said Renata. "He sounds like he's just repeating the same thing over and over again."

This time Michael's gaze focused on her face for a long, dark moment before he turned away. For some reason she could not fathom, Renata knew she'd disappointed him.

Hugging herself for warmth, she stood beside Brick and stared at Michael as he crossed the lawn to join his grandfather. They couldn't have looked more different: young, old; business suit, Indian clothes; utterly contemporary, locked in another space and time. Still, there was a family resemblance, or at least a tribal one, in the coppery skin and straight, masculine nose. The old man's hair was very long and braided, already thin and gray. Michael's black hair was longer than average— thick and straight as it flowed over his broad shoulders—but it was such a magnificent mane that a proud display of it didn't strike Renata as peculiar. In her arty crowd, lots of people cherished eccentricities in their appearance. None of her Milwaukee friends would have looked twice at Michael's hair even if he'd worn it in feathered braids.

"I met Michael when Edward Wocheck came back to town and started talking about expanding Timberlake Lodge," Brick explained sotto voce. "Old man Youngthunder's got some idea that there's a sacred burial ground around here. We drove through your property before but the 'spirits' didn't speak to him."

Renata was astounded. People were right when they said truth was sometimes stranger than fiction! The only burial ground nearby was the family plot out toward the barn, and nobody had been buried there in seventy or eighty years.

"So why do you think he came back here this morning?" she asked Brick.

"Edward's having a ground-breaking ceremony for the new wing of Timberlake Lodge tomorrow. Last night Mr. Youngthunder heard it on the news."

Michael was squatting in front of his grandfather now, meeting his eyes, but Renata found it odd that he still had not spoken. The old man was chanting again, and for some reason Michael's head was nodding ever so slightly as though in time to the distinctive rhythm.

"Why doesn't he say something to his grandfather?" Renata asked. "Aren't they on good terms?"

"Very good terms. Winnebago terms. Don't let the suit throw you. Michael still knows how to be an Indian when he has to, and I think he's going to have to act Winnebago to get through to the old guy."

Brick was right. A moment later the handsome man in the rumpled suit—a suit that looked as though it had fit him magnificently before his night in the police car—folded his long legs and sat down on the mud-soaked blanket in front of his grandfather. Then he held up both hands the way the old man was and started to chant right along with him.

Renata stared disbelievingly at Brick, then back at Michael again. She knew Michael loved the old man, so she wasn't surprised that he was willing to do anything to get him to come inside. She might have been willing to sit in the mud herself, especially in her jeans. But Michael was wearing a suit! And he wasn't just sitting there pleading with the old man. He was joining in the ritual, raising his hands, chanting the same syllables.

It took Renata a moment to realize the symbolism of that simple act. He wasn't feigning understanding. *He knew the chant.* He knew the sounds, the words, the gestures! He knew why his grandfather had come to this place, knew what he was doing, knew why he wouldn't just get up and leave. And he clearly shared some part of his grandfather's way of thinking, something that Renata guessed he couldn't put into English words.

She battled the weird feeling that she was sinking into quicksand. Right before her eyes, this terribly attractive businessman had turned into an Indian! All he was missing was the buckskin and braids.

Suddenly there was a crackle from the cruiser. Brick quickly strode back, picked up the mike, barked a quick response and waved a hand. "Got an emergency," he called to Renata. "Tell Michael I'll be back for him as soon as I can."

In an instant the black-and-white car had pulled away, leaving Renata feeling like an interloper on her own property. It had been strange enough starting the day with one rain-soaked Indian doing eerie chants on her front lawn.

Now there were two of them.

CHAPTER TWO

FOR NEARLY fifteen minutes, Renata stood on the porch, grateful for the overhang, while Michael and his grandfather chanted in the mud. She had no idea what was going through their minds, though she was reasonably certain it wasn't the same thing. The old man was totally absorbed in his ritual, but Michael's eyes were open and his neck muscles rippled with tension. Every now and then he made a mistake in the chanting and had to take a moment to pick up a clue from his grandfather. It was obvious that the ceremony, whatever it was, did not come easily to him.

At last the old man stopped and lowered his arms. It didn't seem to Renata that he was tired or resigned. He just seemed to be finished. At first he did not speak, but at last he opened his eyes and looked at Michael.

A good two minutes of silence passed before Michael began to speak, and even then Renata could not understand him. To her he'd spoken clear, unaccented Midwestern English. To his grandfather he was speaking an unintelligible tongue that she took to be Winnebago. It wasn't an unpleasant sound; it simply surprised her to hear a man in a suit use a language that seemed to belong to another world…another century.

When Michael was done, the old man spoke, his own voice weak and quavery. He sounded calm but stubborn. Michael spoke again, gesturing to himself and then Renata. He sounded angry and embarrassed. She didn't need to speak Winnebago to understand the look on his face.

Whatever he said seemed to impress his grandfather, because for the first time the old one's watery gaze drifted toward Renata. Then he looked down, as though he, too, were ashamed. By this time Renata was shivering with cold and so was the old man. Michael still looked tense. And incredibly handsome.

At last he stood. Muddy water dripped down the legs of his ruined suit. He held out a hand to his grandfather, who ignored it but painfully struggled to rise on his own. The old man had to roll sideways to his knees and use both hands to push away from the ground, and even then he almost fell over. Michael kept his hand outstretched, leaning close to him, but he did not reach out to catch him. Renata was touched by his obvious effort to save the old man's dignity.

When Michael's grandfather stood up and started toward the house, Renata could see that the night in the rain had taken its toll. He looked shaky and cold and exhausted. At once she said to Michael, "Why don't you take him upstairs and warm him up with a hot shower while I find you both some dry clothes."

Michael's eyes met hers with embarrassed gratitude as he nodded just once. Then Renata quickly slipped down to the basement while Michael and his grandfather moved slowly into the house.

It wasn't hard to find clothes for two men; the basement was full of Renata's parents' and grandparents' clothes and keepsakes. She even had a trunk of her great-grandparents' things. Sometimes, when she was feeling lonely, Renata spent hours down here, perusing old photos and letters or rearranging her grandpa's box of artifacts. She had never regretted being raised without brothers and sisters because she'd had so much love from the grown-ups in her life. But one by one, death had claimed them all—tractor accident, cancer, kidney disease. Her grandfather had lived longer than his son; he'd been the last to go. But for four years now, Renata had been the last of her branch of the Meyers in Wisconsin. Until recently she'd been too busy trying to launch a career to worry much about marriage and children, but she knew that she was nearly ready to settle down. The pull was always strongest on the days she came to Tyler.

Pushing away her maudlin memories, Renata quickly dug

out several sizes of men's jeans and T-shirts, plus some old long johns and a heavy jacket, despite the humidity, for the shivering old man. She took the clothes to the extra bedroom upstairs and knocked on the bathroom door. Over the sound of running water she called out, "The clothes are in the room next door. I'll be down in the kitchen making breakfast if you want anything."

She heard a muffled "Thanks," but nothing more.

The instant Renata reached the kitchen she remembered that she hadn't been here for more than a month, and she'd planned to stop at the grocery store after the meeting, on her way back from town. Fortunately she always kept a few staples on hand, so she had no trouble finding some coffee and a box of pancake mix. Normally she added milk and a fresh egg to the batter, but under the circumstances, water would have to do. Pancakes were a better choice than soup at this hour of the morning.

She'd just started dropping batter onto the griddle when she heard footsteps coming down the stairs. She turned as Michael stepped into the room.

He looked different in a pair of old jeans than he had in a suit. Renata's father had been heavier than Michael, so the jeans were loose on him. So was the T-shirt. The casual look did nothing to diminish Michael's attractiveness; if anything, it made him seem more accessible. Renata noticed that his hair was just as appealing wet as it was dry—thick, shiny, the fullness lifting it off his face before it curved under slightly on his shoulders.

But what really drew her to him was the expression on his face. She'd never seen a man look quite like this—proud, grateful and embarrassed all at the same time. When Michael had arrived and found his grandfather, Renata had guessed he was caught up in fear and relief. But since then, a measure of shame had crept into his regal bearing.

"I know Brick introduced us," he greeted her quietly, "but I'm sorry to say I didn't get a grip on your name."

"Renata Meyer."

"Michael Youngthunder." He held out one strong brown

hand, and Renata slipped hers into it. His was still cold, but the chilliness of his skin didn't linger in his eyes. "I want you to know how much I appreciate your kindness to my grand-father. Most people would have called the cops and had him towed away." He glanced toward the front lawn. "I put the slicker on the porch to dry."

"Thanks." Renata tried to give him a reassuring smile, but somehow a smile didn't work at the moment. When he gently disengaged his hand from hers, she realized belatedly that she'd gripped it in greeting and forgotten to let go.

"We're indebted to you," Michael said sincerely. "If there's anything my family can ever do for you, don't hesitate to let us know."

Renata was touched by the offer—and by the sincerity in Michael's beautiful dark eyes. Lots of people, if they'd made the offer at all, would have said "I," not "my family." Obviously his family obligations were important to him.

"I wish I could have gotten him inside sooner, Michael," she apologized. "I only arrived an hour or so ago. For all I know, he could have been out there all night."

"I suspect he was," Michael agreed sadly. He looked absolutely exhausted, but he made no move to sit down.

Abruptly Renata realized he was probably waiting for an invitation. "Please have a seat," she was quick to offer. "I'll have pancakes for you in just a second. Did you have anything to eat this morning?"

Slowly he took a chair, his gaze gratefully brushing her face in a way that made her skin tingle. It occurred to Renata that she must look as bedraggled as Michael and his father. Before, she hadn't minded, but for some reason she didn't want to look her worst now that she was talking to Michael face-to-face.

"I haven't had an appetite since I first found out he was gone," he admitted. "Now that he's in there steaming himself, I'm absolutely ravenous."

This time Renata grinned, and to her surprise, Michael grinned back. His smile took her totally off guard. It was brilliant, almost boyish, utterly charming. What a change from that fierce, anguished scowl!

"Good. I was hoping you'd be too hungry to notice that I'm piecing together a meal from odds and ends," she confessed. "I keep staples here but I always need to get milk and fresh produce when I come to town. But if you're hungry—"

"Ready to eat cardboard. Whatever you've got will be fine."

He gave her another dazzling grin as she handed him a plate full of pancakes, dug in the cupboard for some syrup and rinsed off a clean but dusty fork. It occurred to Renata that coming back to her house in Tyler was sort of like arriving at a neglected backwoods cabin. It was cozy and quaint, but it wasn't set up to entertain strangers. At least she had a phone and running water—the thumps and bangs in the pipes triggered by the old man's shower were proof of that—but that was about the extent of the amenities.

Michael's eyes met hers with an expression that reminded Renata of a little boy in a candy shop in a Norman Rockwell painting. "Are you going to join me?" he asked.

This time Renata laughed out loud. "For goodness' sake, Michael, eat! I can hardly bear to look at you. In another second you'll start drooling."

The smile quickly vanished. "No worry about that. I drooled a lot when I ate raw buffalo in the wigwam, but at Georgetown they frowned on that."

Renata was surprised that she'd offended him and even more surprised that he'd felt compelled to trot out his academic credentials. Honestly, she said, "I was only teasing, Michael, because you sounded so hungry. I wasn't thinking at all about your…heritage."

A dark flush reddened his angular cheeks. "After what's happened outside this morning, I wouldn't think you'd be able to think about anything else."

He was so blunt that Renata decided she should be straight with him, also. "I'll admit that your grandfather took me by surprise. I'm worried about him and I'm damned curious. *You* took me by surprise, too, but that's because I'm having a devil of a time figuring out how a man who looks so comfy in a suit and acts so white can speak Winnebago and think like a traditional Indian.''

She drew a quick breath, but didn't give him time to reply. ''Now I'm wondering if I've done anything to cause you to believe that I've got some Neanderthal prejudice against people who aren't just like me. Since I've spent my whole life as a square peg in a round hole, I'd have to dislike just about everybody if that were true. As it happens, I like people. I like diversity. Until you started making insinuations,'' she finished a bit sarcastically, ''I rather liked you.''

Michael was silent, but his eyes grew dark as he listened to her speech. For a long, tense moment his inscrutable gaze impaled her. Then he rose, abandoning the fork poised to snag a pancake, and slowly prowled across the room.

Renata wasn't sure what to expect of this tightly coiled stranger. She knew he was angry, but she wasn't sure if she was scared. She tried to remember just what Brick had said to her about Michael Youngthunder before he'd galloped off in his police car. He had acted as though Michael were a friend. He'd given Renata no overt or even subtle warnings. Surely he wouldn't have left her alone with these two Indians if he had any reason to distrust them!

Still, Renata shivered as Michael approached her, his lips drawn down in a fearsome scowl. She wanted to duck away from him, to hide or bolt from the room, but she didn't seem to be able to move.

And then he spoke, and she knew by the fresh shame in his voice that his anger was directed inward. And she also knew that the chill that feathered up and down her spine as he touched her wrist had nothing to do with fear.

''Renata,'' he said softly, his voice taking on a low and tortured tone, ''please forgive my rudeness. I am always overly touchy about my…bloodlines. And this morning, I am—'' he shook his head ''—a great deal more embarrassed by my family than usual.'' His gaze met hers, then slipped away, reluctantly swinging back to hers again. ''I've never been in a situation quite like this before, but that's no reason for me to behave badly.'' As the bathroom pipes upstairs stopped banging, he finished tensely, ''You don't have to feed me. As soon as my grandfather gets dressed, we'll go.''

As he turned to leave the room, Renata caught his arm. She seemed to be doing a lot of that this morning—holding on to Michael—but she couldn't seem to help herself. There was something about him that made her want very much to touch him.

''Michael, I'm sorry,'' she said simply. ''I know this whole situation is terribly awkward for you. But it's kind of strange for me, too, you know.''

He turned around, met her eyes again and slowly nodded. A thin layer of tension seemed to leave the room.

''My grandfather lived to be ninety-six,'' she told him, ''and he just died a few years ago. I loved him dearly, but I was the only one left to take care of him near the end, and I didn't always know what to do with him.''

Michael ran a nervous hand through his thick mane. ''Grand Feather's not senile,'' he declared almost defensively. ''I know it looks that way, but he's still sharp as a tack. He's stubborn and determined, but he's not losing a grip on reality. At least, not on *his* reality. It's just that his reality is probably different from yours.''

Again his dark eyes met hers, imploring Renata to understand what he didn't seem to be able to say. She wanted him to go on, to share his feelings, for reasons that went beyond the need to satisfy her curiosity or ease her conscience after their spat. But she knew he was still ravenous and exhausted…and nearly proud enough to leave his pancakes uneaten and go.

''Why don't you sit down and tell me about it while we eat?'' she suggested. Renata wasn't a breakfast person, but she saw no need to mention that to Michael. Grabbing a plate from the cupboard, she filled it with pancakes. ''I'm pretty hungry myself,'' she lied.

It was hard to say whether it was Michael's hunger or Renata's offer to join him that finally did the trick, but he did move back toward the table, where he waited behind his chair until Renata sat down. Only after she took a bite of pancake did he take a forkful from his stack. She tried not to watch him eat, certain that he was holding himself back. Deliberately she kept quiet until he'd consumed three pancakes and she'd discreetly refilled his plate. Mercifully, a companionable silence seemed to fill the room.

Despite her request to have him share the details of his grandfather's reality, Michael didn't mention the old man again. Instead he asked, "So where do you live when you don't live here?"

If Renata had believed he was really interested in her, she would have been pleased by the question. Under the circumstances, she was reasonably certain that he was merely trying to be polite.

"I live in Milwaukee," she answered simply. "How about you?"

"Sugar Creek."

He made no effort to expand on the terse answer, so Renata asked another question. "Does your grandfather live with you?"

Michael exhaled sharply and shook his head. "No, unfortunately. I have begged him and begged him, but he won't leave Wisconsin Dells. He won't even let me buy him a nicer place. Even a little trailer would be an improvement."

"Does he live alone?"

"For all intents and purposes. I have an uncle who owns some land nearby. He checks on him every night."

Renata got the picture. Near the end her own grandfather had been too stubborn to live with anybody, either. She'd had to arrange for a year's leave from the university—while she pretended to her grandfather that she'd dropped out of school— so she could come home and take care of him. Knowing all the hours of worry that Michael surely had to put up with, all the trips back and forth, she said kindly, "But when he's in trouble, you're the one they call?"

He looked surprised at her deduction.

"It's obvious that you two are very close."

Renata was rewarded with another smile—tentative, but beguiling nonetheless.

"He raised me after my grandmother died. He felt he'd failed to teach my father the old ways, so he tried to pass them on to me. That's the only reason I know—" he gestured with his head toward the front lawn "—a few words of Winnebago. Enough to fake my way through a couple of old ceremonies."

Renata was quite certain that he knew far more than "a few words of Winnebago" and "a couple of old ceremonies." His Winnebago conversation with his grandfather had sounded quite fluent, and though he'd stumbled a few times with the chanting, she'd gotten the impression that he'd been struggling to remember something he'd known very well at one time. It took no genius to deduce that his Indian roots made him uncomfortable, and not just because his grandfather had made a scene.

The kitchen became suddenly silent when the old man padded through the doorway, his eyes not on Renata but on Michael. She didn't know if he'd heard Michael's last words. If he had, they had surely hurt him.

He was wearing a pair of her grandfather's jeans, which were far too big and far too long. He'd rolled up the hems several inches in a way that almost made him look like a clown. He'd disdained the heavy jacket, but he was wearing three wool shirts. His hair, soaking wet, had been carefully rebraided. One soggy feather hung from his head.

The old man whispered something in Winnebago, then stood absolutely still. Michael turned around, gazed at him for a moment, then said in English, "This young lady has offered us her hospitality and it would be rude to refuse it. It would also be rude to exclude her from our conversation. If you're not ready to break your fast, come sit down and join us anyway. We can't leave until the policeman comes back."

The old man looked affronted at the quiet reprimand, but he did not move toward the table. He glanced briefly at Renata and said in quavery but perfect English, "I am sorry for the trouble. I am grateful for the clothes. I will wait on the porch until my grandson is done eating."

Shame colored Michael's sharp, handsome features as the old man left the room.

IT WAS NEARLY NOON when Michael helped his grandfather out of Lieutenant Brick Bauer's black-and-white cruiser at the police station, where Michael had left his car. As he shook Brick's hand, he said quietly, "Thank you again for helping me search last night. And assure the young lady that I'll return the clothes just as soon as I can."

Brick waved a negligent hand. "I'm just glad we found your grandfather in one piece, Michael. I'll give Renata your message, but don't worry about the clothes. She's not likely to need them till the next time a soaking-wet stranger shows up on her doorstep."

Michael managed a smile before he slipped into his BMW, but his face was stony by the time his grandfather joined him inside. Forcing the old one to speak English to Renata had demonstrated a measure of filial disrespect, but it had been unavoidable. Tongue-lashing the old man would wait until the white people were out of earshot.

"I have never been so frightened in my life, Grand Feather," Michael snapped in English. "And once I found you, I was ashamed and angry. I spent a *whole night* looking for you with a policeman. We must have made three dozen phone calls. We knocked on doors of strangers and got them out of their beds! And then—" he sucked in a breath, finding it was hard to tackle the worst thing "—you forced that white woman to take us in. To feed us, to get us warm, to give us clothes! And then you treated her with contempt!"

His grandfather looked gray, utterly fatigued. "I was too tired to speak English to a woman whose people stole our land."

"You were rude to a decent person who could have had you arrested for trespassing! You got me so upset that I was rude, too!'' Michael knew that was what bothered him the most. He'd been grateful to Renata, but he hated feeling in debt to her. Not just because she was white, and not just because she was a woman. She was also—how could he put it?—the sort of woman who beckoned to him.

"I want your promise that nothing like this will happen again, Grand Feather," he said sharply, in fluent Winnebago this time.

"I am old," his grandfather answered softly. "It is time for me to go. I want to go to my people. I should not have to explain this to you."

Michael took a deep breath. "You said there was a Winnebago graveyard here. Lieutenant Bauer looked for it. I looked for it. *You* looked for it! We could not find it."

The old eyes bored into his. "That doesn't mean it is not here."

Michael threw up his hands, wondering what he'd do with this stubborn old man when he really did become senile. He hoped he'd spoken the truth to Renata when he'd insisted that the old man was not becoming irrational yet.

"You were lucky you pulled that stunt on land that belongs to a kind woman. If she'd been a different type of person you could have been shot or arrested."

If she'd been a different type of person, I wouldn't feel so ashamed, he added silently. He knew dozens of Winnebagos who would have responded the way Renata Meyer had, but very few white people. She'd gone out of her way to help an old man. She hadn't accused him of trespassing. She hadn't called him a dirty Indian. She hadn't ordered him never to bother her again. She'd fed and cleaned him up and gotten him warm. And she'd smiled…oh, had she ever smiled.…

Angrily he thrust away the memory of that smile. It was the sort of smile that could get a man in serious trouble if he dwelt on it.

Still, as he drove back to the Dells, Michael couldn't seem to put Renata out of his mind. She was not the sort of white woman he dealt with impersonally every day at work. Most of his female customers were professional women who strove to keep their conversation light, and his co-worker, Maralys Johnson, was an aggressive career woman with a sharp tongue and a hard edge. Maralys wasn't a bad sort, but she sometimes got on Michael's nerves. Always jockeying her way to the top, she spoke the language of power and even dressed to look the part of a rising young executive.

There were no hard edges to Renata Meyer. She spoke her mind, but gently. She opened her home to the rain-soaked and wayward. She wore ratty jeans and a paint-speckled T-shirt, and her luscious blond hair cascaded unfettered to her trim waist. She wore no makeup, no jewelry, no power suit. Everything about her was natural and unpretentious.

And she was damn easy on the eyes to boot.

But it wasn't really her appearance that had moved Michael. It was her honesty, her compassion, her warmth. She'd surely felt as awkward as he in their unusual situation, but she'd handled it a lot better than he had. She'd admitted her curiosity, but she hadn't pressed. She'd tried to anticipate his needs and meet them. When he'd botched everything, she'd tried to make amends.

She was a rare woman, and he was sorry—as well as relieved—that he'd never see her again.

Oh, he could return the clothes to her house. He could even call ahead to make sure she'd be home when he got there. He had a hunch she'd be more flattered than distressed. But Michael Youngthunder was not a foolish man, and he knew trouble when it bit him on the kneecap. He'd been clever enough to crawl out of a shack and drag himself through college; he'd been clever enough to get three promotions in the past two years. He was certainly clever enough to remember how painfully he'd learned that he should never, ever, get romantically involved with a white woman.

He'd loved one once—surrendered himself body and soul—and he'd believed, with every ounce of his heart, that she had truly lived for him. When he'd proposed marriage, Sheila had accepted with what seemed like true joy. When she'd taken him home to meet her parents, she had seemed proud of him. But when he'd introduced Sheila to his grandfather and asked that her parents meet *him,* she'd told Michael gently, "Maybe some other time." She'd been so gentle, in fact—so loving and ashamed—that it had taken Michael three full weeks to get the message.

But he'd learned his lesson in the end, and it was not one he could ever forget. He'd mail back those old clothes or leave them with Brick Bauer. He could not deny that he was drawn to Renata Meyer, but that only meant he'd move heaven and earth to make sure he never came face-to-face with her again.

BY THE TIME the two Indians left and Renata started into town, it was almost eleven, the hour the crafts-fair meeting was set to begin at Alyssa's house. It was the first time Alyssa had ever asked her to serve on a committee, and Renata wasn't sure whether to feel flattered or put out. The fact that Alyssa wanted her artistic expertise meant that she didn't see her as a child anymore, and that was good. But since she had plenty of multipurpose volunteers in Tyler, Alyssa most likely planned to turn to Renata for advice that nobody else could offer. Advice that was probably going to translate into boring civic duties that took a lot of time.

As Renata pulled up on the familiar street, she remembered that she had always thought the Ingallses' old house was magnificent. It had trim white columns on the front porch and clusters of wisteria trailing from trellises below the windows. As a little girl Renata had read books about children who dreamed of living in a palace. She'd always dreamed of living like the Ingallses.

"Renata! How nice to see you," Alyssa greeted her when she knocked on the door.

Alyssa was a willowy, elegant blonde in her late fifties who looked a good ten years younger. Today she was dressed as casually as Renata had ever seen her—in jeans and a T-shirt. But the jeans were spanking new with a designer label, and the T-shirt had shoulder pads and some sort of hand-painted design that would have gone for fifty or sixty dollars in Milwaukee. Renata hadn't made a fraction of that when she'd painted some herself.

"You remember everybody, don't you?" Alyssa asked.

I certainly hope so, Renata thought, knowing that all her parents' friends would be offended if she forgot their names. As she glanced around the room, old faces pricked her memory. Dear Anna Kelsey, aging some but looking just as pragmatic as ever. Alyssa's daughter Liza, the hellion, glowingly pregnant and—lo and behold!—proudly sporting a wedding ring. Nora Gates, whose name Renata had recently heard linked with Liza's husband's brother; she'd either married him or was planning to soon. And last but not least, Elise Ferguson, Tyler's beloved spinster librarian.

Nobody ever thought of Elise and marriage in the same breath. Not that she wasn't nice looking—she was tall and slender with a subtle, almost ethereal sort of beauty. Her smile was as sweet as her spirit. But she carried too many burdens on her slim shoulders to indulge herself in romantic fancy. Her sister, Bea, wheelchair-bound for years, demanded a great deal of care and even more attention. And Elise treated the library itself almost as though it were a living thing. It had become her child. For this Renata, along with the rest of the town, would always be grateful. She'd spent more happy hours than she could count poring over art books that Elise had special-ordered for her back in the days when nobody else had thought she had a lick of talent.

Proof of Alyssa's father's faith in Renata was that one of her first paintings, a product of her cubist phase, now hung on a wall in the Ingalles' living room. It was a crush of blues and greens, with no discernible subject matter, though Renata recalled believing at the time that it represented heaven's relationship with earth. Now it represented the fact that crusty Judson Ingalls had been the first person in the world to pay actual money for a Renata Meyer painting. For that reason alone she would always cut Alyssa's dad a lot of slack, no matter what Tyler's rumor mill had to say about him.

"It's good to see you all," said Renata, suddenly enveloped by a sense of warmth for each of them. After the unsettling events of the morning, it was good to feel that she was really back home among people who were always kind and predictable.

"So what have you been doing lately, Renata?" asked Elise with a sparkling smile.

"I'm still trying to make a living from my paintings," she replied, opting not to mention that most of her income came from drawing newspaper ads free-lance. "It's a bit of a challenge out there."

"Tell me about it," said Liza, not with rancor but with genuine, shared frustration. "Oz isn't all it's cracked up to be."

Renata grinned. That was as close as Liza was likely to come to admitting that even for a rebel like herself, there really was no place like home.

For fifteen minutes everybody munched on Alyssa's croissants and swapped tales about who had said what last week at the Hair Affair. Renata listened with one ear while her thoughts drifted back to Michael. He'd said he was going to take his father home first, then report to work as soon as he could. He'd mumbled something about his usual unpaid overtime equaling this morning off, but he'd never gotten around to telling her just what his job was. Brick Bauer surely knew and would tell her if she asked, but she couldn't think of a good excuse to pose the question. Renata had no reason to think she'd ever see Michael Youngthunder again; he'd certainly given her no indication that he was interested in getting to know her. And yet, for reasons that weren't entirely clear to Renata, the man seemed to have implanted himself in her subconscious. Despite the cheery laughter all around her, she couldn't quite seem to join in. She wasn't a woman who normally spent much time worrying about men, but she somehow couldn't get this one off her mind.

"As most of you know, we're in the middle of a fund-raising event to replace our library," Alyssa declared when the meeting finally got under way. "As I understand it, the matching funds we expected to receive have been held up, maybe for years. Elise is going to contact the architect who drew up the plans to see if he can scale them down considerably and still meet our needs, but we're going to need a massive infusion of cash anyway. It is our hope—'' her eyes turned to Renata ''—that this wonderful crafts fair will help meet that need.''

Renata didn't comment, but she couldn't help thinking that Alyssa was dreaming. No crafts fair could produce the kind of revenue the town was seeking, even if the artists paid a hefty commission or made a generous donations from their profits.

''Uh, excuse me,'' she said apologetically, ''but this is the first I've heard about replacing the library. I'm all for raising funds for books, but to be honest with you, I don't think we can get all that much money from a crafts fair. Not on the scale of building a new library.'' She turned to Elise. ''Frankly, I don't see the point. I love the old place.''

Elise shook her head. Her lips tightened in distress. ''So do I, Renata, but Tyler has grown since you were a little girl! We simply don't have enough room anymore. Not for books, not for people, not for meetings that could be held in the public gathering rooms.'' Her voice grew low and impassioned. A hint of desperation darkened her normally cheerful eyes. ''Besides, the building is so old it's likely to be condemned as unsafe at any time, or we could have a disaster that would cost us thousands of dollars in books or even threaten the safety of our patrons. The library needs massive restoration—electrical work, plumbing, plaster, everything.'' There was a tremor of despair in her voice now. ''Originally we just hoped to renovate the building or add on, but it would almost cost more to do that, and we'd still be short on space.''

Briskly, Nora said, ''Renata, we discussed all of this at the council meetings. If you'd gone through all the hassle we have, you'd understand that we really do have to build a new library. The only question is where we're going to come up with the funds.''

''The crafts fair is only one idea,'' Anna chimed in brightly. ''We've got several others in the works.''

They weren't exactly ganging up on her, but Renata got the message clearly enough. *You weren't here when all the planning was done. It's too late to raise objections now.*

Renata maintained a sober silence when Alyssa started to speak again.

"In order for this to come about, we have several ideas. The first is that crafts people will donate part of their proceeds—" her gaze flickered nervously to Renata "—and the second is that we hold an auction of some works by more famous artists, whomever we can impress with the urgency of our cause. Although we'll be offering notable artwork, we're hoping that our publicity of this event as a fund-raiser will inflate the prices considerably."

Again her gaze drifted toward Renata, who was definitely getting edgy now. She didn't have enough money to be generous with her donations to Tyler, even though she loved the old town. She couldn't imagine how she was going to get equally impoverished artist friends to donate their paintings to the cause.

When Renata remained silent, Alyssa started to speak again.

"Of course, we need someone to handle the auction portion of the fair—recruiting the works themselves, I mean. Someone who really knows about art and can assess it fairly. That's why we were so glad that Renata volunteered to serve on the committee."

Volunteered, my foot, Renata thought. But she kept her expression neutral as Alyssa continued.

"Some of you may not remember that Renata started painting when she was a little girl. She sold her first picture to my father when she was thirteen. It's probably worth a fortune now, but he would never part with it." She faced the cubist mass of blues and sighed. "It has such sentimental value."

Renata had to stifle a smile. The only thing Judson Ingalls could sell that painting for was kindling. Still, it was nice that he'd kept the homely thing, even though she suspected that Alyssa had dug it out of the basement to put on display just for this meeting. It didn't fit in a home that had been decorated with such wealth and taste.

When all the other ladies beamed at Renata, she felt the noose tighten. Liza winked at her, clearly reading her apprehension.

"With all of her artist friends and contacts, we're certain that Renata will be able to make the auction an outstanding success," Alyssa continued. "We'll help her store and organize the paintings and sculptures, but of course none of us is in a position to recruit and evaluate artwork as she can." Alyssa smiled hopefully at Renata, who did her best to smile back.

"We were hoping you could bring some of your work to the fair, dear," said Anna. "And possibly donate some of it."

"I know it's asking a lot," begged Elise, "but we so badly need a new building."

Before Renata could answer, Liza suggested, "Why don't you paint us something new for the auction, Renata? You know—the official painting that expresses the theme of the fair? Something Tyleresque but distinctive? Maybe we could capitalize on it in a big way. Reproduce posters for sale nationwide or something."

Why don't you order a painting out of the Sears catalog? Renata was tempted to suggest, not quite sure if spunky Liza was kidding. *I don't do paintings on demand.* Each creation came from the soul and it dictated its own terms. Renata could no sooner make a sculpture adhere to a given theme than Michelangelo could have painted the Sistine Chapel with a paint-by-number kit.

Before she could express this perspective, however, Anna said, "I think a unique theme for the fair is a great idea."

"I thought the library renovation was the theme," said Nora.

"No, that's the reason for the fair, not the artistic theme," Alyssa pointed out, looking truly inspired now. "The physical properties of books makes a very narrow theme, and the subjects books cover is just too broad. I think that the history of Tyler, represented by the library's past and future, might be more appropriate."

Liza didn't look impressed. "How do you draw history? Make a painting of a bunch of pioneers cutting down trees and herding dairy cows? I mean, that might be nice for one painting, but how many can you use in one auction? Besides, we've all seen that sort of thing before."

There's more to Tyler's history than the pioneers, Renata suddenly thought. *Michael's people were here for generations before the first white person set foot on Wisconsin soil.*

As an idea began to form in her mind, Renata cautiously suggested, "I think it might be interesting to feature a different kind of artwork altogether in terms of history. How about bringing Indian arts and crafts to the fair and featuring paintings and sculptures with Native American themes?"

For a moment they all stared at her. Then Alyssa said, "I don't think Indian things will raise much money, do you?"

"Of course they will!" Liza suddenly burst out. "Get with it, Mother! Indians are in right now. The Santa Fe look is everywhere."

"But we're not in Santa Fe, dear," said Anna.

Nora added, "This is hardly known as Indian country. It's not the wild West."

"But there used to be a great many distinguished tribes in Wisconsin," Elise reminded the group, "and I believe there are still some small reservations not too far from here."

Suddenly Anna blinked. "Why, just last night my nephew said the police were looking for some old Indian who'd gotten lost in Tyler. I think Brick said something about an old burial ground."

Renata felt a sudden, curious sense of alarm. For some reason she could not explain, she didn't want anybody in this group to talk about Michael and his grandfather as strangers, Indians who didn't really belong here. Her encounter with the two had been oddly touching, almost spiritual, and she knew she couldn't explain the depth of meaning their visit to her and had had for them. She wasn't even sure she understood it herself.

"All I know is that Tyler's focus has always been on white

settlers. Not that there's anything wrong with that—I'm proud that my great-grandparents helped settle this place,'' Renata was quick to clarify. ''But we all know about pioneer art— quilts and wood carving and knitted goods—and I think it would be an interesting change of pace to focus on the Indians who lived here first. If white artists could use Indian work as a theme and we could persuade some local Indians to sell some of their authentic work, we might be able to really make the fair special.''

''I knew she'd think of something!'' Alyssa warmly concurred. ''Oh, Renata, it's wonderful having you in charge of the auction and recruiting the Indian craft people. I'm just so glad you're here!''

At the moment, Renata was not at all glad to be sitting in Alyssa Ingalls Baron's living room, and not at all glad that she'd been roped into helping work on the fair. But there were perks to the job that none of the other women realized. Surely the memory of Michael's sharp cheekbones or his grandfather's weathered face would inspire Renata to create some of the finest paintings she'd ever done. And as for recruiting Indian artists, well, she'd have to contact every one she knew.

There weren't all that many. She'd taken art classes with Bobby Montero and Judy Hall and got along well with both of them. But Bobby was a mixture of three or four tribes from Arizona and Judy was a Sioux. If Tyler's crafts fair was going to center on Wisconsin history, then surely the committee would have to contact *Wisconsin* Indians. It seemed to Renata that there were a half dozen tribes within the state, but she didn't know which ones they were or where they'd settled. All she knew for sure was that her farm had once been sovereign territory of the Winnebago.

And except for the old man who'd spent the night on her lawn, Michael Youngthunder was the only Winnebago she knew.

CHAPTER THREE

IT WAS NEARLY nine o'clock in the evening when Michael reached the turnoff to Renata Meyer's place. It had been a horrendous day. After spending the whole night in search of his grandfather, finding him at dawn, driving him back home, reporting late for work and working overtime, about the last thing he needed to do was dash back to Tyler again.

And the last thing he wanted to risk was spending an hour alone with this beguiling female.

With great reluctance and more than a little anger at Grand Feather, Michael rang the doorbell. He heard Renata coming, taking her time, probably glancing out the window to see who'd sneaked up on her in the dark. To make it easier for her, he called out, "It's Michael Youngthunder, Renata." And then, belatedly, he realized that she might not find the news particularly reassuring. He could hardly have made a good impression on her this morning. Besides, she'd already done her Good Samaritan deed for the year. If she normally lived in a big city like Milwaukee, she undoubtedly thought twice before opening the door to strangers or casual acquaintances who were men.

Even when they weren't Indians.

To his astonishment, his words had the same effect as "Open sesame." The door was flung open wide.

"Michael!" she burst out, the joy in her voice unmistakable. So was her assumption that he'd hurried back to Tyler just to see her.

For a full thirty seconds Michael simply stood there, dumbstruck. Renata was wearing that same casual outfit he'd seen

her in this morning, although now the T-shirt seemed to sport
a bit more paint. But her face, in the moonlight, looked completely different. This morning she'd been worried, cautious,
offended, hurt. Tonight she looked positively radiant.

She's thrilled to see me, he realized, the discovery swelling
through him with a rush. *I'll be damned. Renata was hoping
I'd come back again.*

It occurred to Michael briefly that maybe his grandfather had
already shown up here again and Renata was just relieved that
someone had come to tow him away. But he hadn't kept his
distance from white women so long that he'd forgotten how to
read the expression he saw on her lovely face. No man in his
right mind was likely to be blind to such joyous anticipation.

Michael swallowed hard and tried to find somewhere to look
besides Renata's welcoming blue eyes. He didn't want to embarrass her and he didn't want to embarrass himself. But today
seemed to be his day for humiliation. Grand Feather wasn't
giving him much choice.

"Uh, Renata, I'm really sorry to barge in like this," he began, pretending he'd missed her delighted greeting. "But my
cousin says my grandfather has disappeared again. He left a
note this time telling me not to come after him, but there's no
way I can sleep while he's missing."

For the tiniest moment Renata stared at him in confusion,
maybe a bit of shock. Then she looked concerned. It was not
for several seconds that she began to blush.

It touched him that she seemed more worried than embarrassed. The very depth and decency of the woman made it
increasingly hard to push away his keen attraction to her.
Fiercely Michael reminded himself of why it was vital that he
keep a safe distance from Renata. To her, their meeting was
probably the beginning of something totally new. To him it
was a replay of a movie he hadn't liked the first time and was
not about to sit through again.

"Michael, I'm sorry, but I haven't seen him since you two
left with Brick this morning," Renata said straightforwardly,

her tone giving nothing away. "It's been very quiet here this evening."

Unhappily he met her eyes, frustrated in more ways than one. He knew this was where his grandfather was heading; it was only a matter of time until he arrived. But what was he supposed to do until Grand Feather got here? Wait in the car? Circle the surrounding farmland? Hang out at that ritzy lodge?

"Do you want to come in and wait for him?" Renata asked politely.

He didn't. He knew it was a bad idea. But he couldn't think of any good way to tell her so without hurting her feelings. And that was the last thing he wanted to do. After all this time he was still cautious with white women, but he'd gotten over the need to be cruel to them.

"Thanks, Renata, but I think I'd better go look for him," he answered reluctantly. "If he's not here he might be on the road or maybe at the lodge."

Renata stepped out onto the porch, her delicate face lit up by the porch light, which was attracting an army of moths. "Do you want me to go with you? Or take my own car? I know all the back ways into this place, Michael. I know the footpaths from the lodge."

He had no ready comeback for that. The truth was, she *did* know the area better than he did, and he desperately wanted to find his grandfather before it got completely dark. The old guy was tough, but it could be dangerous for him to spend another night out in the open. He might still get sick because of last night's exposure.

Michael gazed at Renata and tried to weigh his options. She looked so pretty standing there in the twilight, her eyes vibrant, her skin creamy and pale. But her expression had sobered since he'd explained why he'd come, and now he could read nothing on her face but human concern for a frail old fellow who quite literally didn't know enough to come in out of the rain.

"I'd appreciate your help," Michael said slowly. "I really hate to bother Lieutenant Bauer again. I kept him up all night, you know, and he'd worked half a shift before I even showed up at the station.''

''Just let me get a flashlight,'' she said, then vanished into the house.

As he watched her shapely backside sprint away from him, he loosened his tie and tugged off his jacket. The memory of his air-conditioned car was no help at all in the sweltering evening air, and with Renata by his side, Michael knew that the night was going to get hotter yet.

BY THE TIME she grabbed her most powerful flashlight and locked up the house, Renata felt that she had her feelings pretty much under control. She couldn't recall saying anything in particular that revealed how very glad she was to see Michael, let alone that she'd thought for one foolish minute that he'd rushed back to Tyler with her grandpa's old clothes just so he could see her again. Still, there was always the chance that her feelings had shown on her face. If they had, Michael had chosen to ignore her faux pas, and for that she could be grateful.

The porch was empty when she returned to the door. A classy blue BMW was sitting in her gravel driveway with headlights on and engine running. The passenger door had been left open for her, but Michael was already in the car.

Renata slipped inside and put on her seat belt as Michael pulled out of the drive. Her seat was close to his, so close their knees almost touched, but she studiously braced her body at a safe distance. She was entirely too aware of his proximity. She was also aware that Michael was ignoring her. At least, he was ignoring her as a woman. Since he'd arrived this evening, he hadn't treated her any differently than he would have treated a man.

''Tell me about the back trails from the lodge,'' he ordered, his voice throbbing with concern. ''Maybe that's how we missed him last night. He might have spent part of the night in the woods by the lake. I never thought to ask him how he got here.''

''Even if we knew that, we don't know for sure he'd take

the same route again. I'm not certain why you think he'll come straight back here anyway, Michael,'' Renata pointed out. "For some reason he settled under the oak tree in my front yard last night, but don't you think he might want to check out some other oaks in the area?"

When Michael gave a helpless shrug, his long hair brushed his neck and shoulders. His profile was clean and sharp, stunning in its masculine strength. Renata wondered how he'd look in braids and feathers, then reminded herself that there were some things in life it was better not to find out.

"Frankly, I don't know what he'll do. I would have sworn he would never have come over here in the first place. I would have sworn he'd have had enough sense to do his praying under your eaves or inside your barn. And after I read him the riot act this morning, I would have sworn he'd never have pulled such a harebrained stunt again."

Renata wasn't sure what to say. Michael was frightened. She could feel his fear. And it wasn't just fear because his grandfather was missing. It was fear that the old man truly was losing his grip on reality. He might have decided to run away.

"I don't know what to say, Michael," she said softly. "I'm sorry."

Again he shrugged, with frustration this time. "It's not your fault."

"I didn't mean it was. I just…I wish I could do something to help you. To help you both."

Michael glanced at her, his eyes too dark to read in the twilight. "You already have, Renata. You've done more than anybody could have asked of you." His voice caressed her with embarrassed gratitude. "We have no right to keep showing up on your doorstep. Believe me, if he hadn't run off again—"

Michael broke off abruptly, as though he suddenly realized what he'd been about to say: *You never would have seen me again.* It was tactless, but probably true. Renata swallowed hard and looked out the window. She was drawn to this man, but it was obvious that he did not return her interest in him. Some things just weren't meant to be.

The next half hour was busy but unproductive. Renata showed Michael the shortest way by road to Timberlake Lodge. After circling the main building, he drove through the parking areas while she darted inside to ask if anyone had seen a solitary old man. Edward Wocheck was in the lobby, conferring with his staff in preparation for the next morning's ground-breaking ceremony, and he took a moment to express his sympathy. He promised Renata that he'd tell his people to be on the lookout for Michael's grandfather.

When she got back to the car, Michael didn't touch the door as she opened it and climbed in. Wordlessly he searched her face, then floored the engine when she said, "He hasn't been here."

It was a quiet night on the lake. Only one tourist couple was out for an evening stroll. When Michael made a sharp turn, he caught the startled eyes of deer in his headlights. He slowed down until the deer safely crossed the road, but he made no comment as the BMW approached the highway.

He drove in virtual silence for maybe half a mile until Renata said abruptly, "Stop the car."

Instantly he braked. "Do you see him?" he demanded.

There was a catch in his voice that tugged at Renata. *Oh, Michael,* a tiny voice inside her whispered, *you really do cherish that old man.* She felt a sudden jealous ache as she realized how much it would mean to have anybody cherish her with such devotion.

Especially a man as compelling as this one.

"I don't see anything, but this is the easiest place to catch the back trail to the lodge from the highway," she explained. "Do you want to come with me or keep driving around while I check it out on foot?"

This time when Michael turned to face Renata, he looked astounded. For the first time since he'd arrived, she had the feeling that he realized a real live person was sitting beside him, not just a faceless local guide.

"You are suggesting that I let you wander through these woods alone at night on the off chance you might find a stranger who was trained in the Winnebago art of hiding?'' he asked incredulously.

Renata was touched by his concern, even though she realized that his protest might be an instinctive macho reaction. "I was born here, Michael," she reminded him. "I know these woods like my own backyard."

"And that lodge is filled with city people, all strangers," he retorted. "I've got enough on my plate looking for Grand Feather. The last thing I need is to report to Lieutenant Bauer that I've lost you, too."

"Gee, thanks, Michael," she snapped, not at all appreciating his sharp tone. "I'm sorry I'm such a burden to you."

He glared at her for a moment, then exhaled a mighty sigh. His dark eyes were intense as he apologized. "I didn't mean that the way it sounded. I just don't want you to get hurt because of me or mine."

"This is Tyler," she pointed out patiently. "Nobody ever gets hurt walking in the woods."

"Renata, a woman was killed here! Right here at the lodge!"

"That was forty years ago." She was surprised that he'd heard about Margaret Ingalls, but since he'd spent a good twelve hours in Brick's police car last night, he probably had heard everything that had ever happened to anybody in Tyler.

"If they never found the killer, it might as well have been yesterday," he insisted somewhat irrationally. "Whoever did it might still live near here. How many of the farms around your place have been sold since then?"

"Michael, you don't honestly think that one of my neighbors—"

"I don't know your neighbors. I only know you. And I don't want anything to happen to you." His voice was low…too low for a casual statement. It caused a strange vibration that sensitized Renata's ears. She felt herself leaning toward him again; she felt his grip tighten on her hand.

Was it possible that he felt a fraction of what she did when they touched like this? Was there some reason beyond fraternal concern that he was still holding her hand?

"Then I guess you'd better walk back to the lodge with me," she suggested, not at all averse to taking a moonlit walk around Timber Lake with Michael, especially when he seemed eager to keep her close to him. "I really do think we need to check out the trail."

This time when Michael's eyes met hers, Renata saw something she hadn't noticed before. He was torn. For some reason he was struggling to protect her from something more than Timberlake Lodge's out-of-town guests…something he hadn't put into words.

For the first time she wondered if, in some strange way, he was trying to protect her from himself.

IT WAS AFTER TEN when Renata suggested that they check the house again. They had walked from the road to the lodge, from the lodge to the house and from the house back to the road again. They had listened for the sound of chants; they had watched for any ghost of motion. They had alarmed some Timberlake guests, dislodged one ring-necked pheasant hen and startled a ruffed grouse. Other than that they had seen no one.

The instant Michael pulled into Renata's driveway, he knew that he was wasting his time. Grand Feather had outfoxed him again. The old man hadn't sneaked off just to come right back to where Michael had collared him the first time. He was hiding somewhere different this time.

He must be working on a new plan.

"Oh, my God," Michael said aloud as the implications of that thought crystallized in his mind.

"What?" Renata's voice echoed his alarm.

"I'm so stupid! I can't believe I didn't think of it before!"

"Michael, tell me!"

He shook his head. "Renata, Grand Feather came over here in the first place because of that damn ground-breaking ceremony. He's going to show up there tomorrow and make a scene. I know it!"

"Oh, Michael." She didn't try to tell him he was wrong. "If we go there early, maybe we can stop him."

Again he shook his head. "I doubt it. The best we can do is try to keep him from getting hurt. He is a stubborn, stubborn old man, Renata. I told you he was not senile. He's got a mind like a steel trap, and you'd better believe that he's thought up a plan worthy of a Winnebago chief. Damn it! He's going to take Edward Wocheck and all the rest of us by surprise."

Renata took a deep breath, then laid a hand on his arm.

He knew it was meant to be a comforting gesture, but his instantaneous response was anything but platonic. All night he'd been far too aware of the proximity of this terribly appealing female. "If he's planning something in the morning, he must have planned somewhere to spend the night," he told her, trying to place some distance between them, at least in his mind. "Unless he's broken into one of the unoccupied rooms at the lodge, he's going to take shelter in some other empty place."

"Why don't we check the barn?" asked Renata.

It was the best idea he'd heard all night. Quickly he bolted out of the car and followed Renata past the house. A single feeble light bulb announced the barn's location. It wasn't more than fifteen yards to the beat-up old building. Although there were no animals inside, it had six large stalls and half a load of moldy hay in the loft.

Michael hurriedly checked every stall and every corner of the tack room while Renata shinnied up to the loft. They met in the center of the barn two minutes later, ready to concede their defeat.

"I'm sorry, Michael," Renata told him. "It was just an idea."

"Not a bad one, actually. Do you suppose he might be hiding out in somebody else's barn around here?"

"He might, but if he is, then he's already safe for the night," she assured him. "This time of year he won't get cold as long as he's dry. But we could go visit all my neighbors…"

Michael shook his head. "No, it's too late to get everybody in the county out of bed. Besides, Grand Feather would hear us coming and take off anyway. He's probably better off in some haymow than he would be chased off into the night.''

Wearily he plopped down on an old milking stool and faced Renata. He felt engulfed by the silence of the empty building. Its lingering scents of leather, hay and horses reminded him of his childhood. After a moment he mused, ''There's something terribly lonely about an abandoned barn.''

Renata seemed to bristle. ''I'd hardly call it abandoned, Michael. I still live here.''

''I thought you lived in Milwaukee.''

''Well, I do. At least most of the time. I rent an apartment so I can work there.'' She gestured toward the empty stalls. ''But my family has lived here since 1840. This will always be my home.''

Michael didn't answer. He wasn't sure he wanted to find out just how her family had come to own the land.

''It's hard to believe I used to spend half of every day out here,'' Renata mused, fingering a rein that hung from a harness tacked up on the wall.

Michael studied her in the dim light. God, she was a beauty. So natural, so unfettered. Like a filly in the spring. ''You had a horse?''

''I had three.'' She grinned at him. ''We had chickens and a milk cow, too, when I was little.''

A tired smile crept onto Michael's face. ''A real country girl, huh?''

She chuckled. ''I was raised on a farm. What else could I be?''

I was raised in a shack, but it might as well have been a wigwam made of bark or hide, he felt the urge to tell her. But that would open up old memories and new concerns. This wasn't a date; it was no time to get better acquainted. Renata was a stranger helping him look for his grandfather. That was all.

Seeming to sense his discomfort, Renata prosaically suggested, ''I suppose we could check the basement, Michael, if you think he might be able to break a lock or find some other way to sneak inside.''

Michael fought back the urge to ask if she was making assumptions about sneaking Indians, but restrained himself. Renata didn't deserve that kind of crack. The woman who did was a thousand miles away. She probably didn't even remember his face anymore. He wished he could forget hers.

''Sure, why not,'' he agreed wearily. ''I don't think he's there, either, but he sure as hell isn't here.''

Silently he followed Renata back toward the house, taking note of the way her hips swayed just a little bit from side to side. She made no special effort to put on female airs. She was just herself—bold in some ways; in others, understated. Whatever the combination was, it spoke to Michael in some quiet nameless fashion.

With great effort, he turned a deaf ear.

Renata dug a key to the basement out of her pocket and opened the door. There was no indication that anybody had fussed with the lock. When she flipped on the light, Michael was surprised at what he saw. The barn was almost empty, but this protected room was stuffed to the gills with the remnants of a century of farm life. There were stacks of boxes, stacks of lumber, stacks of old paintings crammed together wall to wall. A cat could hide in here for a lifetime, but he didn't think a human could even squeeze inside. It made his grandfather's tiny shack seem downright spacious.

''Your family sure doesn't believe in holding on to things, do they?'' Michael teased Renata, surprised that he could come up with a joke.

Renata turned around, her eyes big and happy. For a moment he felt happy, too. Then he remembered what he was doing here.

''I should have taken him back to Sugar Creek this morning,'' he said soberly. ''I can't believe I lost him again.''

She took a step toward him. ''Your grandfather ran off to feel like a freewheeling adult. You've been treating him like a child. I don't blame you for that,'' she assured him. ''I understand your obligations. But I don't blame him, either, Michael. Wouldn't you hate to be in his position?''

He felt a fresh well of feeling for this white woman who so quickly seemed to grasp the heart of Winnebago ways. She didn't fully understand what drove his grandfather, but she understood the part of the proud old man that still ached to call his own shots, who was not yet old enough to surrender. Grand Feather was still a warrior, or longed to be. And that would be true for the rest of his days.

Suddenly Renata seemed entirely too close. Michael could smell the soft female scent of her, a blend of paint, shampoo and woman. He tried to step back before it grew intoxicating, but behind him there was a pile of bricks. To either side, there were boxes.

''I'm the only one left,'' she said quietly, her eyes looking sadder now. ''Each time one of them died, we'd pack up everything because it hurt too much to look at it, but we couldn't bear to throw their things away.'' She gestured toward a giant crate in the corner. ''My great-grandmother's wedding dress is still in there. I always hoped I'd wear it one day.'' As she turned toward another box near the steps, her shoulder brushed Michael's, electrifying his senses. ''This is Grandpa's collection of Indian artifacts. He was so proud of it. I know I ought to donate these old arrowheads and moccasins to a museum, but I just can't bear to give them away.''

Michael didn't want to think about Indian artifacts, painful memories of another space and time. He didn't want to think about Renata, either, or feel touched by her loneliness. He didn't need to know how many brothers and sisters she'd had or how many extended family members were part of the Meyer clan. The bottom line was that Renata was all alone now, and despite her spunk and cheery nature, the emptiness wore on her from time to time.

He was sorry he'd made her come down to this sad room.

He was also sorry that he was trapped so close to her, close enough to smell that clean womanly scent again. Close enough to kiss. Close enough to reach out and slip an arm around her waist to offer comfort and…whatever followed.

It was one of those moments when a man and woman find themselves alone together and they both know that it's time for something intimate to happen. Michael suddenly wanted very much to kiss Renata. He was sure it was what she wanted, too.

"I'm going about this all wrong," he said abruptly, desperately hoping that his panic wasn't evident in his voice. He had to get away from her, had to break the mood before he did something he would surely regret. He didn't want to hurt her, but he had no choice. "I've been thinking what *I'd* do," he babbled quickly. "I've been thinking white."

Renata licked her lips. Her eyes could not entirely conceal her disappointment, but she discreetly stepped away. "You need to think Winnebago?" she asked, as though the tender near-miss had not just happened.

He nodded, grateful for her tact. And surprised that this confession did not embarrass him as much as it would have just this morning.

"Do you still know how?"

He'd hoped she wouldn't ask him that. Now that she had, he found himself unable to tell her anything but the truth.

"I can when I really work at it, but it's a challenge when I'm hungry and wearing a suit and it's the end of a long day."

Renata gave him the sort of smile a hardworking man gives up bachelorhood to come home to. "I can find some more of Grandpa's old clothes to fit you, Michael," she offered, "and I can drum up something for you to eat, too. I went to the store today, so it ought to be an improvement over breakfast."

He was so tired that he found himself laughing. "You've given me food and clothes and tour-guide service, Renata. Next you'll be opening a bed-and-breakfast inn so I can spend the night."

He regretted the words the minute they were spoken, but he could not call them back. Suddenly Renata seemed entirely too close again—too ready, too willing. Her lips seemed to beg him for a kiss, and Michael feared he didn't have the willpower it would take to pull back.

But Renata abruptly stepped around him and headed toward an open box of clothes. "In the old days Grandpa always took in tired travelers," she said nonchalantly. "You need to sit down and take a load off. I've got a spare bed."

He knew she did. He'd been in her guest bedroom this morning, upstairs beside the small bathroom. He'd also seen Renata's room, right across the hall.

Anticipation suddenly tightened his groin. It was a keen warning of why it would be foolish to spend the night in this house. Renata was only offering the guest room, and he had no doubt that she expected him to sleep there tonight. But a fresh kind of intimacy lurked in the darkness nonetheless, a drawing together that tomorrow or next week or next month would surely spell nothing but trouble.

"I think I've imposed on you enough," Michael said tightly. "I really should go."

"Where?" Renata asked, turning back to face him. "You're not going to leave Tyler until you find him. The lodge is jammed to the rafters with all Eddie Wocheck's people who came in for the ground-breaking ceremony tomorrow, and your only other choices are way back in town."

Her logic seemed impeccable, but Michael knew he had to find a flaw in it.

"Even if you drove back," she continued, "you know you couldn't sleep. You'd be waiting for me to call with news, or you'd be driving by here every hour."

He couldn't really argue. Staying here was the reasonable choice, and she was kind to invite him. She'd be insulted if he offered to pay her, but at least she'd know that he considered it a purely practical arrangement.

"Renata, I'd feel a lot better if—"

"Michael Youngthunder, if you even suggest paying for my guest room, I swear I'll make you sleep in the barn."

Again he laughed. It wasn't funny. Nothing was. But he

hadn't slept in thirty-six hours and he was punchy as hell. "I'm not looking for a roll in the hay," he joked.

At least it seemed like a joke to him. But Renata didn't seem to find it humorous.

"Barn, hay—you get it?"

Stonily she gathered up her grandpa's jeans and thrust them into his arms. "Michael, you don't need to spell it out for me. I have no intention of throwing myself at a man who's made it clear that he hasn't got the slightest interest in me as a woman."

He flushed. "Renata, I didn't mean—"

"Yes, you did. You've been giving me 'no way, lady' signals ever since you got here tonight, and now your alarm is working overtime. I know you wish you could get away from me, but until we find your grandfather we're stuck with each other."

He was speechless. And absolutely mortified.

"I get the message, Michael. No problem. What makes you so damn sure that I'm hot to trot with you, anyway?"

Just like that, his confidence vanished. Had he read her all wrong? Was she reminding him that compassion was one thing, attraction to an Indian quite another?

"I'm sorry," he said lamely. "I don't know what I'm thinking. This has been such a bizarre day. When I got here you seemed so glad to see me that I—"

"Of course I was glad to see you. I need your help on a project and your arrival saved me having to track you down. You did tell me, didn't you, that I should give you a call if I ever needed a favor?"

Confused and embarrassed, he said, "Yes, I did. I would be happy to even the scales, Renata. It…" *It's the Winnebago way,* he'd almost told her. There had been a time in his life when every thought was Winnebago. Then there'd been a time when every thought was white. Now there were surprises like this one.

He'd been disappointed when he'd thought she wanted him. Now he was upset to learn he'd been wrong. It didn't make sense, but nothing about this crazy day did. And things were getting even worse.

Ever since he'd arrived tonight he'd been afraid of hurting Renata, but she'd just turned the tables. She'd shut him down and turned away. Surely that would be the end of it.

But as Michael watched her sashay up the basement stairs, a flush of arousal warned him that he was far too tired to lie to himself. Getting close to this woman would be stupid. Spending the night here was unwise. Sorting out in her presence the parts of him that were Winnebago would be akin to opening a Pandora's box of trouble.

He was going to do it anyway.

CHAPTER FOUR

IT WAS THE SOUND of a door opening that woke Renata. No woman living alone in a big city fails to develop a certain wariness about unexplained sounds and movements in her own home. The clack was enough to jolt Renata out of her grogginess in a flash. Her heart was pounding crazily before she remembered where she was…and that she was not alone.

There had been a change in Michael after her little speech in the basement. Before then he'd been alternately warm and distant. Since then he'd been apologetic, almost meek. When he'd thanked her—profusely—for putting him up for the night, his tone had been decidedly impersonal. But his intimate gaze hadn't left her face until she'd shut the door to her own room.

With her mind so full of worries—about the old man, the crafts fair and Michael—Renata hadn't expected to doze off. But after an hour, even the gripping spy novel she was reading couldn't keep her awake. Now, in the darkness, she seized the hardback book as though it were a weapon.

She stood up, crossed the room and groped for her own door, still securely shut. She opened it and whispered, "Michael?" When he didn't answer, she turned on the light in the hall. The door to the guest room was open, but there was no one inside.

Quickly Renata grabbed a robe—the lightest one she owned, since it was a humid night—and hurried downstairs. There was a light on in the kitchen, revealing an open pickle jar and an unwrapped pack of bologna on the counter she'd cleaned off a few hours before. She called Michael's name again, but there was no answer. Hoping his grandfather had finally shown up,

Renata opened the front door and peered out at the porch. There was no sign of Michael…or his grandfather.

Resigned to the fact that Michael must have gone off searching again without her, Renata turned to go back inside. She almost didn't hear the quiet, reluctant voice that said, "I'm over here, Renata."

Her pulse pounded in a second's quick fear before she recognized Michael's voice and sought his virile face in the darkness. He was sitting on the lawn in the shadows. Right about the spot where he'd first joined his chanting grandfather.

Tightening the sash of her robe, Renata crossed the porch to the railing. Between the porch light and the moon, she could see him and he could surely see her, but somehow Renata felt they both welcomed the emotional barrier the hand rail provided. She'd invited Michael the yuppie to spend the night in her guest room. It was Michael the Indian who was sitting on her front lawn.

"Sorry if I woke you," he said in a troubled tone. "I did my best to be quiet." Then, with an apologetic smile, he reminded her, "You told me to make myself at home. I was hungry."

"I'm beginning to believe that's a permanent condition with you," she teased.

He chuckled. "Maybe it's because I hadn't eaten for nearly a day when I first showed up here. Maybe it's because I had to fast when I was young. Maybe it's because I don't have a squaw to cook for me."

Renata wasn't sure how to handle a line like that. Every time she'd broached the subject of his background, Michael had gotten a bit testy. She wasn't at all sure what to say when he was the one who brought it up. She wasn't at all sure he was teasing.

Uneasily she asked, "Why were you fasting?"

"My grandfather was determined to give me a traditional Winnebago upbringing," he explained, "even though most Winnebagos don't honor the old ways very strictly anymore. When he was a boy, Winnebago youths were trained to fast as part of their vision-quest ceremonies.'' He gave an expansive gesture that seemed to embrace the world. ''Personally, I think they also did it as training for times when food was scarce, so they'd be accustomed to starvation and still be able to hunt or fight or whatever.''

''I guess it worked,'' Renata said. ''You were ravenous when you got to Tyler, but you still carried on.''

He laughed again. It surprised Renata to see him so relaxed; he'd been stiff as a board earlier tonight. Maybe his change of demeanor had occurred because he'd gotten a few hours of sleep, or because his face was largely hidden in darkness, or because Renata herself was a fair distance away. In any event, he was in a completely different mood than she'd seen him in before. Chatty. Mellow. Expansive.

''I'm surprised that Winnebagos still practice fasting at all,'' Renata commented, hoping to draw him out. ''I mean, I thought most of the tribes were pretty much assimilated by now.''

He shook his head. ''That's a popular misconception. I think it would be more accurate to say that most tribes have been forgotten. Most white people never see an Indian unless he's become so white he just mixes in. They have no idea how things are on the rez.''

''The rez?'' Renata repeated. ''You mean the reservation? Did you grow up on one?'' For some reason the notion horrified her. It made Michael seem…well, so distant. *Too* distant. Too far away for her to ever reach.

You can't reach him anyway, Renata, she tensely reminded herself. *He's made it perfectly clear he doesn't want you.*

It was a long time since Renata had been so keenly drawn to a man, a long time since she'd been this hurt by a man's rejection. She often went out with male friends, but she'd been in love only twice since high school. She had planned to marry Ray, a wonderful boy she'd met in college, but he'd been stricken with leukemia shortly after they got engaged. She'd loved him till the end, desperately hoping there was some way to alter his destiny, but day by day she'd watched him slip away.

It had taken her years to recover from Ray's death, and when she finally had, Vic, another artist, had splashed into her life in a riot of sexual energy and brilliant colors. They'd had a joyous affair, one that Renata had been certain would last for the rest of her life. But one day Vic had blown out of her life as tempestuously as he'd blown in. Bewildered, wounded and cautious after that, Renata had not been eager to plunge into any other relationship, even though she'd met several nice men since then.

Her interest in Michael troubled her—not because of any lack in his appeal or shortcoming in his character, but because it had been so obvious right from the start that he didn't return her enthusiasm for him. It was bad enough to be drawn to a man who *might* lose interest down the road a piece. It was foolhardy to fall for one who didn't even want to join her at the starting gate.

"The Winnebago reservation is in Nebraska," Michael explained, "and I spent a fair number of summers there with cousins when I was young. But I grew up in Wisconsin Dells."

Renata asked curiously, "Why is the reservation in Nebraska? I got the impression the Winnebago homeland was in Wisconsin."

"It is." Michael grimaced, then clarified, "Every time the whites yanked away more of our land, they shipped us off to some new place and pretended it was our homeland. We got cheated once too often, and the last time—the alleged "treaty" of 1832—some of our people dug in their heels and just plain refused to go to Nebraska. They scarfed up enough money to purchase homesteads in Wisconsin like white folks—Congress had passed a law allowing Indians to own private land by then—and staked out a slew of small communities across the state. Wisconsin Dells was one of them." He turned away, almost as though he were talking to the night and not to Renata. "I've got relatives scattered all around, but my grandfather has always been one of those traditionalists who tried to preserve the old ways after everybody else had pretty much forgotten them. When my father dumped me with him, Grand Feather was determined that I would carry on the traditions.'' After a long, quiet moment, he confessed, ''I've been a big disappointment to him.''

Renata wasn't sure how to respond to that. She didn't know a lot about Michael's life, but she certainly had the impression that his career was successful. His devotion to his grandfather was exemplary. Uncertainly she said, ''I'm sure he loves you, Michael.''

He turned his head and stared at her for a minute. The warmth in his voice abruptly vanished. ''You don't know a thing about me, Renata.''

''I was trying to be kind!'' she flared, taken off guard by his change of mood. ''If I don't know anything about you it's only because you refuse to talk about yourself. I don't want to be pushy, but there's a lot about you I'd like to know.''

His eyes focused on her in the moonlight, and she felt the strange power of his strength. She had a sudden sense that he was going to open up to her, and the knowledge filled her with an inexplicable thrill.

''I was engaged to a white girl once,'' he said abruptly.

A curl of alarm tightened Renata's stomach. She'd ached to know Michael's secrets, but *this* secret could only mean bad news for her.

''She wanted to know all about me, too. Found what she called 'all that Indian stuff' downright fascinating. I suppose you find it fascinating, too.''

And then she knew. In that one sentence, spoken with an undertone of bitterness, Renata realized what had gone wrong between herself and Michael right from the start. It didn't have anything to do with her, Renata Meyer, personally. He didn't have a clue who she was and he didn't care. She was white. End of story. She might as well have dressed like a biker and had green hair.

''Good night, Michael,'' she said stiffly. ''I'm going back inside.''

She'd barely turned around before he was on his feet, light as a cat, rushing barefoot across the lawn to touch her arm from the other side of the porch railing. "Renata, wait," he pleaded. His fingers wrapped around her wrist, warm and beseeching. "Please. I'm sorry."

The heady impact of his skin on hers was both startling and overpowering. Never before had she been rendered helpless by the mere brush of a man's fingertips. But in that instant, if Michael had kissed her, she would have surrendered her soul.

Renata turned around uncertainly, not at all sure it was wise to stay but utterly unable to go.

Michael's eyes dropped to the weathered railing between them as his fingers slowly kneaded her sensitive wrist. "I'm sorry," he repeated, his voice low and slightly hoarse. "I don't usually have trouble like this with white people, Renata. All this chaos with my grandfather has me so upset." In a near whisper he tacked on, "So ashamed."

"Michael, you have nothing to be ashamed of," Renata told him gently. "He's the one who's doing these odd things, not you, and he's just an old man with a dream—"

"You don't understand."

Boldly, her eyes met his. "Then tell me. Tell me what you think I don't know. I'm teachable."

He gave her the ghost of a smile. "Renata…"

Whatever else he was going to say was lost in the unspoken communion that suddenly roared between them. Renata knew when a man was about to kiss her, and suddenly she was certain that the moment was just right. Of course, she'd had the same sensation in the basement before Michael had tried to escape. But this was different. His grip gently tightened on her wrist. A flush of anticipation surged through Renata. She found herself leaning toward him, rising to her tiptoes.

But Michael—damn him!—turned his head slightly. He closed his eyes and released her arm.

"I'm ashamed," he said huskily, "of the fact that I am ashamed."

For a long moment Renata grappled with this pronouncement, knowing that even though he'd thrust her away as a woman, he'd somehow embraced her as a friend. He had revealed a dark ripple of his inner pain to the light of her compassion. He'd entrusted her with a gift. But what did he mean, exactly? Was he ashamed of his grandfather and so felt disloyal because of it? Or was he ashamed of something else?

"Do you understand?" he whispered.

Badly torn, Renata opted for the truth. "Not quite," she admitted, "but I want to, Michael. I'm trying."

He shook his head, but he did not step away. He was so close that a lock of his thick black hair brushed her face. "Grand Feather embarrasses me not because he is old and acting foolish, but because he is acting Winnebago in front of white people. I am white enough to be ashamed of this. But enough of me is still Winnebago that I know I should be proud of him for holding out for what is ours."

It was a catch-22 if she'd ever heard one. Renata's heart went out to him. "Oh, Michael," she said simply.

To her surprise, he reached out for her again, and this time he slipped his broad hands over her shoulders, palms resting near the top curve of her breasts. It could have been a platonic gesture, but to Renata it didn't feel like one.

"He's right, you see. This is *our* land. It's part of that last so-called treaty." Abruptly, he seemed to remember his audience. He didn't step away, but he did release her shoulders with an expression that might have been on his face if he'd stepped in something unclean. "I don't know how your family got it and I don't care. That's not the point. The point is that there *is* a Winnebago burial ground around here somewhere, Renata. Whether they're going to start digging it up tomorrow or somebody dug it up already, it's still not right that it should be neglected, unmarked, uncared for."

The flare of anger faded from his eyes, and to Renata's surprise, his fingertips brushed hers once more. This time she didn't give him a chance to escape; she gripped his fingers tightly.

Michael tugged her closer, until her hand rested against his ribs. He leaned so near to her that his lips, full and moist, almost brushed hers as he whispered, "Grand Feather's great-grandparents are buried there, Renata. *My* ancestors are buried there!" His lips tightened, but he did not pull away. "I'm young and strong and I've got all the skills to fight the system, but I've turned my back on them. He's old and feeble and bewildered by most of the white man's ways, but he's still doing his damnedest to make things right for the ones who've gone on before. He's following the true Winnebago way."

Renata laced her fingers tightly with Michael's. She wanted to put her arms around him, to kiss away his hurts and fears, but she was still getting mixed signals. She was only sure that, at this moment, he was willing to share a tiny piece of his soul. She wanted to cherish and protect what was being entrusted to her.

"I wish I could help you, Michael," she whispered. "But all I've got are rumors."

"Rumors?"

"Of a burial ground. Somewhere north of Tyler. That's all I've ever heard. We always thought somebody made it up. Nobody in town ever dreamed it was true."

He stood so close to her that she could smell the grass on his jeans and the faintest hint of fresh rain in his hair. There was another scent, too, uniquely Michael, uniquely male. It tugged at her, urged her to press herself closer. But the porch railing stood between them. A host of other barriers, some obvious and some still unnamed, stood between them, too.

"If he finds the burial ground, what will he do?" she questioned.

"Stop them from building. Keep them from desecrating the earth."

"Can he do that?" Renata asked. "I mean, is there a legal precedent for that sort of thing?"

"There's a precedent, in fact there's a federal law now, but that doesn't mean it's a sure thing," Michael told her. "It would be a lengthy court battle involving the whole tribe. I doubt he'd live to see it through."

She squeezed his fingers, hating to see his fear for the frail old man. Still, she understood the true battle Michael was waging. It was inevitable that Grand Feather would die someday. At his age, someday soon. Michael hadn't yet accepted that fact emotionally. The real question was, would he pick up the banner when it fell?

Renata wasn't certain that Michael knew the answer yet, but tonight, as she studied the torment in his beautiful brown eyes, she herself was sure what he would do. "You'd carry on the fight for him, wouldn't you?"

At first he didn't answer. He didn't move. Then, very slowly, he nodded.

"I don't want to. I don't want to do half the things he makes me do. But when he looks at me and says, '*Hitkunkay,* you are still Winnebago,' I can't seem to argue."

It was an awesome moment, one Renata feared would change Michael's life. But she didn't think it was her place to say so. It was risky to even stroke his tantalizing hand.

Wanting to keep him talking, Renata asked, "What does *hitkunkay* mean?"

"It means 'grandson' in Winnebago. Or rather, it means 'son of my son.' We have separate words for all kinds of relationships that are just lumped together or ignored in English." As his eyes met Renata's once more, Michael seemed to be asking if she wanted to hear more about his people. He must have read the interest on her face, because he went on talking. "We even have separate rules about how we're supposed to relate to different kinds of relatives—sisters, brothers, mothers-in-law, that sort of thing. At least, we used to. Nobody pays that much attention to them anymore. But the one thing that hasn't changed is our respect for our old people." Again sadness took over his voice. "It's funny that as a teenager, I was perfectly willing to defy my teachers, but I never lashed out at Grand Feather."

Cautiously, Renata asked, "You said he raised you, Michael. What happened to your parents?"

He took a deep breath. "My father served in Germany in

World War II. It changed him, Grand Feather says. He turned white. When he came back, he married my mother, who'd gone to a white boarding school and was turning white herself. Then Dad left Wisconsin to go into business in California with a white guy he'd met in the army." He revealed this information the way Renata would have confessed to having an ax murderer in the family tree. "When I was about a year old, my mother died of some sort of complication in early pregnancy. At first I thought she might have had trouble stemming from an abortion, but I'd rather think it was something like an ectopic pregnancy." His eyes flicked down to Renata's. "We don't believe in abortion."

"We?"

"Indians in general. Not in the twentieth century. We've got to cherish every one of our babies, nurture every chance to hang on to our people." Abruptly he stopped. "I just know she wouldn't have done it, Renata. She hadn't turned that white. She was still writing to her parents, planning to come home."

"For a visit, you mean? Or without your father?"

"Neither. I mean…" He ran a hand through his thick black hair. "Renata, Indians don't look at going away from home to work as *moving* anywhere. It's like, well, hunting for game. You go out, you find food for your family, you bring it home. In the 1990s, or the 1950s, for that matter, a person goes out hunting work, whatever type, to take care of his family. But sooner or later he comes home. He never intends to stay anywhere else forever."

Renata wondered if Michael had gone to work in Sugar Creek with the same point of view. It wasn't all that far from the Dells, and he returned there fairly often. Did he, too, intend to return to his grandfather's home one day?

"But after my mother died, my father brought me back here. My grandmother was still alive then. It made sense to everyone that I should be with her. In those days fathers didn't usually raise babies alone. My grandfather tried to convince my father to come home to live, too, but he wouldn't have any of it."

He paused, and when he spoke again, his tone was bitter. "Two years later he married a white woman, his partner's sister. I met her once. Her husband had been killed in the war, and she had four children. My father adopted them." His tone grew very low. "Even after my grandmother died, when I was three, he didn't come back for me."

Renata could hardly suppress her need to put her arms around him. Michael was a man now, not a child, but the rejection of his youth—of his heritage—was a grief she knew would always wound him.

Suddenly he straightened and glanced down at her hand. He'd been gripping it tightly for a good five minutes, but now he seemed surprised to see their fingers looped together.

Somewhat sheepishly he released her, then half turned away. In the moonlight his profile looked sharp and sad and unbearably virile. It hurt Renata to see his pain. What she felt for him was part compassion, part desire and part rising respect. But she hadn't a clue what Michael truly felt for her, let alone what he'd be feeling in the morning.

"Anyway, the point is that from the time I was a tiny thing, Grand Feather raised me on his own," Michael informed her, his tone almost businesslike now. "He wouldn't let any of his female relatives take me, though several of them were willing. When my father married a white woman and turned his back on me, my grandfather said he had lost a son the same as if he'd been killed overseas. I had been sent to replace him."

"Replace him?"

He thrust both hands in his pockets, increasing the distance between them. His eyes were trained on the oak tree that had sheltered his grandfather that morning, but Renata had the feeling his thoughts were far away. "It's another Winnebago tradition, Renata. In the old days, when a mother or father lost a child and saw another child who looked somewhat similar, they believed it was their child in another form. Another life. They could ask the parents for that child and the child would be handed over. It was a form of adoption."

"Adoption!" Renata was appalled. "That's fine for an orphan, but what about a child who has parents who love him? If I had a baby, I wouldn't give it up to anyone!"

Michael smiled sadly. "Neither would I, but you have to understand that things were different then. Everybody lived, well, more communally. The original parents still saw their child a great deal, and sometimes he even ended up living with them. It just meant the little one had another set of loving parents." When Renata didn't look convinced, he added, "In the old days, a woman's sisters all referred to her children as 'son' or 'daughter' just as she did to her own. The Winnebago vision of family is more…" he struggled for the right word "…expansive than the white one. There's room for everyone."

Renata smiled at him and was rewarded with one of his beautiful grins. After the last dark half hour, she was thrilled that he was feeling better again, even though losing their brief moment of intimacy was the price she'd had to pay for it. Determined to cheer him up, she teased, "Then there ought to be room for a Winnebago boy who went to college and made good."

To her astonishment, Michael's smile began to fade. Why did she keep making mistakes with this man? Was it really so hard to relate to him?

"There's a place for me, Renata," he confessed, "but at times it's sort of a chilly one."

Renata knew there was a lot more he could have said, but the tight set of his mouth told her the subject was closed. In fact, the whole episode on the porch—the sharing, the touching, the meeting of hearts—was suddenly no more than a memory.

"I'm going back to bed," said Michael, heading for the door.

He didn't wait to see if Renata followed him.

"I'm sorry I ran on like that last night," Michael told Renata the next morning while she served him scrambled eggs and toast. He'd had a terribly restless night, both before and after their talk on the porch, and he was almost more tired than he'd been the day before. Worse yet, he knew he'd shared some private things, much the way a drunk confides in a bartender, and he hoped Renata didn't think that meant he viewed her as anyone special.

Give it up, Youngthunder, he chastised himself as he recognized the lie for what it was. *You would never have shared those thoughts with anybody else. You're lucky that the whole scene didn't get out of hand.*

All in all, it seemed like a miracle that he'd made it through the night without kissing her...or ending up in her bed. But he'd survived somehow, and now all he had to do was get through the next few minutes without tipping his hand.

"I don't usually talk about...well, family things," he tried to explain. "It's just that Grand Feather was on my mind last night and—"

"Michael, you don't have to explain. I understand. I'm worried about him, too."

After that the conversation seemed to die, and fresh tension filled the small room. Michael knew that if he didn't fill the air with pointless chatter, he was going to find himself staring into those honest blue eyes again, and if he did, he would end up telling her the truth.

"Last night in the basement you said there was a project you wanted me to help you with. What did you mean?"

She glanced up uncomfortably. "It's kind of complicated, Michael. Maybe some other time..."

Michael glanced at his watch. "The ground breaking doesn't start for two more hours. We've got plenty of time." Secretly he hoped it was a *very* complex story.

But it wasn't. In less than five minutes she'd explained Alyssa Baron's plans for a crafts fair to raise funds for the about-to-be-condemned town library. He wasn't surprised to hear that Renata had been recruited to serve on the committee. The only thing that took him off guard was her proposed Native American theme.

"It just seemed to me that it would be interesting to feature Indian arts and crafts for a change," she explained. "I know some Indian artists in Milwaukee who might be able to help me contact other professional painters and sculptors who work with Native themes, but I don't know anybody involved in traditional crafts. Beadwork, barkwork, quill embroidery, that sort of thing. I was hoping I might be able to get some names or ideas from you.''

Michael studied her lovely face for a long, quiet moment, trying to imagine her long hair in feathered braids. Somehow he couldn't put the blond color and the feathers in the same mental picture. Still, he managed to say, ''There is an old woman in Wisconsin Dells named Lydia Good Heart who teaches the young girls how to tan leather and do beadwork. She is truly gifted in her craft. She lived next door to me when I was small and is…like family.''

''You mean she's part of your clan?''

Emphatically, he shook his head. ''No, she's Bear Clan. Traditionally the policemen for the whole tribe. It's an important clan but…'' he paused, feeling a curious mixture of apology and pride ''…all the clans are secondary to Thunderbird.''

''Thunderbird?''

Uncomfortably his eyes met hers. ''My clan, Renata. My grandfather's clan. It's more than a…cluster of distant kin. It's sort of a legacy.'' He swallowed hard. ''It's the reason he's fighting this burial ground thing so hard. Traditionally, it's our obligation to solve problems that affect the whole tribe.''

''I see,'' said Renata. But he could tell she didn't really see at all.

Uneasily Michael turned the conversation back to his elderly friend. ''Lydia is a traditional woman and she's wary of outsiders. She may seem a little cool to you at first, but if you tell her that Thunder Eagle sent you, she'll welcome you with open arms.''

''Thunder Eagle?'' Renata asked, her tone curious but guarded. ''Is that your grandfather's real name?''

Slowly he shook his head. As a rule he didn't share his tribal name with whites—they either found it grandiose or ridiculous—and he already regretted mentioning it to Renata. It was too personal to share with a stranger. And he desperately wanted to believe she was still exactly that.

"No, Renata. It's my tribal name, chosen with reference to my clan." He fought a sudden urge to explain why he was so proud to belong to Thunderbird Clan and, ironically, so ashamed to admit it. Unable to overrule his need to share himself with this white woman who, despite his rejection, kept reaching out with a silent heart, he blurted, "I have a business card in my wallet that says I'm Michael Youngthunder, manager of the Sugar Creek retail branch of Katayama Computers. Next to it I've got a card that says I'm a registered tribal member of the Winnebago nation." He swallowed hard and looked away. "The first card is the reason my cousins call me whenever there's a problem with my grandfather. It's also why they call me a half-breed." At last his eyes met hers, his heart willing her to understand why he had to keep her at arm's length.

"The second card is the reason why the woman I planned to marry tossed in the towel three weeks before our wedding day, Renata. She wanted to take home the man who managed Katayama Computers to meet her mother." He swallowed hard against the lingering bitterness. "She wouldn't take home the one whose grandfather still wore feathers and braids."

"ARE YOU ALL RIGHT, Alyssa?" Anna Kelsey asked as they waited for the ceremony to begin. Her kind, round face wrinkled with concern. "I know this ground breaking is supposed to be a grand affair, but it's got to be hard on you."

Alyssa gave her friend a tight smile. Anna was right, of course. This beautiful old lodge, replete with the joys and pains of Alyssa's childhood and Cliff and Liza's courtship, no longer belonged to the Ingalls clan. It had passed on to a new owner, the hometown boy from the wrong side of the tracks who'd made good.

The boy who had once passionately loved Alyssa.

In some ways Alyssa was immensely proud of Edward. She'd always told her father that he'd be a man to be reckoned

with someone. But when push came to shove, she hadn't
proved to Edward that she'd believed it.

She wasn't sure that he cared that she believed it now.

Together she and Anna watched the preliminary festivities
of the morning. Fortunately, she had no duties here today except those of unofficial cheerleader. No one was likely to comment on her presence, but her absence would have definitely
raised a few eyebrows. Everybody knew how she'd once felt
about Edward; everybody knew that their breakup thirty years
ago was the reason he'd left town. It was a cruel irony that his
triumphal homecoming involved taking over her father's lodge,
the scene of her family's greatest joys and despairs.

But today the joys would all be Edward's, and the despair
of the past would be set aside.

Everybody who was anybody in Tyler had shown up today.
For that matter, the grounds were full of total strangers, too.
Some of them, sleekly suited, looked like business associates
of Edward's. Some probably were from the press. The handsome, bronze-complexioned young man with Renata Meyer
must have been one of her friends from Milwaukee. Nobody
in Tyler let his hair grow to that length. The hippies were long
gone and the punk crowd was into short hair in different colors;
none of them would have worn a suit while sporting that flowing mane.

Anna's nephew, Brick Bauer, was also skirting the crowd.
He was wearing his uniform, which meant he was keeping an
eye on things as a cop as well as enjoying the local affair. She
loved Brick dearly, but ever since the new, hard-nosed female
captain had come to town—not to mention married him—
Alyssa had kept her distance from him. In the past Brick had
always protected any member of her family who was in trouble.
But Karen, his wife, was an outsider, one who believed that
Judson had somehow been involved in his wife's—Alyssa's
mother's—death. Alyssa was sure that was impossible, but she
wasn't sure her dad could prove it. She desperately hoped he
wouldn't have to.

"Let's move over that way," Anna suggested. "I want to ask Brick something."

Alyssa followed her friend, but before they reached Brick, he'd started off in another direction. By the time they caught up with him he was standing next to Renata, talking to her friend.

Renata didn't look quite like herself today. Of course, it was always hard to tell with Renata. No matter how formal the occasion, she always carried a knapsack, big enough for a sketch pad, instead of a purse, and like Liza, she dressed to suit herself. Though her clothes tended to be more avant-garde than risqué, Alyssa often shook her head at some of Renata's fashion choices. Today she was wearing a flaming orange jumpsuit that should have been all wrong for her coloring but somehow made her look dashing and beautiful. Her hair was long and loose, as usual. The light wind brushed it freely, causing a few blond strands to mix with her friend's dark mane.

Alyssa forgot about Renata and Brick the minute the ceremony got under way. She didn't really hear her father's words as he told the history of the lodge or gave Edward the key to the city. Her gaze was on Edward, dressed in an impeccably cut suit, his eyes dark and proud as ever. Oh, he'd aged some since high school, but the changes only made him seem more debonair. Alyssa stifled the memory of the first time he'd publicly claimed Timberlake Lodge. It had been at Christmas, when the combination of matchmaking friends and mistletoe had forced him to kiss her. It was not a memory she wanted to linger over, but neither was it one she could banish.

"I'm so proud of him, Alyssa!" Anna whispered in her ear. "I wish Johnny could be here to see this." Anna's husband, Edward's best friend, had planned to come to the ceremony, but had been held up at the last minute by an emergency at Ingalls Farm and Machinery. It seemed, Anna had lamented, that that was the story of his life.

But as soon as Edward began to speak, Alyssa forgot about Anna, about Johnny, about everything but him.

"This lodge has always had a special place in my memory,"

he started graciously. "My father was employed at Timberlake for many years, so this was my home, too. I can't tell you that it was always my dream to own this lodge, but I feel I've come full circle today."

Everybody clapped with more enthusiasm than was absolutely necessary.

"As most of you know, massive renovations were already under way when I bought the lodge, thanks to Liza Forrester. But we at Addison don't do anything small if we can help it, so we decided to expand the lodge to meet the high standards of resort accommodations in this country today. When we break ground—"

He stopped in midsentence as an eerie war whoop echoed across the spacious grounds. Everybody turned toward the noise. Edward stared disbelievingly across the compound at the scrawny brown horse charging his way.

It was adorned not with saddle or bridle but with feathers in its mane and tail. Red paint had been ritually painted on its side. On its back perched a leathery old man dressed in buckskin and beads, wobbling so precariously that Alyssa was afraid he'd fall off before he got halfway to Edward. Feathers and strips of rawhide hung from his long, braided hair. He was carrying a lance and a shield.

"Oh, my God," whispered Renata's friend.

"Oh, Michael," said Renata.

A few people let out startled gasps, but everybody else stood rooted to the ground, absolutely silent as the quavery, high-pitched war whoops echoed across the lake and back again.

The horse pulled up in front of Edward. The old man hurled the lance toward the ground. It hit the shovel and fell over harmlessly. The gesture certainly didn't have the dramatic impact of similar scenes Alyssa remembered from the movies.

The old man began an impassioned speech to Edward, but Alyssa couldn't understand a word of it. She understood the gestures though—once to the east, once to the west, once north toward the lodge and south to the lake. At the end the old man thumped his fist on his chest, rattling the bone-and-bead breast-plate.

"Oh, my God," Renata's young man murmured again.

This time Brick laid a hand on his shoulder. "Michael, if you think you can move him faster than you did yesterday, I'll give you first crack at it. But we've got a big crowd here—outsiders who aren't going to understand. For his sake as well as Edward's, we've got to get him out of here right away."

Slowly, very slowly, the young man shook his head. His neck and shoulders grew rigid with tension. "You do what you have to do, Lieutenant Bauer. I can't go down there and throw down a lance beside him, but I'll be damned if I'll raise my voice against a Winnebago warrior." His voice was low and strained. "Don't you understand? All he's got left is his pride."

Abruptly he turned and marched past Alyssa to the parking lot, with Renata scrambling to keep up with him. Alyssa didn't know the young man and couldn't guess just how things stood between him and Renata, but she could hardly bear the thought of her own son wrestling with the anguish she saw in his eyes.

CHAPTER FIVE

THE NEXT FEW HOURS were terrible for Renata, and she could only begin to imagine what they were like for Michael. They waited by the police cruiser until Brick literally took the reins out of Grand Feather's hands—gently but firmly—and led the scrawny brown horse back to the black-and-white car. Brick's voice was low as he spoke to Grand Feather, but he was all policeman now.

"You have violated a number of laws here this morning, Mr. Youngthunder," he said firmly. "You trespassed and you disrupted a public event. You may have stolen this horse, and you threatened a man with a weapon in front of dozens of witnesses. I'm going to have to check you out for sobriety and—"

"I am a warrior, not a drinker," the old man said belligerently, his voice crackling like November leaves. "I did not do something rash because I could not think straight. I had a warrior's job to do, and I did it." A heavy cough rattled his frail body. "Do you think you can shame me with white men's laws? The shame belongs to my grandson. He is so white he does not even see the task that lies ahead of him."

Michael's lips twisted in inner pain that he could not conceal. Renata hadn't a clue what she could do for him.

About all she could do was take the horse's reins from Brick. Quickly she checked over the painted gelding, ascertaining that it was tired but uninjured. To her relief, it wasn't a horse she recognized. While there was still a chance that it belonged to one of her neighbors, someone who might have bought a new horse in recent years, she thought it was also possible that

Grand Feather might have ridden all the way from Wisconsin Dells, in which case the horse might not have been stolen.

"Does your grandfather own a horse?" she asked Michael.

He shook his head. "No, but there are plenty of Winnebago horses he could have borrowed with the owner's blessing."

Grand Feather turned on him. "Which is more than I could have expected from you!" He suddenly switched to Winnebago, his tone furious and scathing. Michael answered in similar tones, but Renata couldn't follow any of it.

At last he turned to Brick and recapped the conversation. "I believe the horse belongs to one of my cousins. He didn't ask permission for it ahead of time, but that's only because he knows she would have called me. There's no question of rustling." His lips tightened as he explained, "My grandfather says he rode the horse all the way here and sees no reason not to ride it home."

"I do not need you to speak for me!" the old man barked. "I would have listened if you had prepared yourself to be a warrior and ridden here beside me. But all I saw when I arrived was my grandson in his white clothes with his white friends!" He glared at Renata, then studied Michael's face again. "Did you learn nothing from your last white woman? Could you really be foolish enough to shame your clan with one again?"

He said the words as though Michael had taken up with a prostitute or a drug dealer, and his bitterness made Renata feel unclean. She'd never experienced racial prejudice before. As a white person, she hadn't really thought about being on the receiving end of it, especially since she'd never done anything to anybody of another race to make them feel anything but friendly toward her. It was an eerie, miserable sensation that she felt hopeless to confront.

"As soon as the police are done with you, I'm taking you home," Michael stated. "And then I'm going to call a lawyer to see what we need to do to protect you from yourself if Edward Wocheck presses charges. If you keep this up I'm going to have you declared incompetent!"

For a moment the old man did not speak. He looked as

though Michael had slapped him in the face. Then he said slowly, "You will never do this, *hitkunkay*."

Renata remembered the word for "son of my son" that Michael had mentioned was always his undoing; she recalled last night's anguish on his virile face. She saw the same wave of feelings now—love, gratitude, defeat.

At last Michael turned back to Brick, his tone unsteady, his frustration clear. "Do you need to take him to the station, Lieutenant?"

"Yes, I'm afraid I do. At least until the festivities here are over and we get this all straightened out."

Michael looked sick, but his grandfather lifted his chin defiantly. Mercifully, the old man did not speak again.

Renata jumped into the breach, volunteering to take the horse back to her place until somebody was ready to collect it, even if it took a couple of days. This comment brought a glare from Grand Feather, a brisk "Thanks, Renata" from Brick and a humble nod from Michael.

It was, in fact, the last time Michael Youngthunder acknowledged her. When Brick tucked the old man into his police cruiser, Michael headed back to his own car. Renata expected him to turn around, to say goodbye or thanks or "I'll see you later," but he didn't even glance at her before he drove away.

IT WAS NEARLY NOON before Michael left the police station with his grandfather, and this time he didn't leave the old man in the Dells. "You are coming to stay with me for a while," he ordered, his voice dark with unspent thunder. Despite his grandfather's sassiness in front of strangers, the old one offered no protest now that they were alone. But neither did he come in and help Michael pack his things once they reached Grand Feather's shack. Instead he remained in stony silence in the BMW.

Michael picked up the clothes Renata had loaned to his grandfather and added them to those she'd lent to him, which were still in the trunk of his car. Then he drove to the home of his cousin, the one who owned the horse, and left the clothes and a healthy wad of cash. Sarah was several years older than Michael and he was not especially close to her; in fact, they'd seen each other only at a few family gatherings since Michael had moved to Sugar Creek. But despite his black-sheep status with the more traditional members of the family, he knew that his cousin would follow his instructions to the letter. When it came to Grand Feather, Michael was the undisputed chief of this branch of the clan.

"You'll find your horse at a farm run by a woman who has been very good to our grandfather," he told Sarah, using the Winnebago term for "our" that referred to the Thunderbird Clan. "The clothes should be washed and returned when you go to collect the horse. Take her something to eat, something special. Tell her we will always be grateful for her help in this awkward family matter." Then he took a moment to sketch a map showing how to get to Lydia Good Heart's house. "Give this to her also, and remind her that she must tell Lydia she comes with the blessing of Thunder Eagle."

Sarah asked a few questions about Grand Feather's health, then took a minute to say goodbye to the old man. Before Michael climbed back into the car, she said to him sotto voce, "He is too old to survive away from his people, Michael. Do not try to pen him up in Sugar Creek."

"He's too old to live alone," he snapped back. "Unless he moves in with one of you, I don't think he should keep on living here."

"If you came back, we would have no problems," she answered.

He didn't bother to point out that the problems would all be his.

They drove in silence to Sugar Creek. Michael had missed another day of work, and though his assistant manager, plucky Maralys Johnson, would keep things running fine in his absence, he didn't want to press his luck. So far his regional supervisor, based in Chicago, hadn't paid a great deal of attention to his ancestry or to his recent "family sick leave," and he intended to keep it that way.

But that was not to be. As Grand Feather walked stonily into Michael's apartment and planted himself in the recliner chair, Michael stuck two packages of fettuccine Alfredo in the microwave and turned on the news. Within five minutes the announcer was talking about a tiny Wisconsin town where an Indian attack had been reported for the first time in more than a hundred years.

Although the reporter made light of the whole event, he did explain the history of the land and treaties, and the local legends about the Winnebago burial ground. Some cameraman, already in place for the ground breaking, had captured shots of Grand Feather throwing his war lance and Michael fleeing the scene. The last picture was one of Renata in her flaming-orange jumpsuit, long hair streaming as she rode the painted brown pony bareback away from the lodge.

Michael vowed he would not look at her beautiful face, but he could not look away. He'd sent her presents and a tribal display of gratitude, but he knew what she really longed for was a phone call or a handwritten note from him that just said thanks.

But he knew it wouldn't stop at that. He'd escaped from her in the nick of time, and if he made any attempt to see her again, he couldn't expect to escape unscathed. All last night they'd been hovering on the brink of a precipice, and with the tiniest shove, he knew he'd fall over the edge.

When Michael turned back to his grandfather, he found the old man grinning ear to ear. He looked absolutely delighted with the broadcast. Suddenly Michael understood the old one's intention. Michael had thought he'd been acting like a Winnebago—avenging the past—but his motivation had been closer to white tradition. He wanted to get his cause on the evening news! And he'd achieved his objective admirably.

"Are you happy now?" Michael snarled. "The whole damn state knows what you've done!"

"Now the state will pay more attention to our claims of a burial site," Grand Feather answered stoutly. "Now maybe something will be done."

"I'll tell you what will be done!" Michael snapped, feeling furious and impotent at the same time. "I'll go to work tomorrow and spend the whole day listening to redskin jokes from Maralys and answering to 'chief' from everybody else. And I'll tell you, Grand Feather, I had enough of that when I was young."

"It is time for you to remember who your people are, *hit-kunkay*," Grand Feather answered unsympathetically. "You sat down in that white woman's kitchen yesterday as though you belonged there. Have you forgotten everything I taught you?"

Michael snapped off the television. "Of course not."

"You do not pray as a Winnebago. You do not sing. You do not even dance, Thunder Eagle."

"I can't dance anymore," Michael said lamely, thrusting away the memory of the years when he'd danced the old way in feathers and beads for hours and hours nearly every summer night. "You've got to be fifteen to keep that up."

"You are only thirty-seven, Michael! A child yet. You have lost the privilege of dancing at our sacred ceremonials—for now—but you could still dance at a tourist powwow. It would be a start." His voice grew strong as he added proudly, "You once won all the prize money and everyone was jealous of you. Nobody could fancy-dance better than you."

"I needed the prize money to get through school."

"Ha! You could have found another way to earn it. You chose to go the way of your people."

"And you know how that turned out." It was an acerbic reference to the trail Michael had followed until he'd come to a rock—a rock that splits every adolescent's road into two paths, one of reality and one of ideals.

"You have been no happier since you were whiteman-ized."

Pushing away the tug of memories, Michael said, "Look, Grand Feather, this is a new world, a different one than you grew up in. I'm not turning my back on the old ways. I still respect what they mean to you. I'm just trying to find a way that works for me."

The old man harrumphed, then he said tightly, "Your hair is almost long enough to braid again. At least a feather—"

"I can't wear feathers at work."

"You are not working now."

"Only because of you! If you keep this up I'll be out of a job! Now I want your solemn promise—" he switched to Winnebago to make sure his grandfather took it as a vow "—that you won't leave this apartment while I'm gone tomorrow."

His grandfather glared at him. "I want your solemn promise that you will someday dance again."

Michael shook his head. The hair…well, it was a start. A token statement, no more. After Sheila had left him three years ago, he'd felt the old tug again, a tug he couldn't really explain, and he'd let his hair start to grow. Until recently he'd kept getting it shaped professionally, so it had only looked fashionably—and then unfashionably—long. If he'd dressed like Renata, people might have mistaken him for a leftover hippie. With his complexion, sharp features and crisp-cut suits, however, the hair had now become a mute declaration of his proud heritage.

"It's too late for me to dance," he said harshly. "I can no longer hear the beat of the drum." The drum was sacred, the heart of his people, and he knew that his bald statement wounded his grandfather to the core. Yet his blunt pronouncement was true. It *must* be true. Why else, after all he'd been through, would his mind be so full of a white woman's face?

RENATA REACHED Wisconsin Dells around three o'clock on Wednesday afternoon and found Lydia Good Heart's house within twenty minutes. It was hidden among some willow trees on a back road that had no name, at least no name that Renata saw posted. Michael's map had been accurate, but the irregular landscape prevented it from being precise.

She hesitated once she turned off the engine of her truck. She felt awkward going to a traditional Indian's house without an invitation, and she wished she could have called or written first. Most of all, she wished Michael had come with her.

And not just to make her visit with Lydia easier.

Her anguish had not abated in the least since she'd received his message, delivered by the cousin who'd come with her husband to collect the scrawny horse. The woman had delivered the map, half a dozen baskets full of sweet, homegrown berries and a stack of Renata's grandpa's clothes, washed and neatly folded. She had been the soul of courtesy, stressing the entire family's gratitude for everything Renata had done. She had emphasized their willingness to repay Renata's kindness if there was any way they ever could. Although Renata suspected it was just Winnebago custom that caused the woman to repeatedly refer to Michael as "my cousin" instead of using his name, the habit added to Renata's sensation that Michael had deliberately distanced himself from her.

He'd done everything in his power to express proper gratitude without exuding the tiniest bit of intimate man-woman warmth. He was a bright and sensitive man, so she found it hard to believe his omission was an accident. In the middle of a tense, hot night, he'd confided, with quiet words and soft, erotic touches, a well of unspoken feelings. He had come a breath away from kissing her. She'd been certain he had fantasized about sharing her bed.

Renata could not believe she had imagined all they'd shared. But in hindsight, she realized that Michael had never really touched her as a lover, never spoken a lover's words. He had scrupulously said nothing he'd have to take back and had done nothing he had to apologize for. In short, he'd made her no promises she could expect him to keep. He'd given her no reason to hope she might ever see him again.

But he had given her his tribal name as an entrée into Lydia Good Heart's house. Despite everything that had happened— perhaps because of it—Renata was more excited than ever about using Indian art as a theme for the crafts fair. Alyssa had told her Grand Feather had provided Tyler with the kind of publicity that would encourage tourists to flock in and buy Indian crafts. In hindsight, the town's imagination was inspired by Grand Feather's brave defiance, which struck Renata as odd, because she thought most of the people at the ground-breaking ceremony had been rather intimidated by his display.

Giving herself a mental shake, Renata parked the car and started to walk up to the little house. It was not as dreary as Michael's description of his grandfather's shack, but it was hardly a lakeside condo, either. Lydia's place was about the size of a studio apartment, with the pipe of a wood stove poking up from the back. Wildflowers encircled the place in their own untamed pattern, yet they looked so healthy that Renata had the feeling they'd been cultivated. Surely somebody made sure that water and fertilizer found their way into the soil.

She tried to step around the petaled faces as she approached the door, knocking in a firm but unaggressive manner.

At once she heard the sound of a chair creaking, but it was a long time before the heavy footsteps reached the front of the house. When the door edged open, all Renata could see was an eye through the crack.

"I'm looking for Lydia Good Heart," she said, suddenly wondering if Michael's old friend spoke English. "Is this the right house?"

The door opened fractionally, and an old woman's quavery voice answered, "This is Good Heart house."

Renata swallowed hard, wishing she could at least see a face in the dark interior. She had only one more chance. "I'm Renata Meyer. Michael Youngthunder sent me."

The door opened an inch or two more. Suspiciously, the woman asked, "What do you want with Michael?"

Now that's a loaded question, Renata thought to herself. But the tone of the woman's voice indicated that she thought Renata might be a reporter or a cop, either of which, she gathered, would get precious little information. Especially if it might be damaging to Michael.

She wanted to say, "I'm a friend of Michael's," but she wasn't sure that was accurate. She could have said, "I want to be his lover," but she knew that wasn't wise. After a moment she remembered what Michael himself had told her to say. "Thunder Eagle said you were like family to him."

Like magic, the door swung open. The woman said a long, undecipherable word that sounded as though it might be a name—Michael's Indian name?—but Renata couldn't reproduce so much as a syllable. She still couldn't see the woman's face as she took hold of her arm and cheerfully tugged her inside.

"Michael does not tell his tribal name to strangers," Lydia explained. "Forgive me for being slow to welcome you. After all the trouble in Tyler, there have been nosy reporters asking questions about both of them."

Renata knew she meant Michael and his grandfather, and she ached as she thought of the trouble they'd been through. "I last saw Michael on Wednesday, when he left the horse with me," she said. "Has anything else happened since then?"

Lydia shook her head, but the look in her eyes revealed that she knew about the horse and the white woman who'd briefly taken charge of it. "Michael took the old one away with him. We are not sure when he will be back. Michael has always wanted him to live with him. He does not want him to stay alone in an old shack."

Renata wasn't sure what to say to that. She didn't think she'd want one of her relatives living in this tiny house, either, but at least it was neat and clean. A true homemaker obviously lived here. Renata had the feeling that Grand Feather's place was something else again.

She tried to remember what Michael had said about Lydia, but she couldn't recall very many details. He'd described her as one of the few Winnebagos left who remembered things almost as keenly as his grandfather did. She'd found a way to bring in some white man's money to support herself, but according to Michael, she still honored the old Winnebago ways.

"Michael said you were very special to him," Renata finally said, figuring that said it all.

Lydia seemed to understand. "He is a special boy, that one. He just does not know who he is yet."

It seemed like an odd comment to make to a stranger, yet Renata thought it was a perspective that had some merit. Michael reminded her of a man she'd seen in a science fiction movie once, painted white down one side of his face and black down the other. Michael was just as cleanly split between two cultures, and he didn't seem to know how to live with both of them in the same skin.

"I think he's very special, too," Renata answered, not sure what else to say.

By now her eyes were adjusting to the light, and she saw that Lydia Good Heart was a large woman wearing a calico camp shirt and a denim skirt that hung loosely to her calves. She wore long beaded earrings and a bone-and-bead choker with a feather in the center. Not a trace of makeup brightened her dark, wrinkled skin.

"Come, sit. Are you hungry?"

Renata shook her head. She was, truth to tell, too nervous to eat. She hoped she wouldn't offend the old woman by refusing the offer of food.

"Coffee, maybe?"

Renata didn't really want coffee, either, but she graciously said, "If you've already got some made."

Lydia gave her a warm smile and quickly crossed the room. She moved well for a woman of her size and age, though Renata really couldn't guess how old she was. She appeared younger than Grand Feather, but he looked about 130, so that was nothing to go on. Belatedly Renata realized that she'd never gotten around to asking Michael how many centuries his grandfather had been walking the earth.

As the old woman ushered Renata into the main room and urged her to sit in a mended straight-backed chair, she tried to decide how best to explain why she had come. Although she was proud to be supporting Indian art at the fair, she suddenly knew she couldn't ask this woman to donate part of her meager earnings to a white man's cause. Alyssa could charge admittance, or raise prices somewhere else. If Renata could get Lydia and some of her friends to provide authentic Winnebago work, that would have to be enough.

As her glance fell on a uniquely whittled stick with the

carved design of a bear, Renata said, "How interesting! My grandfather collected Indian artifacts like this." At the moment they were fresh in Renata's memory, since she'd pored through the box just this morning before she left Tyler, hoping for some inspiration for the paintings and pen-and-ink drawings she wanted to create for the fair. Grandpa's collection had some marvelous items: an exotically quill-embroidered moccasin, a half-petrified woven basket and a tiny baby's rattle in the shape of a war club.

Now Lydia said proudly, "This is Bear Clan stick. It is my duty to protect it for the whole clan."

Renata smiled uncertainly. Every time Michael had mentioned his own clan, she'd felt as though she were sinking into an abyss of cultural confusion. She wasn't at all sure that she wanted to start off her visit with Lydia the same way.

Lydia urged her to sit down, then disappeared for a moment and returned with coffee and homemade oatmeal cookies that tasted like the ones Renata's grandmother used to make. She talked about the look on Michael's face when, as a boy, he'd first seen a gopher. It was a small story, quickly told, but the tone of Lydia's voice while she told it revealed a great deal of affection for the small child she had known.

"We do not see him much these days. Always he is driving that fancy car and wearing those fancy clothes. You should have seen what he looked like when he was young!" Before Renata could ask what she meant by that, the old woman said, "But you did not come to hear me talk. There is some reason Michael sent you to me."

It was the best opening Renata could hope for. Leaning forward slightly, she said, "I am an artist. Michael told me that you are an artist also."

Lydia smiled almost shyly. "I am a beadworker. And I am not so bad with leather."

Renata grinned. "Michael said you know all the old ways and are teaching them to the young women. He said some of you might like another place to sell what you make."

Lydia pondered this a moment, then nodded slowly. "It would depend," she said.

Carefully Renata explained about the crafts fair, omitting Alyssa's original plan of taking a donation from each crafts person. She did mention the library, however, because Lydia was sure to find out it was a fund-raiser later and might think she'd withheld something.

When Renata was done the old woman said, "This is a white crafts fair. It is to raise money for a white building. Why did you come to me?"

Feeling flustered, Renata told her the truth. "After I met Michael and his grandfather, I gave some hard thought to where I live. All of Tyler used to be Winnebago land."

Lydia's lips tightened.

"When a friend on the committee mentioned that we should celebrate the history of the area, I thought it was only right to celebrate the Winnebago history as well. It seems to me that we—I mean, white people—forget about the Indian part of our history too often." When Lydia remained silent, she added truthfully, "Besides, I've always loved beadwork. When I was little I bought a beadmaking kit, and once I tried to tan a hide to make an Indian dress for myself." How desperately she'd wanted a genuine Indian dress! For a whole summer she'd struggled with the tanning process before she'd given up all hope. "It was a disaster. I decided that tanning was a job better left to the experts."

It seemed to be the right thing to say. Lydia's lips curved back into a grin. "It is an ancient art. People think they can do beadwork on white-man-tanned skin, but they can't even poke the needle through. You need to learn the Indian way to tan hide. Sometime I will show you."

"I'd love that, Lydia," Renata said sincerely. She didn't think anything would ever come of the courteous offer, but secretly she was thrilled at the very thought of learning this process at the feet of a traditional Winnebago. It would be like learning to paint from Picasso.

"I sell my work at the Winnebago outlet in Wisconsin

Dells,'' Lydia told her after they discussed the fair some more, ''but there are many of us here and we would like to sell much more. I would rather have a place to sell more beadwork all the time instead of just one weekend. But every little bit helps. I will talk to some other people and see what we can arrange to sell.''

''Thank you so much, Lydia,'' Renata said. She felt a curious sense of relief, so keen that she realized with surprise how much this mission had really meant to her. She wasn't sure why—after all, the fair could carry on without Winnebago crafts—but after everything she'd said to Michael, she didn't want to botch things up with the one contact he'd given her. She could have borne it if Lydia had said no, but not if she'd been upset when she'd sent Renata on her way.

''Would you like to see what I make? Then you can decide what sorts of things you want at the fair and how many of them.''

Renata nodded eagerly. Aside from the fair, she was itching to see genuine Winnebago beadwork herself. When the old woman stood and beckoned to her, Renata followed her to a small back room. In an instant she realized that she hadn't given nearly enough credence to Michael's claim that this woman was a genius in her craft.

In one corner of the little room was a hat rack draped with unfinished deer hides. Next to it a wooden table stood beneath a dozen tiny shelves built into the wall. Each little cubbyhole had a different color of beads inside it. It was a minute but flawlessly organized workshop, as impressive as any artist's loft. More impressive yet was the wall that sported the finished products—rows and rows of beaded necklaces, hangers that sported beaded buckskin. One shirt had a stunning pattern of red and gold beads that looked something like the one Grand Feather had worn on Thursday. Next to it was a white buckskin dress with exquisite turquoise beadwork and majestically draping fringe.

''Oh, Lydia, that's absolutely magnificent!'' Renata burst out without thinking. One finger stroked the incredibly supple leather and lingered on the beads. "I've always wanted a dress like that."

To her astonishment, the old woman took the dress off the hanger and held it out to her. "Take it with you. It is yours."

FOR NEARLY A WEEK, Michael left work for home each night afraid that he would not find his grandfather waiting for him. The old one had promised he would not sneak back to Tyler, and in the old days, his word would have been enough. But his behavior had been so odd lately that Michael wasn't sure what to expect.

Michael had made an appointment to talk to someone at an Indian support center in Milwaukee the next morning, so he figured his grandfather would stay put until then. There was a chance—not a very good one—that someone there could find some way to help him. Unless he could find proof of the burial ground other than his grandfather's urgent hope and hazy memory, he didn't think there was anything anyone could do. But as long as Grand Feather insisted on being laid to rest in the Winnebago burial ground near Tyler, Michael couldn't turn his back on the whole affair.

"Hey, chief," a sharp voice hailed him from across the store. "Where did you want that new load of printers put?"

Wearily he turned to Maralys Johnson, the superefficient young woman who'd been his right hand for the past six months. She was excellent at what she did. She knew as much about computers as he and was just as good with people, especially the men. She didn't have quite Michael's knack for business, though, so he knew she was no immediate threat to his own position. Normally he welcomed her efficiency and no-nonsense attitude. They got along well most of the time, but that was partly because their relationship was professional and superficial. Michael didn't believe in bringing personal joys or sorrows to a job.

Now, with reluctance, he said coolly, "Clear a space for them on the right-hand side of the back room. And if you want to keep working here, find another way to address your boss."

"Touch-y!" she squeaked.

Michael glared at her. "Maralys, I'm just not in the mood."

She took a step closer and studied him with care. In a rare serious moment, she said, "No offense, Youngthunder. I just like jerking your chain."

"I know you do. But this particular chain has been jerked so many times in the past week that I just—" he exhaled impatiently "—I just don't want to hear it anymore."

At the moment, he didn't want to hear about the store, either. He liked computers, liked dealing with the public, liked the heady sense of knowing he was very good at what he did. But after his grandfather's last lecture on tribal obligations, Michael was having trouble feeling good about his career. He made money, and he provided excellent service. But what did it really mean in the long run? What had he done for his people in the past fifteen years? Did it really matter that he wasn't helping them, as long as he wasn't hurting anyone?

His grandfather had decided to take advantage of his time in Sugar Creek to drill Michael on the four sacred Thunderbird songs. His performance at Renata's had reminded them both of how much he'd forgotten. Grand Feather had reminded him rather pointedly that when it came time for his own burial— not too far in the future—Michael would have to sing the songs and carry out the specific clan burial rituals. Michael didn't want to admit to his grandfather that he didn't remember all the details of the traditional procedure, but on the other hand, he didn't want his grandfather to die before he brushed up on it, either. No matter how he felt about his own heritage, there was no doubt about Grand Feather's feelings. Any grandson who loved him would bury him according to his own traditions.

And the one thing Michael had always been sure of in his shifting cultural world was that he dearly loved this old man.

Maralys, mercifully, was silent as Michael pondered his situation. He thought she was worrying about where to place the shipment when she surprised him by saying, "You've never said much about being Indian. I figured it didn't bother you."

"It doesn't bother me to *be* Indian," he retorted. "It bothers me that ignorant white people think my heritage is some kind of a joke.''

It was the most personal statement Michael had ever made to thorny Maralys, who was long on wisecracks and short on depth. To his surprise, she said with genuine regret, ''I'm sorry, Michael. Really. I never meant to hurt your feelings. I just never thought of it that way.''

He nodded, feeling somehow cleansed and foolish at the same time. ''Forget it. No big deal.''

As she gave him a tight smile and headed off toward the back room, Michael tried to remember what he'd said to Renata about how it felt to be an Indian. He knew he'd been prickly with her, too.

Her image was seldom far from his mind since he'd driven off and left her with the horse. It was done—there was no reason to see her again—and yet the temptation lingered.

No…it *burned*.

Tomorrow he'd be driving to Milwaukee, and unless Renata had some reason to stay in Tyler, she'd be back in Milwaukee.

RENATA WAS just stepping out of the shower when she heard the phone ring the next morning. She didn't know if it had been ringing for five seconds or five minutes, but she did know, as she grabbed a towel and rushed blindly toward the bedroom phone, that the air-conditioning in her Milwaukee apartment was set too high for someone who was stark naked, dripping wet and groping for the phone.

''Hello?'' she shouted breathlessly into the receiver, hoping she'd reached it in time.

There was a pause, as though somebody had forgotten why he was calling…or maybe given up.

''May I speak to Renata Meyer, please?'' said a deep male voice. It was an educated voice, a sexy voice, a voice that struck a deep chord of response in Renata even before she consciously placed it in her memory.

''This is she,'' she said formally, while another part of her mind cried out, *Michael, Michael, is that really you?*

"Hello, Renata," he continued with professional decorum. "This is Michael Youngthunder. We met last week when my grandfather, uh, planted himself on your front lawn."

Renata was astounded that he felt the need to identify himself. How many men did he think she met in an average week, anyway? Especially men who spent the night at her house, nearly kissed her and gave her their tribal names as a password that guaranteed a welcome into the homes of their friends? Guiltily she glanced at the beautiful beadwork dress hanging in her closet, knowing that the gift had been more a tribute to Michael than to her. Renata had been utterly unable to refuse it without offending Lydia, yet she felt guilty that she'd unwittingly erred in some aspect of Winnebago protocol, triggering the old woman's obligation to give it to her in the first place. The dress was magnificent, and Renata would be incredibly honored to wear it, but she knew it was worth a bundle and that she would have to find a diplomatic way to repay Lydia.

Maybe Michael was looking for such a way to repay her for her own gift; maybe Lydia's dress had been repayment along the same lines as the boxes of tasty berries. But secretly Renata hoped that Michael's call had nothing to do with meeting debts and obligations. She desperately hoped that he just wanted to see her again.

"Of course I remember you, Michael," she said as evenly as she could manage. "How is your grandfather?"

"As stubborn as ever, I'm afraid. He's been staying with me this week. I had my doctor check him over to make sure he hadn't hurt himself with his shenanigans. Apparently he's fit as a fiddle…for his age."

He didn't mention the possibility of senility and Renata didn't ask, but she had a hunch that it was a question Michael had privately posed to the doctor.

Somewhat awkwardly, Renata said, "I'm glad his exertions and exposure didn't have any serious aftereffects, Michael. I'm just sorry we couldn't find him sooner."

"So am I," he said quietly, his voice sounding a bit more

like the Michael she remembered. They had shared so much!
Why had he felt the need to identify himself to her, as though
he were some pesky stranger? "Renata," he continued after a
lengthy pause, "I've got an appointment in Milwaukee this
morning and I'd like to take you to lunch afterward if you're
free. It's the least I can do to pay you back for all you did for
us."

Renata wasn't sure what to say. The fact that Michael
wanted to see her at all was surprising…and a reason to rejoice.
But she didn't want to see him just to fulfill some sort of
obligation—Winnebago, male or otherwise—that he was feeling. She wanted him to want to see her, period. Because he
was a man drawn to her as a woman.

Apparently she hesitated too long, trying to come up with
the right way to express her feelings, because before she could
speak, Michael jumped back in.

"I know you're very busy, and if you can't spare the time
I certainly understand. I simply wanted to make the offer."

His sudden capitulation made Renata angry. "Does that
mean you were hoping I'd say no? That you could say you did
your duty even though you didn't have to see me?"

This time the silence stretched out even longer. Michael's
voice was quiet, deadly quiet, when he finally replied. "It is
the custom of my people to return a favor when the time is
right. Since I'm not likely to be around next time your family
is harvesting cranberries, I thought I'd take a leaf from the
white man's book. I did not mean to offend you by making
the offer. If I did, I apologize. I did not get the impression that
you'd be uncomfortable being seen in public with an Indian."

Stung, Renata snapped, "This hasn't a damn thing to do with
you being Indian, Michael. This is a man-woman thing. I just
want you to be straight with me. Are you or are you not asking
me out?"

When he didn't jump right in with an answer, Renata knew
she'd made a terrible mistake. Why, oh, why hadn't she been
able to still her tongue? The man was simply fulfilling his own

sense of obligation. She'd been surprised that he'd called her in the first place. Now she was certain he'd never call her again.

In a softer voice, Renata said, "Michael, I'm sorry. I didn't mean to snap at you. The truth is, I don't want you to ask me out because you think you owe me a favor. I want you to ask because…you'd really like to see me again."

The silence was truly awesome now. Renata knew that a lot of Caucasian guys would be put off by such a blunt confession. She had no idea what to expect from this very educated Indian.

But she knew what she wanted, and suddenly she knew that she couldn't bear to have anything less. All the banked feelings she'd ever felt for Michael had flared the instant she'd heard his voice. She couldn't see him as a casual acquaintance. She couldn't even enjoy him as a friend. What she felt for Michael was keen, urgent…and frightening. If he wasn't interested in pursuing a romantic relationship with her, she just couldn't bear to see him again.

At last he said huskily, "Renata, maybe I…maybe I did ask you out sort of as a date. I probably could have found another way to repay your kindness to my grandfather. But now that you put it so…" he struggled for a discreet word "…directly, I feel obliged to give you a direct answer back." He paused again. He cleared his throat. He exhaled deeply. "I thought I made my feelings about this sort of thing clear to you in Tyler. I'm sorry, Renata, but I don't date white women anymore. Nothing personal."

"How can it not be personal?" she replied sharply, feeling as though he'd aimed a karate chop at her solar plexus. "I'm not just a generic white woman, Michael, any more than you're a generic Indian. I'm a person, I'm Renata Meyer, and I thought I was…becoming your friend."

"I'm sorry," he said lamely. Frustration radiated in his deep voice. "I…I do feel friendly toward you. If that's all I felt, we could be friends. Under the circumstances—" she heard him swallow a harsh breath "—I just don't think it's a good idea."

"What circumstances?" she pressed, angry and hurt and hopeful all at the same time.

"Renata, you know what I mean."

"I'm white. I don't know anything about you, remember?"

"You know too damn much!" he flared. "I never meant to tell you all the things I did. Everything was odd about the time I spent in Tyler. You know that. It doesn't change the truth of the matter. I don't want to get tangled up with a white woman. I don't need that kind of trouble ever again."

What kind of an answer could she offer to that? Before she'd met the Youngthunders, she'd never encountered that sort of prejudice, never felt slapped in the face not by her behavior or her income or the way she dressed, but simply by her race. Struggling for dignity, she said, "I've paid dearly for getting involved with some of the men I've known, but I haven't sworn off the male sex for life."

"This is different."

"No, it's not. It's judging somebody by something that has nothing to do with him or her. If I told you I wouldn't date you because you were an Indian, you'd call me a bigot. What do you think that makes you?"

He swore under his breath. "Please, Renata, don't make this any harder than it has to be. I don't hate anybody. I don't hate any race. I've just got too many Winnebago problems to juggle right now. Trying to do that while I'm dating a white woman could only make things worse."

"I was talking about lunch. You sound like you're talking about marriage."

"In the past, talking about one has somehow led to talking about the other."

"Michael, forget the past. Live in the now! There's something between us. Something new, something fresh. I felt it the first minute you walked into my house. You can't tell me you didn't feel it, too."

He was quiet for a long moment before he said huskily, "It doesn't matter, Renata. I don't want to get involved with a white woman. That's the bottom line."

Sudden tears sprang to Renata's eyes. How could she be so mad at him and so desperate for his affection at the same time?

"If that's how you feel, why did you call me? Why didn't you leave well enough alone?"

She heard him swear before he confessed, "Because I was lying to myself. I never meant to lie to you."

Renata swallowed hard. "So where does that leave us, Michael?" she whispered, knowing the answer but unable to accept it. "Couldn't we get together for lunch and just…see how it goes?"

The silence was long and terrible, so long and terrible that Renata knew what he was going to say even before he started to speak.

"I'm sorry, Renata. I think the answer has to be no."

"I see." Her tone was bitter now. He'd made his decision—a coward's decision, in her view—and she was too deeply wounded to spare him. "This has been a real learning experience for me, Michael. Imagine. The next time I meet a charming Indian man, I can say, 'Gee, I can't date you, because the last time I was attracted to an Indian he was cruel to me.'"

"Renata, please—"

"Goodbye, Michael. Don't worry about my feelings. I think this is going to turn out for the best. I misjudged you," she barged on sarcastically, unable to keep from lashing out at him, unable to stanch the bleeding of her own heart. "I wanted to get to know the man I thought you were—strong enough to brave the world, wise enough to see me for myself. Now that I know how small-minded you really are—" she paused, then hurled one final barb "—I don't think I could ever love you after all."

CHAPTER SIX

RENATA HUNG UP the phone in a state of shock. *Michael, Michael, how could you?* she cried silently as the anger subsided into naked hurt. Wasn't it bad enough that he'd left her with such an impersonal goodbye in the first place? At least she'd begun to accept that. The healing would have to start all over again now that he had phoned.

Why had he called at all? He'd already done enough to thank her! Surely he could have figured out it would end like this!

Blinking back fresh tears of wounded rage, Renata did what she always did when she was hurting—she turned to her work.

Her first drawing came to her easily, spurred on by pain and anger. She sketched a white woman, a pioneer, staring with fear and curiosity at a magnificent Winnebago brave. Renata was not sure what a Winnebago would have been wearing 150 years ago—though she could copy some of her grandfather's relics to add interest to the picture. But she knew what his face would look like. Mercifully, Michael would never see her artwork, so she could give her subject his striking features.

She made another sketch. This time the woman had a rifle. The brave had a bow and arrow. They were enemies. Hatred and prejudice had grown from the fear. But Renata couldn't capture the brave's hostility on Michael's kind and handsome face. The Michael she remembered was not a bigot. After all they'd shared, how could he tell her he had no use for white women and just leave it at that?

Renata reminded herself that there were some things she could not tolerate in a man she loved, and racial prejudice was one of them. In the long run, what did it matter, anyway? Michael had made his decision. Her needs and feelings didn't enter into it.

Suddenly Renata knew she couldn't just sit there gnashing her teeth. She had to take action—any kind of action—and under the circumstances, there seemed to be only one thing to do. If she could track down Bobby or Judy, she could get moving on the crafts fair…and bounce her feelings off somebody who cared about her and also understood the Indian point of view.

She headed first to Bobby Montero's, since his apartment was only a few miles away. To Renata's dismay, Bobby's neighbor told her that he'd taken a job with a gallery in Chicago a month ago. Her luck was better with Judy. Judy wasn't home, but her cheerful, redheaded roommate gave Renata directions to the art school where she taught young students.

Judy was a tall woman with dark brown eyes, a short pixie haircut and an upbeat, competent demeanor. Although she and Renata had never been intimate friends, they'd always been friendly during the classes they shared in college. The last time they'd seen each other was at a mutual friend's wedding about six months ago. Judy had seemed very glad to see her then.

She was certainly glad to see her today. When Renata walked into the studio after Judy's last class, Judy glanced up, said hello automatically, then did a double take. "Why, Renata! What brings you here? Are you giving lessons also?"

Renata shook her head, grateful for the warm greeting after Michael's glacial call. "No, Judy, I was looking for you."

"Well, here I am," she answered cheerfully. "What can I do for you?"

Renata had hoped to ease into the conversation gradually, but that didn't seem to be possible now. At the moment, she couldn't even recall where she'd first heard that Judy was a Sioux. Belatedly it occurred to her that Judy herself had never claimed her Indian heritage—though her features surely would not allow her to deny it—and she might possibly be uncomfortable discussing the subject.

"Well, actually, I have an idea that might be to your benefit as much as mine, Judy,'' Renata said truthfully. ''I've been asked to coordinate a crafts fair for my hometown in Wisconsin. They're holding a big fund-raiser to build a new library because the old one is about to be condemned. They asked me to help because of my background in art, and when I suggested Indian arts and crafts as a logical historical theme, they suggested that I talk to my Indian friends.''

Renata's heart dropped when her friend's eyes took on a decidedly chilly cast. ''And I'm the closest Indian friend you've got?'' she challenged.

''Well,'' Renata hedged, ''you're an Indian, you're a friend and you're involved in art. I thought you might like a chance to sell your work.''

''With a hefty chunk for your library lopped off the top?'' she snapped. ''You think I just crawled out of a tepee?''

A week ago Renata would have been startled at Judy's uncharacteristic prickliness. After her recent encounters with Michael, she realized that she shouldn't have been surprised.

''I'm sorry, Judy,'' she backpedaled, realizing that she'd made a big mistake in approaching her friend about the fair...especially today, when she was running on empty. She was beginning to wish that Alyssa had never roped her into helping with the fair at all. ''It was just an idea. I thought you'd either be pleased or not interested. It never occurred to me I might actually offend you.''

''Very little about Indians ever occurs to whites,'' Judy responded darkly. ''I don't suppose you even realize that I've spent the past ten years trying my damnedest to shake off the dust from the rez. I'm an Indian who happens to be an artist, and I'd just as soon the art-buying public would forget the Indian part. The last thing I want to do is show my stuff at a white wingding with feathers in my hair.''

''I'm sorry,'' Renata repeated. She felt helpless and confused. The last thing she'd ever wanted was to hurt Judy's feelings...or to get kicked in the teeth again herself. The pain of Michael's rejection stung afresh. ''I know you don't use Indian themes in your work, Judy, but I didn't realize you were

trying to hide your background," she said apologetically.
"There's so much I don't understand about Indians—"

"You can say that again."

Renata felt a fresh burst of tears coming on. In some ways,
Michael was a stranger, but Judy was a longtime friend. She'd
never heard Judy raise her voice to anybody, never heard her
cut another person off cold. It was obvious that Renata had
poked her in a very tender place, and for that she was sorry.
But today she had tender places of her own.

"I just don't know what's wrong with you guys!" she burst
out, the hurt of Judy's rejection on top of Michael's overriding
her own common sense. "I know that white people have done
Indians a lot of damage over the years, but *I* never have! I'm
just a human being, Judy. I never meant to hurt you. I never
meant to hurt *him!* Why is it so damn hard to be friends?"

Her sudden tears seemed to get through to Judy, who suddenly took a deep breath and slumped in shame. "Aw, Rennie,
I'm sorry," she murmured with a sigh. "You just stabbed me
in my Achilles tendon, but I know it's not your fault." She
reached out and patted Renata on the shoulder somewhat awkwardly. Then she said, "Sit down. Tell me more about the
crafts fair. And tell me who you were talking about when you
said 'him.'" When Renata didn't answer at once, she
prompted, "Another Indian artist?"

Renata shook her head, sat down and started to cry again.
Somehow Judy's sympathy broke down the floodgates even
more than her hard words had. Suddenly Renata recalled every
word of her morning's conversation with Michael, and the echo
of them in her memory was even more painful than they'd been
the first time around. "He's Winnebago. He likes me. He admitted it. But he won't go out with me because I'm white,
Judy!" She couldn't hide her hurt and dismay. "He only wants
to date another Indian."

This time compassion filled Judy's bronze-hued face. She
shook her head and patted Renata's shoulder again. "Oh, Renata, I wish I could help you, but I can't," she said sadly. "I've
found a different way to deal with the problem—I'll date any-

body who *isn't* an Indian—but I understand your friend's position. It's pure hell being an Indian in this country today, and each one of us has to deal with the situation the best way we can.''

Judy stood up and straightened her shoulders. She seemed to be mentally leaving Renata, moving to some other time and place. ''I want to forget the rez, Renata. I just want to fit in. It sounds like your man's gone back to the blanket. I know lots of people like him.''

Vigorously Renata shook her head. ''No, he hasn't. That's the thing, Judy. He's a successful businessman, a first-class yuppie. He drives a BMW and wears suits nobody in my family could afford. But his grandfather is a traditional Winnebago who keeps embarrassing him. I don't think Michael *wants* to be an Indian. He's fighting it like crazy!'' She tried to dry her tears, but didn't do a very good job of it. ''I don't care whether he acts like an Indian or not. I just want to be with him.''

Sympathy darkened Judy's pretty eyes. ''I really am sorry, Renata,'' she repeated gently. ''I'm sorry about your Winnebago friend and I'm sorry that I snapped at you. There're only so many times you can be the white crowd's token Indian before you just...'' She exhaled deeply and shook her head. ''Look, Ren, I can't speak for your boyfriend, but I can give you a glimpse of what's in his mind.''

Her eyes met Renata's, as if in question. When Renata nodded, she began.

''As long as you stay on the reservation, you're going to be poor. You're never going to get an education. You might even starve. You'd think everybody would cheer if you finally made it in the outside world, but somehow it doesn't turn out that way.''

As Renata's tears began to dry, Judy stood up and walked toward the window. She stared at the children outside, speaking softly as she watched them play. ''At first they're proud of you because you're one of them, and you scored something *against* the whites. The occupation forces, some of the more radical types call them. But if you stay out there, you start scoring points the same way everybody else in this rat race does.'' She lowered her chin, as though in shame. ''Gradually you stop ridiculing the white life-style and start wanting a chunk of it for yourself. It's sort of like an undercover cop who blends in so well that after a while he becomes one of the very people he's supposed to bust. Each time you go home and feel a bit more strange. Finally you realize that home isn't home anymore. The new place is. And you realize that secretly it's what you always wanted.'' There was a long silence before she muttered, ''But when you come face-to-face with one of your old friends again, it doesn't seem to be what you wanted at all.''

Renata wasn't sure how to reply. The whole situation—for Michael as well as for Judy—was far more complicated and sensitive than she'd ever imagined. ''I'm sorry, Judy. I really wish I'd never brought it up. Let's just forget the whole thing.''

Judy waved a hand. ''I know a number of Indian artists in Milwaukee, Renata, and I've got artist friends in Chicago as well. They should be allowed to make their own decisions about your crafts fair. I'll make you a list and earmark the ones who'd rather not make a big deal about their bloodlines so you don't accidentally stir up a hornet's nest, okay?''

Renata nodded.

''I'll call you next week and make a date for lunch. We can go over everything then.'' Judy glanced at her watch, then said, ''I hate to rush you, Renata, but I've got a meeting in five minutes. Is there anything else I can help you with before I go?''

''No, Judy. You've been a big help.'' After a second's pause, she reached out to give her a hug, and Judy hugged her back. ''Thanks.''

As they walked out into the hall together, Judy asked softly, ''Was it just a passing thing, Renata, or do you really have it bad for the guy?''

Bleakly Renata met her friend's eyes. With it put so bluntly, she had to face the truth.

''I'm not sure I can forget him,'' she confessed.

MICHAEL REACHED the Milwaukee Indian Support Center a few minutes before ten and took a moment to assess his surroundings—a habit ingrained in him by his grandfather. Of course, Grand Feather used it primarily when he was hunting or fishing—his primary source of meat until quite recently—or when he was sizing up white people. Michael did it with everybody.

Oh, how carefully he'd sized up Renata Meyer! How carefully he'd tried to analyze her, then process his own feelings and file them away.

How had everything gone wrong this morning? He'd called the damn woman because he knew he had to see her again! But somehow he'd ended up disinviting her to go out with him, and she'd told him she didn't want to see him again. It only made him want to see her more.

He knew she was right. It wasn't fair to judge her by her culture, to see only her white skin. Hadn't he given the same speech to a dozen friends? But he couldn't ignore his own past, either, or the dreams he had for the future. He was tired of living alone. He was ready to settle down. And he *couldn't* settle down with a white woman! He wanted children who would revere his grandfather and honor their past.

He shut out the memory of Renata's shining blue eyes, pushed away the sensation of her hand on his arm. He'd come to Milwaukee to put this burial ground thing to rest once and for all. Worrying about a woman he didn't want and couldn't have was the last thing he needed.

"Michael Youngthunder?" The young woman who greeted him was dark-eyed, dark-skinned and beautiful, probably twenty-five. He knew she wasn't Winnebago, but he had no doubt she was Indian. "I'm Sandra Jordan. Why don't you come into my office so we can talk."

He took the hand she offered him, murmured an appropriate greeting, then followed her into a small but nicely furnished room. He took the chair opposite her desk and watched her carefully, trying to gather clues that would tell him her tribe.

"Cree," she said with a smile.

Michael laughed. "Sorry. I didn't mean to be obvious. I'm Winnebago."

"Full-blood?"

When he nodded, her smile broadened. "I wasn't sure you were going to admit that. Usually when we get Indians in here in suits, they're trying pretty hard to pretend they were born anywhere but on the rez. But I still shouldn't have made any presumptions."

Michael wasn't sure how to answer that. She'd pretty well hit the nail on the head, but he wasn't sure he wanted to share his mixed feelings with a stranger. If he owed anybody an explanation about his painful past and foggy future, it was Renata.

And now more than ever he knew he didn't dare risk seeing Renata again.

"To be perfectly accurate, I didn't grow up on the rez, but that's only because when our people were shipped off to Nebraska way back when, my great-grandparents refused to go. They weren't alone. There are thousands of us left in Wisconsin—"

"In little communities peppering the state," she finished for him, embarrassing Michael with her obvious knowledge of his people when he knew nothing of hers.

They shared a smile as Michael realized that he didn't need to give her the Winnebago history lesson he'd given to Renata. He simply said, "My grandfather lives near the Dells," knowing she'd realize what he hadn't said. *I no longer think of it as home.*

But it was home, in an odd sort of way, because it was still where the heart of his family resided. Although he'd roped his grandfather into coming back to Sugar Creek after the groundbreaking fiasco because he'd felt he had no choice, Michael couldn't bear to watch the sadness that seemed to weigh down Grand Feather a little more every day. He knew it was only a matter of time before the old one had to go back to his pitiful little house—with or without Michael's permission.

Sandra swept a lock of long black hair out of her face, reminding Michael of the way Renata's lush blond tresses flowed over her shoulders. "How can the Center help your grandfather, Michael?" she asked.

He lifted his hands in a helpless gesture. "Frankly, I'm not sure you can. I only know that I've done everything for him I can think of, and he's still…" He tried to think of an appropriate word to describe his grandfather's state of mind and failed. "He thinks they're building a resort on a sacred Winnebago burial ground, the one where his great-grandparents are buried. He insists that he's been to the site many times, years ago, and he'll recognize it by a horseshoe of oak trees."

"Which are gone now?"

Michael thought about that for a minute. "It never occurred to me that they might be gone. I just figured we couldn't find them, or his memory has…changed."

Sandra took a pad of paper from the edge of her desk and started taking notes. "How old is he, Michael?"

He shrugged uncomfortably. "At least a hundred. He says he remembers going over to Wounded Knee to see the last Ghost Dance as a child, riding his own pony on the journey for the very first time. I figure that makes him somewhere between 104 and 107. Any way you look at it, he's been alive a long, long time."

Michael felt a curious sense of gratitude that he was sharing that information with another Indian. Imagine telling a white bureaucrat that his grandfather had no birth certificate! Grand Feather had been born in a bark-and-hide wigwam, for Pete's sake, in the middle of a snowstorm! It was a miracle he'd lived through the first night.

Without missing a beat, Sandra asked, "And this burial ground…is it more or less where his clan would have lived or hunted?"

Michael nodded. "Yes, I checked that out. It's Winnebago country, all right, and the resort and the surrounding farms are built on former Winnebago land. There's not a lot of development near the resort—it's a remodeled hunting lodge—and even the nearest town is pretty small. You'd think people would want to preserve a set of oak trees, but as you suggested, they could have died or been cut down.''

"You've looked?''

"God, have I looked!''

When she glanced up, Michael grew silent, embarrassed by his outburst. She said nothing as she went back to her notes, but Michael felt he owed her an explanation.

"When he first heard about the expansion of this old lodge, I went to the local police department to get permission to look for evidence of grave sites. The captain ordered a lieutenant to take my grandfather around—''

"You went to the police for help?''

Michael was feeling sufficiently Indian to understand her need to pose the question. The police—the army, the marshals, the sheriffs throughout the West—were lifelong tormentors of Indian peoples, and a traditional Winnebago would never have approached them for assistance. The fact that Michael had— the fact that he actually was growing to think of Lieutenant Bauer as a friend—was another sharp reminder of how far he'd gone from his roots.

A sudden vision of his adolescence made him shudder. Defensively, as though to prove his own credentials, he blurted out, "Things have changed in recent years.''

"Have they?''

With an anger that surprised him, Michael suddenly unbuttoned his right cuff and rolled up his sleeve, exposing a small but ugly bullet scar. "I was in D.C. on the Trail of Broken Treaties while you were still in grade school, Sandra! Don't preach to me about the cops. I've learned to see good in lots of people I hated when I was young.''

The young woman across the desk said nothing, but her eyes flashed in surprise and disapproval. Belatedly Michael realized that she had not been challenging him. Nobody was asking him to prove his loyalty to his grandfather or to his tribe. It was his own problem, unsettled and unnamed, always simmering, stewing, brewing. Brought to a boil by his smoldering need to see Renata.

And his absolute assurance that it would be fatal to his peace of mind to get involved with a white woman—especially now, when he could feel the voices of his people valiantly trying to call him back.

He could almost hear the beating of the drum.

AFTER SHE LEFT JUDY, Renata spent several hours window-shopping, then took a swim in her apartment pool. When she came back inside, she took off her suit, slipped on her coolest seersucker robe and curled up with a cheerful romance novel, knowing she needed the lift it would give her.

Despite her best efforts, she was suffused by her memories of Michael—Michael with his long hair and long lashes, Michael with the frustration in his beautiful dark eyes. It hurt so much to know that he didn't want her—wouldn't even take the risk of seeing her when he'd called up expressly to do just that. Maybe she should have played it cool and kept things casual until his feelings had had a chance to grow. Maybe she should have pleaded a little bit instead of getting angry. Maybe she should have been smart enough to read between the lines all along.

Renata had listened carefully to Judy Hall's explanation of what life was like for a late-twentieth-century Indian, and she thought she understood it a little bit. But there was a big difference between Michael and the other Native Americans she had known. Judy was comfortable living as a white person. Lydia was totally Winnebago. Bobby Montero, who danced between the cultures, did so with a lively step and a whimsical heart. Poor Michael couldn't seem to decide just who he ought to be, so he couldn't dance at all.

Renata could still picture Michael's face the first time he'd bolted out of Brick's police car. She could still see his long hair wet from the rain. She could even see his eyes the morning of the ground-breaking ceremony, when he'd reached for her with cautious fingertips after breakfast, biting his lip with the effort it cost him to turn away.

She was bleeding at the memory of that moment, the most

bittersweet moment of all, when she heard the doorbell ring. Relieved to see almost anybody who might take her mind off Michael, Renata rose quickly and peered through the peephole.

Was it just her imagination, her own longing, or was she staring at Michael's face?

She felt a sudden swirl of hope and confusion, tinged with a sudden rush of desire. She was naked under her seersucker robe, and she toyed with the notion of getting dressed before she let him in. But suddenly she knew she couldn't take the time. It was a miracle he'd come to her, for whatever reason. She didn't dare give him a chance to slip away.

Swallowing hard, she pulled open the door with one hand while she tightened her sash with the other. "Come in," she muttered, not really looking at him. Whatever they had to say to each other was going to be easier to express if they didn't do it out in the hallway.

Michael came in silently, his wingtip shoes squeaking on the polished wood floor. He was wearing a suit in a beautiful deep shade of navy blue that dramatized the color of his hair. His eyes were both ashamed and angry, and his sensuous lips were moist and tight. For a long, aching moment he simply stared at Renata, his expression the most potent mix of fury and frustration that she'd ever seen on a man's face.

"Tell me you didn't mean it," he ordered, his husky voice rendering the words half command, half plea. "Tell me you didn't mean you never wanted to see me again."

Renata wasn't sure how to answer. As an icebreaker or an apology, it left a lot to be desired. But if he was going to skip the amenities, so would she.

"A bigot is a bigot, Michael, no matter what the color of his skin," she managed to whisper, trembling with the need to touch his face. He was so close, so very close, and the expression he wore was not the one she suspected he reserved for strangers. "I don't choose friends or lovers who judge other people by their race. If that's the only way you can look at me—"

"Renata!" he begged, cutting her off as he took a forceful

step toward her. For a long, tense moment he said nothing, poised between surging forward and holding back. Then he laid a strong, gentle hand on her face.

Renata couldn't believe how much that simple touch moved her. Instinctively she bowed her head.

"Can't you see how it is for me? Can't you see how I feel about you?" His voice ached with frustration, throbbed with unbanked need.

Renata felt the same ache within her. She quivered where Michael touched her skin. All her anger and common sense washed away like summer heat during the rain. She felt weak. Subdued. Utterly unlike herself.

Slowly she reached out and touched his chest, her questing fingertips grazing the sensitive hollow of his throat above the loosened tie. With a new seed of hope growing within her, she raised her gaze to his.

"Michael," she confessed, ashamed of the quivering of her voice, "I know who you are." Her fingertips brushed his chin. "I know that you're the man I want."

Michael's own fingers caressed her cheek tenderly, potently, and his thumb brushed across her lips. When his free hand cradled the small of her back, she shivered with sudden, unexpected need, certain he was ready to relieve her suffering.

But Michael still looked angry. He still kept himself stiff.

"You don't know me," he countered. "Not really. Not in any way that counts. You don't have any idea about my past, let alone my future."

"I know you're having some problems sorting out both, Michael." She lifted both hands to cradle his shoulders. Her eyes never left his face. "If anything, it makes you easier for me to relate to, because you know how it feels to not fit in. I've spent my whole life being a bit of an oddity. Do you think I could love a conventional, conservative man, the type whose ancestors came over on the *Mayflower?*"

"Renata," he said with a groan, "you don't know what kind of man I am. *I* don't even know! I know who I was when I was young and stupid, and I know that what I did then was a mistake. That's why I ended up selling Japanese computers and turning my back on my heritage. But I know that wasn't the right path, either, not when I feel my grandfather's eyes boring into my back everywhere I go.''

His hand stroked Renata's spine longingly, unleashing a furl of need within her woman's core. Michael braced her nape as he tipped her head back and dug his fingers more deeply into her hair. ''I don't know where I'm going now, Rennie,'' he pleaded, his lips just centimeters from hers. ''I don't know what I want. I only know that I've come to a fork in the road. If I follow you, I'll never be sure it's the right road for *me*.''

Renata didn't know what he'd done when he was ''young and stupid'' and she didn't care. ''There's not an adult alive who doesn't have something in his past he wishes he could do over, Michael'' she pointed out, pressing closer. ''And I don't know a soul who doesn't have questions about where he's headed next. I don't want to tell you what path to take. I only want to walk alongside you.''

He bowed his head until their foreheads touched. The hand on her back pulled her closer, so close that her pelvis brushed against his, setting off another electric, sexual rush. ''Renata, there's room beside me only if I walk in the white man's world. In my grandfather's world, there is no place, no place at all, for a woman who is not Winnebago.''

Renata lifted both hands to cup his face. She was desperate now, desperate for his body…desperate for his love. ''I'm not falling in love with your grandfather, Michael!'' she pleaded. ''I'll paint us a whole new road if we can't find a way to walk on any of the other ones. I'm used to making up my own rules as I go along. Aren't you?''

She was all out of arguments. But it didn't matter because, quite abruptly, Michael seemed to give up the struggle, too.

''Renata—'' he began. But whatever he was going to say was lost when he suddenly claimed her mouth with lips as hot as flame and as sweet as morning dew.

Renata didn't try to think, to reason; she didn't try to fight him. All of her burning questions were left on hold. She wanted this man, wanted him terribly, and at the moment she could do nothing but rejoice that he was finally willing to admit how desperately he wanted her, too.

Michael's kiss was deep, total, both a conquest and a surrender. Suddenly he was clinging to her shoulders, pressing his body against hers. Renata stifled a cry of need as she felt his tongue lick flames along her open lips, inviting her tongue to dance with his.

As his tongue plunged inside the soft reaches of her mouth, Michael's fingers kneaded the willing flesh of her hips. He was hard and hot as he surged against her. She was hot and soft, melting wildly as she surged back.

''Rennie!'' he whispered. Then his lips claimed hers again, claimed her soul with a fiery brand of urgency that belied all of his protests and filled her with hope and untethered need.

Instinctively Renata wrapped one ankle around Michael's, overcome by the need to wrap the rest of her body around his, too. Her robe worked its way open, and she felt her nakedness keenly as Michael's hands slipped down her hips and then up again beneath the fabric. Everywhere his skin touched hers she felt a trail of flame.

Renata felt her body open to his, felt herself prepare for what would surely come. If she'd ever needed a man this badly, she could not remember it. And the desperate fire of Michael's kisses as she reached for his belt told her that his need for her was potent, too.

It was at that exact moment—because of that moment?—that he suddenly wrenched his mouth from hers. For a second Michael still held her close, while he took a great, shuddering breath. Renata was absolutely shattered when he slowly stepped away.

The only thing that kept her from breaking in two was that he didn't abandon her totally. He still clung to one of her hands as though to soften the blow. It didn't do a thing to ease the storm in her body, but it helped ease the hurricane in her heart.

''Renata, don't...don't look at me like that,'' he begged. Apologetically, he shook his head. ''I'm not...I'm not ready for this. I can't…do what feels natural. Not so soon. Not without getting this straight in my mind. I don't want to make love with you tonight and call you tomorrow and say it was a mistake.''

Abruptly, Renata dropped his hand, wounded so badly she could hardly speak. ''You've got a real way with women, Michael,'' she snapped. ''I can't think of when I've been more flattered.''

His eyes darkened, and this time he deliberately moved away. ''I realize that modern white women are accustomed to casual sexual liaisons, but I was raised—''

''Oh, stuff it, Michael!'' Renata burst out. ''This doesn't have a damn thing to do with modern sexual standards or old Winnebago ways. What makes you think I give myself to any man casually? I'm twenty-nine years old and I've slept with only two men in my whole life. The first one died of leukemia while we were engaged and the second left me for another woman when I thought he'd come to change my life.'' She glared at him, trembling now with a mixture of frustrated desire and unadulterated angst. ''I want to make love with you because I'm ready to make a commitment,'' she angrily confessed, ''while the proud warrior is running from it like a frightened rabbit!''

Renata watched Michael straighten in an almost predatory fashion that was somehow scary. It occurred to her belatedly that calling the descendant of Winnebago warriors a coward was not a good idea. She couldn't think of many men who would be thrilled by her accusation, and she couldn't imagine that Michael would like it much better.

''Would you prefer for me to use you when I know we have no future?'' he challenged her.

Angry tears sprang to Renata's eyes. ''Why did you come here, Michael?'' she replied. ''Did you have to make things worse? Didn't we already say goodbye?''

Michael slumped and took a deep breath. The fire seemed to go out of him in a great whoosh. ''I didn't come to say goodbye,'' he admitted in a low, strained tone, his eyes anguished as they met hers. "I came because I couldn't bear the thought of never seeing you again." He sucked in his lower lip, exhaled again, then slowly reached for Renata's quivering hand.

For a moment she kept her fingers stiff, unable to switch moods so easily. But she didn't have it in her to fight him long. As his strong fingers kneaded her skin, he managed to gentle her again.

"I met a Cree woman at the Center today," he confessed. "Bright, educated, beautiful. Just the sort of wife I thought I had in mind."

Hurt anew, Renata would have pulled away, but Michael's grip on her hand grew tighter.

"I was back in my car and halfway across town before I realized that it never even occurred to me to ask her out. I'd actually *forgotten* that I was supposed to be on the lookout for an Indian woman. There was no room for her in my heart." He couldn't face Renata as he confessed, "Damn it, Ren! Since the first time we met, I knew it'd be impossible to forget you."

Renata didn't know how to respond. It was wonderful to hear him say he wanted her, but he still wasn't saying what she needed to hear. "So where does that leave us, Michael?" she asked more gently. "Where do we go from here?"

"I don't know where we're going—" he tugged her closer "—but please don't give up on me while I figure it out. Let me try to get my grandfather's problems out of the way. Let me come to grips with my own." He stroked her face with a beseeching hand. "The next time you're in Tyler, let me take you out."

Renata wanted to believe he'd turned the corner, but she wasn't sure just where he was heading yet. Tensely she told him, "I'll be in Tyler next weekend. I have a crafts-fair committee meeting."

Michael looked surprised; she knew he'd been hoping for more time to solve his dilemma. Still, his gaze was steady as he said, "Okay, Rennie. I'll call you."

Renata knew a sensible woman would have left it at that.

But she also knew that she couldn't bear it if he left her hanging, if "I'll call you" meant she'd never hear from him again.

"If you change your mind," she whispered, feeling humble and achingly vulnerable, "please let me know. The cruelest thing you could do would be to just leave me hanging."

Tenderly, Michael reached out to touch her face once more, his fingers slipping deeply into her hair. "I will take you out to dinner Saturday," he vowed. "That's a promise." There was a long, tense silence as their eyes met. Then he added, "A Winnebago promise."

Renata found herself fighting tears again. She wanted to kiss him so badly, to feel his passion, to know that the aching need he'd aroused in her was something they shared, not a torment that was hers alone. It hurt so much to know she wanted him so deeply, when he was willing to just walk away.

When Michael leaned forward, she thought he was going to kiss her lips. But to her surprise, his hand slipped down to her throat and his fingers edged under the collar of her skimpy robe. In one smooth motion he pushed the robe off her shoulder, exposing one aching breast. His strong brown hand swept over Renata's white skin, electrifying every inch of it, bringing the tightening dark center to a shimmering peak.

Renata gasped as he bent down and kissed her taut nipple. She could feel him trembling with need as he sucked it into his mouth. She started shaking almost uncontrollably.

Renata's hands slipped into his thick hair, tugging in urgency as much as for balance. "Michael," she pleaded, "you don't know how much I want this. Please don't start if you're still going to leave."

At once his mouth left her nipple, but he covered it with the palm of his hand, pressing gently as he claimed her lips once more. It was a deep, potent, promising kiss that filled Renata with hope and a flash flood of desire. By the time it was over, she knew she'd completely surrendered her heart to him.

But the surrender wasn't mutual. When Michael finally broke off the searing kiss, he stroked her breast one last time and headed for the door.

CHAPTER SEVEN

"SO WHAT DO YOU THINK about Renata's plans for bringing Indian crafts to the fair?" Alyssa asked Anna as they sat in the Kelsey's kitchen munching brownies and sipping tea one warm, breezeless evening. "Do you think people will buy their handiwork?"

"Oh, certainly," said Anna, ever the optimist. "I think the bigger question is whether the Indians will be willing to come here to sell their things. Tyler isn't exactly known as a Winnebago enclave."

Alyssa smiled. "Well, after that free publicity we got at Edward's ground breaking, anybody who reads the news knows that this was once Winnebago territory. That ought to help bring in tourists. I just don't know if it will bring in more Indians." After a moment Alyssa frowned and asked, "Whatever happened to that old Indian Brick towed away? I know he caused quite a ruckus for everybody, but I have to say I felt rather sorry for him. He seemed so—" she struggled for the right word "—sincere."

Anna nodded. "I think he was. Brick knows his grandson. Apparently the old man has some fixation on the land near the lake. The night before the ground breaking, Brick found him out on Renata Meyer's place. He seems to think the burial ground might be near there."

"Well, he could be right. You know we scared ourselves silly with ghost stories about an old Indian graveyard out there when we were children."

"But that's all they were, just ghost stories. The only people buried out near the lodge that I know of are Renata's great-grandparents. The rest of the Meyers were buried in town." As Anna stood up to refill their teacups, Alyssa had a sudden thought. "Anna, if Brick found that old Indian on Renata's place just before our meeting, I wonder why she never mentioned it? She was certainly thinking a lot about Indians when she came to my house."

"That's a point," Anna concurred. "Maybe I got the day wrong. I'll ask Brick when he comes down."

"Is he here? I didn't see the cruiser out front."

Anna gestured toward the stairs with her shoulder. "He's up there clearing some space in Phil's closet for me." A thump from the ceiling confirmed Brick's location. "Since his marriage, I really miss having him live here, but I'm glad he still makes a point of dropping by and giving me a hand occasionally."

A moment later Alyssa forgot about Brick as another man— tall, lean and just as handsome as he'd been thirty years ago— sauntered into the kitchen, with one thumb lazily hooked in the belt loop of his tennis shorts. It was the first time since he'd come back to town that Alyssa had seen Edward looking so casual, and the impact of his informality struck her with a rush of nostalgia, tinged with long-forgotten desire. His legs had been those of a skinny young man the last time she'd seen him in shorts. Now they were strong and virile.

He looked surprised to see her, too. "Uh...Alyssa," he said quietly. "I didn't realize you were here."

"I walked," she said, as though she owed him an explanation. "It's a lovely evening, don't you think?"

Suddenly she remembered the dozens of summer evenings the two of them had walked Tyler's mock orange–scented streets together. Alyssa stifled a quiet ache at the realization that they'd never do that again.

"A lovely evening," Edward answered, his eyes on her hair.

Alyssa was hoping that Anna would break into the conversation when footsteps sounded on the stairs and Brick marched in. Normally Anna's nephew was a sunny soul, always quick with a joke or a kind word. But at the moment he looked frozen in some sort of anger that rocked Alyssa. By the look on Edward's face, Brick's arrival rocked him, too.

But not because of Brick's expression. The real problem was what Brick was holding in his hand.

"I was moving an old box in the back of your dad's closet for Anna. The bottom gave way and this fell out," he said to Edward, gesturing with the blue-black pistol that suddenly seemed to bring menace to the room. "It's a .32 caliber. The same size as the bullet Liza found in her grandmother's room."

Edward took a step back as though Brick had hit him. "My dad doesn't own a gun, Brick! And even if he did—"

"Oh, I don't think it's his." Now he took a step toward Alyssa, pointing with his free hand to the initials engraved on the side. J.T.I; her father's initials. Surely not her father's gun? "Alyssa, have you ever seen this gun before?"

In that instant, Alyssa remembered a gunshot, felt herself vibrate with the explosion even though Anna's kitchen remained utterly still. Suddenly she felt a raw and aching terror, a fear of Brick Bauer, as she imagined his face distorted and hateful, seeking to kill.

It only lasted a second, and then he was once again the kind young man she knew. Even in her panic, Alyssa knew that Brick had not threatened her. But somebody had. A thousand years ago, on the night her mother died, she *had* seen this gun…in the hand of an acquaintance who'd suddenly changed into a foe. She remembered its shape and color, its fancy initials on the barrel, its terrible proximity and booming voice. And she remembered something else.

A man—a man she knew—running into the shadows.

The only other thing she could remember from the jumble of images was the beat of her own childish heart, thudding with absolute dread.

MICHAEL SAT on the three-legged stool in his grandfather's shack and leaned against the wall, grateful that he'd remembered to change into his oldest jeans before coming over to visit. When he'd returned from Milwaukee last weekend, the old man had been packed and waiting. He'd made no excuses. He did not beg or plead. He waited until Michael had recapped his failure at the Indian support center, then said softly, "*Hitkunkay,* I cannot live in this city. It is time for you to take me home."

Michael had not argued. For days he'd watched the sorrow on his grandfather's face, and he knew that the old man would rather die in his own shabby little house than live penned up in Michael's luxury apartment. Michael had decided to talk to the family again and see if somebody else could come check on Grand Feather every morning. With Michael's uncle dropping by after work, the old man would have a clan member visiting twice a day. It was all Michael could do short of moving back to this hovel.

As he looked sadly around the dump and cast a mournful eye on the squalid barnyard, he could not imagine any circumstances that would bring him back here to live. There were lovely places in Wisconsin Dells, of course, and even splendid Winnebago farms nearby. But Grand Feather would not move an inch; he wouldn't even let Michael build him a place on this same land or bring in a nice new mobile home. Michael had had trouble even convincing the old man to let him repair the forty-year-old furnace when it had finally died last winter.

Grand Feather had been staring quietly at Michael, but now his eyes narrowed and he focused with care. "I do not have much time left, Thunder Eagle. Do not deny me the one thing that will give me the peace I need to die."

"You're not going to die, damn it!" Michael burst out. The mere thought of losing his grandfather caused an aching pressure in his chest. Things had been tense, terribly tense, between them since that scene at the ground breaking, but that in no way diminished his love for the old man. "You're healthy as a horse, Grand Feather. The only thing likely to kill you is another summer without air-conditioning or a winter without decent insulation! For Pete's sake, if you can't bear to stay in Sugar Creek, why won't you let me fix things up out here?"

"You want to help your grandfather?" the old one asked. "Then help in the Winnebago way."

"Look, I can't go hunting for you," Michael protested. "I can't just chop up logs and stack them for the winter. It's different now. I want to do my duty, but you make it as hard for me as you possibly can."

It was rare that he talked back so forcibly to the old man, and he always felt guilty when he did it. But Michael felt helpless and irascible today. He'd told Renata he was too Winnebago to give himself to a white woman, but he wasn't anywhere close to being Indian enough to satisfy his grandfather. To do that he'd have to give up his job and go back to the blanket.

But he knew that his anger was greater today because of what he planned to do next Saturday. He'd promised Renata to take her out, and take her out he would. In the meantime he knew he ought to call her to firm things up, but he didn't know what to say. Nor did he know what had happened in those few feverish moments he'd spent in her apartment in Milwaukee. They hadn't had a date, or even a conversation. He'd just barged in, begged for her forgiveness, claimed her body and her heart, then run away. He was not proud of any of it.

But when he recalled the look in Renata's eyes when he'd touched her face and felt the quivering tip of her breast, he knew he'd do it all again if he had the chance.

Absolutely nothing about Michael's behavior had made sense to him since he'd first met Renata, and he knew that once he saw her again, the last of his common sense would simply drain away.

There was a long, painful silence in the shack, while Michael thought about Renata and his grandfather thought about... buffalo? Sweat lodges? Medicine ceremonies? At last the old man said, "We could make a deal, *hitkunkay*."

Michael studied him suspiciously. Grand Feather always called him "son of my son" in Winnebago when he was determined to get his own way. He knew that Michael couldn't fight him when he spoke to him in the traditional manner. "What kind of a deal?"

"I do something for you. You do something for me."

Michael straightened up. "What will you let me do for you? Build you a new house?"

The old man sighed. "I cannot go that far. But you can buy me a little one that moves. I will live in it now to make you happy, but it will not be a waste because you can sell it when I die."

Michael was astonished. It was the biggest step his grandfather had ever taken toward letting Michael care for him. He was even thinking like a modern person—reselling the trailer, no less! What had happened to change his mind? Had his recent bizarre antics frightened even *him?*

"I would be honored to buy you a mobile home, Grand Feather," Michael said seriously. He didn't know how much they cost, didn't know how the hell he could afford one on top of his apartment and car payments, but he knew that he'd move heaven and earth to get his grandfather into decent housing. "I can have something here for you next weekend. Air-conditioning, heating, electric stove, the whole works."

His grandfather didn't look too happy about it, but he slowly nodded. "I will live in this place you bring to me. But first you will keep your promise to me."

"What promise?" Michael demanded, truly on his guard now. He knew this capitulation had been too easy. His grandfather was going to ask for something outrageous...like promising to move the damn trailer to Renata's backyard.

"I want to see you dance again. I want to know my grandson is still a Winnebago."

Michael threw up his hands in exasperation. "Grand Feather, I told you, I don't remember the steps! I don't remember the words."

"You did not think you remembered the words to the ancient clan prayers, either, but when you found me on the white woman's lawn, they came back to you."

Michael couldn't deny that. Nor could he deny how ridiculous and awkward he'd felt chanting in the mud in front of Renata.

"Since then we have practiced many times, and you are sure again of the four sacred songs of our clan."

Michael could not deny it. But neither could he deny how embarrassed he'd been as they'd practiced the ancient chants on his living-room floor, sandwiched between the CD player, the cassette tape collection and the VCR. How afraid he'd been that one of his yuppie neighbors would hear them.

"I no longer have the right to take a Thunderbird role at any regular clan ceremony, Grand Feather," he reminded his grandfather.

"No, but the trade fair powwows are open to everyone. There are lots of white people there to buy our things—and city Indians like you who come to dance. It would be the easiest trailhead for you to start your way back."

There was a certain logic to Grand Feather's reasoning, but that didn't make Michael any more willing to risk a public display. "I can't do the steps," he insisted. "*I can't hear the drum.* I have to feel it. Live it. Breathe it. You know what it takes. You're the one who taught me how to dance!"

His tired old eyes speared Michael. "And I will teach you how again."

"Come on, you're too old to dance!"

"I do not need your young legs, Thunder Eagle! *I* still have a Winnebago heart!"

Michael looked away as Grand Feather vowed, "And I will help you find your people's heart again. I *must* do this one last thing before I die." He stood up and stared down at Michael as though he were the tiny boy who'd come to live in this shack when his own father had abandoned him. "My soul will never rest until I know you can once more hear the drum."

RENATA WAITED until Saturday morning to drive to Tyler, hoping all week that Michael would call her before she left. He'd promised to take her out to dinner Saturday night; surely he'd call to confirm his plans before then. If he was anxious to make her a part of his life, he'd be as eager to talk to her as she was eager to talk to him.

Before he'd kissed her breast, it would have broken Renata's heart to have had him vanish from her life. If he did it now, she'd feel even worse—cheap and tawdry as well as crushed. And she'd wonder about his values, too.

Nothing that happened would have felt wrong to Renata if she'd been certain that Michael shared her feelings. She'd been ready to ride off into the sunset with him—why not ride off to her bed? But Michael was still trying to decide whether to wear moccasins or Nikes, and he wasn't ready to ride anywhere with anyone. He'd told her that—she couldn't pretend he hadn't made it clear—but his eyes and his hands and the heated crush of his body had told her something else again.

She found no message from him when she got to the house, no scrawled note lurking in the mail. There was no sign that his grandfather had returned to her land again on horseback or on his own two feet. No sign that she'd ever met a Winnebago.

No, she corrected herself, *that's not true.* The one Winnebago in her life who truly seemed to delight in her company was dear old Lydia. She'd checked back with the old woman a couple of times and received a glowing welcome each time. Lydia had made progress recruiting other Winnebago bead-workers for the fair and was working on some contacts from other tribes. During her last visit, Lydia had reiterated her offer to teach Renata how to tan deerskin, and they'd agreed upon a date to start. Now Renata owed the dear old woman two massive favors instead of one.

When Renata reached Tyler, she had a few hours to kill before the meeting at Alyssa's, and she realized instantly that she had to keep herself busy or go crazy waiting to hear from Michael. In Milwaukee she had an answering machine, which she'd checked every time she walked in the door. In Tyler she had no such luxury. There would be no way of knowing if Michael called while she was out.

It would serve him right if he couldn't reach me to cancel, she told herself, by now almost certain that was what he would do. *Maybe he'll have to drive over here in person to tell me to forget the whole thing. Surely he wouldn't be tacky enough to just not show up!*

Renata was feeling utterly dismal by the time she headed into town, deciding to stop at the library before the meeting. Her knowledge of Indian art was still sketchy at best, and if she was going to expand the Indian crafts at the fair, she knew she'd need more information on all the local tribes, not just the Winnebago.

As she parked her truck in front of the two-story structure, Renata felt a swell of nostalgia for the old place, which represented so many joyful memories. All the warmth she still felt for Tyler enveloped her as she walked up the sidewalk.

She spotted Elise the minute she walked in the door.

"Well, hello, Renata!" Elise greeted her cheerfully, looking cool and calm as always. "I didn't expect to see you for a couple more hours."

"I decided to do some research while I was in town," Renata explained, feeling brighter already. "There's a lot I still don't know about the Indians who used to live around here." *Or the ones who still do,* she might have added.

"Have you made any progress on getting Native crafts people for the fair?"

"Well, yes and no. I've got some Winnebago beadworkers coming in with marvelous clothes and jewelry, but I'm still working on crafts people from the other tribes. And my leads on Native American artists have been…not quite as promising as I'd hoped." Judy had joined her for lunch a few days ago and shared her thoughtfully compiled list of Indian painters and sculptors. But Renata had had difficulty finding some of them, and several had already turned her down. The general consensus seemed to be that Tyler was too small and insignificant to make the fair a good use of their time.

Deciding it was better to reveal her financial bombshell to one committee member before she had to face all the rest of them, Renata admitted uncomfortably, "It turns out that the Indian beadworkers will just be helping with the fund-raiser by bringing in more tourists to the fair. Except for the regular price for a booth, I found out that it would be…'' she struggled for a word ''…inappropriate to ask them to donate to our library.''

For a long, tense moment Elise just stared at her. It was the first time Renata could ever remember Elise being at a loss for words. She looked gray-faced, almost stricken.

She recovered quickly—Elise always did—straightening as she busied herself with a pile of books. When she'd recovered her composure, Elise said kindly, ''Well, yes, I can see how that might be, Renata. I suppose it wouldn't mean all that much money for the library, anyway.''

Belatedly Renata realized the reason for Elise's hesitation. Everybody in Tyler knew that the library was Elise's whole life, and the town had no worries about it as long as it rested in Elise's capable hands. Renata had naively assumed that Elise herself would take care of any problems. But now she was getting the true picture that Nora and Alyssa had tried to paint for her: the library's finances were in such bad shape that not even Elise could fix the situation.

''Alyssa said you were going to talk to the architect about scaling down the plans,'' Renata said, trying to think of anything at all to make Elise feel better. ''How is that coming along?''

Fresh anxiety flickered across Elise's tense face. ''Not very well, I'm afraid. The gentleman says he's too busy to take on any work, and I'm afraid he's not too happy that, after all his labor, we've changed our minds.'' She looked embarrassed as well as unhappy. ''Johnny Kelsey says he's trying to reach another architect who might have some time this summer. Apparently he's a university professor, so he's free for the next two months. Johnny tried to call him last week, but the departmental office wouldn't give out his home number, so we'll have to wait until he checks in again, rather an iffy thing at this time of year.''

Renata didn't know what to say. Cheery Elise had always been able to pull her out of the doldrums. In hindsight she realized that, subconsciously, that was part of the reason she'd decided to come to the library this morning.

But now the tables were turned, and Renata felt a keen desire to cheer up Elise. Though her uncertain situation with Michael was heartbreaking, she still had her art, her friends and her home in Tyler. But Elise lived for the library; she had nothing else. It flourished because of her. It was the thing that made her Elise instead of just a spinster trapped in the lifelong care of a petulant crippled sister.

Renata had seen Elise cope with Bea's attitude with optimism. She handled every crisis with a sure and steady hand. But this morning, for one unguarded second, Renata had seen something in Elise's eyes she'd never seen there before.

It wasn't greed. It wasn't professional pride. It was fear.

MICHAEL POSTPONED calling Renata until the last minute, hoping that the longer he waited, the better chance there was that some solution would come to him, some way to do what was right for himself, his grandfather and Renata all at the same time. But now it was Saturday afternoon—almost Saturday night, really—and he'd waited as long as he dared. If he didn't call her right now, he'd botch things up so badly that she'd never want to see him again.

He knew it was foolish to see her tonight. He knew it was cowardly to break things off. He knew that he desperately wanted to hold her in his arms, to make her smile, to feel good when she made him laugh. He also knew that whatever they did tonight would just make it harder for both of them when he finally told her what he simply had to say.

"Hello. It's Michael," was all he could come up with when he finally got Renata on the phone.

There was a long silence—disappointment, or just surprise?—before she answered, "Hello, Michael." That's all she said, but he heard the rest in her stiff voice: *I didn't think you were going to call.*

He took no refuge in apologies or excuses. "Last time we

talked, we agreed to go out to dinner tonight. Is that still okay with you?"

Again that pause, that tension. Her voice was low but sharp when she asked, "Is it with you?"

"Renata, I said we'd go out and we're going to go out. What more do you want from me?"

"I don't want you to do me any favors, Michael." Her voice was stiff but not rude. "If you're planning to see me tonight to break things off in person, why don't you just do it now? It'll make things easier in the long run."

Michael swore softly under his breath, then swore again out loud. "Damn it, Renata, do we have to go through this every time we talk to each other?"

"Michael, just tell me the truth. Did you forget to call till now, are you just clumsy with social etiquette or were you hoping you could think of some way to get out of going to dinner with me?"

He swore again, then blurted the first words that entered his mind. "Nothing's changed, Renata! I still think this is stupid. It's not going to lead anywhere. But I want to see you more than ever. I've thought about you all week long." He took a deep breath, then said before she could cut in, "It'll take me about an hour to get over there."

He held his breath while he waited for her answer. The silence went on so long he wondered if she'd left the phone.

At last she whispered, "Michael, I want to see you, too. I want to see you so much it hurts."

He swallowed hard and muttered, "I'm on my way. You wait right there."

RENATA WAS READY in fifteen minutes, but she spent most of the next hour picking a cluster of fresh baby tea roses and pinning them in her long hair. She didn't know what she should say to Michael when he got there, didn't know if she should plan on him spending the night. She wanted a quiet evening alone with him, but she had a feeling he'd want to take her somewhere snazzy—to prove that he could—so she'd dressed the part in a sleeveless, hot-pink clingy knit that showed off every curve to best advantage. She'd considered wearing the magnificent dress that Lydia had given her—what better way to show her acceptance of his heritage?—but she decided it would be smarter to let that wait for some other time. If there was another time. Tonight she didn't dare say a word about Michael's Winnebago background unless he decided to broach the subject.

Renata didn't want to think about the hard feelings that had stemmed from their last Indian-white discussion, but she also knew that if they didn't talk the subject through and put it to rest, there was no way that they were ever going to be able to go on together.

He showed up fifty minutes after he'd hung up the phone, wearing a beautifully cut black suit with a sober gray-and-black tie. Besides his overly long but terribly attractive black hair, the only indication of his background he sported was a small tie clip in the shape of a feather. Renata wondered if it was a silent statement of rebellion that he wore all the time. If it was, she had never noticed it before.

"Hi," she said simply.

Michael looked at her eyes, her throat, her breasts and all the rest of her. Then he shook his head and ever so slowly smiled at her as he teased, "You're cheating, Renata."

A tiny rush of desire flamed within her. "I know." She grinned and he grinned back, and suddenly everything was all right between them.

Michael leaned forward to kiss her lightly, his lips just barely grazing hers. "I'm very, very glad to see you," he whispered, "but I want to talk tonight. It's important. Please don't do anything to distract me."

"You mean like dance naked on the restaurant table?" Renata asked, grateful that she could joke with him again.

His eyes narrowed suspiciously. "Have you done that before?"

"Well...not exactly. But—"

"I don't think I want to know." His bright, teasing tone

made Renata feel so good she wanted to wriggle like a puppy. Was it possible, truly possible, that things were going to work out between the two of them at last?

Michael was still standing close enough to touch her, and he looked as though he remembered the way they'd parted as keenly as she did. Her nipples were peaking just at the sight of him.

"I was going to invite you in for coffee, Michael, but maybe we should just go."

He closed his eyes, swallowed hard and nodded. "Good thinking, squaw."

They exchanged an intimate grin as Michael ushered her out to his BMW. This time he opened the door for her, and Renata dropped a quick kiss on his mouth before she slipped inside. Squaw, he'd called her! From some other man, it would have been an insult. From Michael it was a sign of acceptance…maybe even respect. *I could get used to it,* she told herself. *I could get used to anything he called me in bed.*

To her surprise, Michael wanted to take Renata to Timberlake Lodge for the evening. She would have thought he'd want to avoid it like the plague. But as he ushered her inside, acting every bit the gentleman, she realized that he needed to erase the impression his grandfather had made on these people. Oh, there were different individuals there tonight, and probably none of them realized that Michael was the grandson of the old man on the horse. But Michael knew it. Renata could see a glimpse of angry pride in his beautiful eyes.

But they didn't talk about his grandfather over dinner. They talked about his prosaic job and her faltering career, his rapid promotions and her reluctant acknowledgment that it might be time for her to find permanent work in some field related to art and keep painting on the side. Michael asked about her progress on recruiting artists for the crafts fair and Renata told him about her growing friendship with Lydia. When she mentioned doing research on Indian crafts at the Tyler library, he told her he had some books on the subject that he'd be happy to lend to her.

It was starting to cool off by the time they left the restaurant, so when Michael suggested a walk along the lake, Renata didn't argue. She wanted to be alone with him, but she knew that too much privacy might be more than they could bear.

"When I was a boy, we went to powwows by the lake near the Dells on summer nights like this," Michael told her as they walked hand in hand. "Grand Feather would sing and beat the drums with the older men, while the younger ones danced." He gazed across the lake, but he did not look at Renata. "That was before powwows turned into tourist affairs. It was a private thing for our families. Winnebago. Not even intertribal."

Renata tried to imagine an eight-year-old Michael in feathers, whooping it up around a campfire. The image wouldn't come into focus.

"By the time I was a teenager, Indians were in vogue and we started earning money dancing for the tourists who came to the Dells. It was my summer job in high school. I got a scholarship or I never could have gone to college, but dancing gave me spending money." The set of his shoulders was stiff and proud, with a dose of lingering defiance. "Feathers and war paint, Renata. I looked pretty much the way my grandfather did the other day."

Renata tried to imagine an eighteen-year-old Michael in dramatic feathers and war paint, but she couldn't do that either. The man beside her was dressed in a classy, sober suit. She couldn't really think of him as a traditional Indian, though the image rather appealed to her.

"The other day my grandfather said he had one dying wish besides being buried with his people on your land." At last he turned to Renata, eyes dark and sad. "He wants to see me dance again."

Instinctively Renata squeezed his hand more tightly. His fingers tightened over hers as he tugged her a little closer.

"If that's all it takes to make him happy, Michael, surely you could do it for him."

He shook his head and looked away. "I knew you wouldn't understand."

Renata flushed. She'd been so certain that she'd said the right thing! How could she have muffed it again? "Don't shut me out, Michael," she begged him. "This Indian stuff is all new to me, but that doesn't mean I'm not listening with all my heart. If I don't understand, don't put me down. Just explain it to me."

His eyes met hers for a long, tense moment. Then he squeezed her hand and started to walk again.

Several minutes passed before he started talking. His silence would have alarmed Renata more if she hadn't watched the way he'd talked to his grandfather and observed the way time had passed during her conversations with warm-hearted Lydia. Silence didn't seem to mean the same thing to white people as it did to some Indians. If any other man Renata dated had remained silent that long after such a question, she would have been certain he was angry. With Michael, there was a fifty-fifty chance that he was merely showing respect for her feelings as he tried to sort out his own.

"I haven't fancy-danced in fifteen years, Renata," he finally said. "I'm not even sure I remember how. You could tell me I could brush up on the steps and it would come back to me quickly, and you'd probably be right. But a mechanical rendition of an old dance or two wouldn't do a thing for my grandfather. When he says he wants to see me dance, he means he wants to see me *dance*." Again his eyes met hers, imploring her to understand. "He wants me to *feel* Winnebago."

Renata laced her fingers with his more tightly. "Michael, you can't be somebody you're not just to please him."

Quietly he replied, "And I can't be somebody I'm not just to please you."

The gently spoken words speared Renata. Had she imagined that they'd been growing closer? Had the evening's early laughter and later openness been nothing but a mirage?

Feeling helpless and depressed, Renata turned away. Her hand left Michael's and he didn't try to pull her back. For a long moment she simply stood there by his side, pretending to watch the beauties of a Wisconsin summer night, pretending he hadn't torn her up inside.

It was a clear and lovely evening. She could smell the rich scents of cedar and pine. Off to the south, she heard an owl calling. Tiny creatures scurried away in the night.

Breaking the silence, Renata said, "Michael, I know you've got some things to sort out about being Winnebago. I know there are bits and pieces of your life I can't ever hope to understand. I wasn't raised the way you were. I don't have the same background to work through." She turned to face him. "But I'm a person, too. I have my own old war wounds, my own dreams, my own conflicts. They don't keep me from loving somebody else. They won't keep me from loving you."

His eyes met hers. He swallowed hard. Again he looked away.

"Don't you understand, Michael? I don't care how Indian you are or aren't. You've got one foot in each world—I can see that. I don't care. I'm not trying to make you act more white. Good heavens, look at me! Nobody would ever accuse me of being conventional. If you were totally straitlaced I wouldn't know what to do with you. I like you just the way you are."

"I don't know what way I am!" he ground out, his hands balled into angry fists by his sides. "Don't you understand that? How can you say you accept me the way I am when I don't know who I am anymore? I keep wobbling from side to side, Indian to white and back again. I feel like two different people inside the same skin!"

The agony in his voice was terrible. What was more terrible yet was that there was nothing Renata could say to help him.

"When we talk about each other, all you see is that you want me and I want you. Maybe it ought to be that simple, Rennie, but it's not. Not for me."

Fresh tears were welling up inside Renata, but she fought them back. She knew where he was heading. She'd seen him march to this drumbeat before.

"Sooner or later I've got to make a decision that's much

bigger than whether or not I'm attracted to you. My people are dying off. There's such a small group of us left! Your people keep talking about overpopulation. They feel an obligation to control the number of babies that come into the world. But *we* feel an obligation to the ones who've gone on to keep rebuilding the race. We treasure every child—not just as an individual, but as part of a collective whole. Each one lost is more than tragic. It's one more step toward our total elimination." His eyes met hers, terrible eyes full of pain. "We've been victims of genocide ever since your people got here, Renata. If—"

"Stop right there!" she burst out, suddenly overwhelmed at the bevy of accusations. She'd been patient and supportive just as long as she could. "I am sick to death of hearing about what 'my people' did to the Indians! Somebody—people of my race, people of my government—did some terrible things to the Indians here. I feel awful about it, Michael, and so does every other compassionate American living today. *But I didn't do it.* I wouldn't have done it even if I'd been alive back then! It's grossly unfair of you to blame me for the crimes of thousands of strangers who've been dead for a century!"

His lips tightened as he took an angry step toward her. "I know it's unfair. But it's there. It's in me." He thumbed his chest with his fist. "It's in all of us. We've been kicked and killed in so many ways for so many years that we can't ever get rid of all the bitterness."

The breeze picked up, cooling Renata's skin, but it couldn't cool the sting from her inner wounds.

"Besides, you're wrong when you say the crimes were committed by strangers who've been dead for a century!" Michael railed. "Some of the criminals are still running the government, still robbing the reservation people blind. What do you think happened at Alcatraz or Wounded Knee? Why do you think we went on the Trail of Broken Treaties to Washington, D.C.? Not that it did any good. What's changed in the past twenty years?"

It was at that moment that Renata saw, as if painted in bright neon letters, the message that Michael had been trying to tell her. She'd thought his grandfather was a relic of another time, an anomaly, a half-senile old man whose problems worried Michael only because he was Grand Feather's grandson. The burial ground he kept worrying about hadn't been used in generations. But now, quite suddenly, she realized that Michael was talking about problems that had occurred in his lifetime. In *her* lifetime! She'd heard of the Indians' occupation of Alcatraz Island back in the seventies when she'd been in high school, though she couldn't remember anything about the issues involved. She remembered hearing that a radical group had taken over the tiny village of Wounded Knee, the same place where the U.S. Cavalry had massacred Sioux women and children during the famous Ghost Dance a century earlier. But she didn't know *why* they'd holed up there—either time. And she certainly didn't know about the incident in Washington he'd mentioned.

"Renata, I was a radical when I was in my twenties. I had hair down to my waist. I wore it in braids. With feathers and rabbit skin, damn it, and not just when I was dancing for spending money. I was super-Indian! I was going to change the world, reclaim the whole damn state for my people. My father had left us, left all of us, and become a businessman somewhere in California. My grandfather was ashamed of him. But I went back to the blanket, back to the old Winnebago ways. The whole country was in an uproar then. You remember— Vietnam, Cambodia—protest marches were closing down lots of schools. And I joined the movement. I was inspired by the standoff between the cops and the traditional Sioux at Wounded Knee. I had a friend who was badly beaten there. When he asked me to go to Washington with him on the Trail of Broken Treaties, I was thrilled. I put on war paint. I was ready to drop out of school. I was going to become a man! My grandfather was so proud of me."

Renata didn't dare make a sound. Michael was still angry, but he was pouring out his soul, telling her who he really was. No matter what he had to say, she wanted to hear it. She wanted to embrace the real Michael Youngthunder, whoever he turned out to be. But as he spoke, she began to realize that it might be impossible.

"We were going to take Washington by storm. We were ready to make the B.I.A.—the Bureau of Indian Affairs—atone for a zillion wrongs. We were told that the church people were going to help us out, give us a place to stay. We were told that the government was willing to listen.

"None of it came true. The government put so much pressure on the church people that they backed off. We were given a squalid dump to stay in, an abandoned church. Our leaders got together, made decisions. They decided to take over the B.I.A., which was rightfully ours. It wasn't until we marched in there and people started smashing things just for the hell of it that I realized I'd made a mistake."

His voice began to change now. Through his memory, Renata got a glimpse of the angry teenager, the frightened young man. But she still couldn't see the buckskin or the braids.

"It was a free-for-all after that. I knew why everybody was angry. I knew why they were upset. But I knew my grandfather would never countenance destruction of property, anybody's property, and I was ashamed of what was happening. I told myself that's why I left and hitched a ride back home. But the truth is—" he swallowed hard "—I was also afraid."

He started to walk more briskly along the shore, and Renata mutely scrambled along beside him. She scrambled even harder to find a way to ease the rapier-edged memories that still sliced his heart.

"I wanted to help my people as long as it didn't involve any sacrifices on my part," Michael continued abruptly. "That's the long and short of it. I knew that I was smart enough to get through school and make something of myself in the white man's world. I told myself that once I did that, I could help out some other way. Some legal, quiet, dignified way. I cut off my braids and packed up my feathers, and I never danced again."

There was a long, anguished silence before he continued, "I've never done a thing for my people since then. Not one damn thing. I've worked for white men, sold computers to whites, dated white women—some who tried to ignore my blood, some who thought it made me more exciting, who displayed me like some exotic sex toy to their uptown friends. Some white women won't have anything to do with an Indian, of course—even one in a suit—but at least they're honest about it. In some ways I find it easiest to deal with them.''

At last he faced Renata. Stiffly he leaned back against a giant oak and took a deep breath. His face was twisted in torment, but his anger seemed to fade some as he confessed, ''I've never slept with a Winnebago woman. When I was still Indian, no Winnebago girl would have me. I was too wild. Now I'm a man, but I'm too white.''

Sorrow and frustration battled in his eyes as he said, ''Renata, I want to make love to you desperately. I want to make love to you tonight.'' He cupped her face and kissed her with a rough and urgent kind of tenderness that moved her unbearably.

Then he whispered against her lips, ''But I can't get Grand Feather's teachings out of my head. He wants me to date a Winnebago woman. He wants me to marry one. And when the time is right, he wants a Winnebago woman to bear my child.''

CHAPTER EIGHT

THEY DROVE BACK to Renata's place in silence. Michael was sorry that he'd said things that might hurt her—and scared that he might have presented her with a dilemma that was more than she could handle. But he also felt a certain amount of relief. He'd finally shared his true feelings with this wonderful woman, told her who he really was. At least, who he thought he wanted to be. He knew it didn't make sense, not even to himself, so how could it make sense to her? He'd chosen the white man's road and most of the time he was pretty happy walking it. He would be happy walking it with Renata if only he could solve his tribal dilemma. And he wanted to. Desperately. What was it that made him keep looking back? Was it worth giving up the one woman he was sure he'd never be able to forget?

As he pulled up in front of Renata's house, he said quietly, "I was honest with you, Renata. You said that's what you wanted." But that had been before his blunt declaration. She had not said a word since they returned to the car.

She stared straight ahead, her body stiff but still beguiling in that skimpy pink thing that outlined every tantalizing curve. Michael knew he'd hurt her badly, but he couldn't think of anything to say that would take the sting away. He reached for her hand and tried to squeeze it, but it was as stiff as cardboard and as cold as Timber Lake on a winter's day.

"Michael," she said valiantly, "I told you I'd accept you the way you are. I do. But I never really thought that your Indian struggle had anything to do with us, not really." At last she met his eyes. She was crying, crying silently, with enormous tears that whipped at his heart. "I was wrong. You were right all along, and I was wrong to press you. If you can look at me and tell me that your future still lies with some nameless Winnebago woman—" she swallowed fresh, choking tears "—then there's nothing left for me to cling to."

Michael was horrified. He'd tried to tell her the problem straightforwardly; he hadn't meant to throw down a gauntlet she couldn't pick up. "Renata," he whispered, tugging her stiff hand to his chest. "I told you what Grand Feather wants for me. I'm still struggling with what I want for myself. Please help me find a way to—"

"I can see you imagining such a woman in an ideal world if you weren't…dating anybody special," she told him, her voice breaking on the last word. "But if you feel that way tonight, after everything that has and hasn't happened—" she swallowed a terrible sob "—then I don't think there's anywhere for us to go from here."

Urgently Michael laid one hand on her nape and pulled her closer. He hated to see Renata cry, hated knowing he was the cause of her tears. He had to make her see that he desperately wanted to find a way out of his dilemma. He wanted to find a way to shed his guilt while he savored life at her side. "Renata, there has to be some middle ground here."

"Where? How can you possibly give yourself to me and still make your grandfather happy?"

Honestly he answered, "That's the problem. I'm not sure I can. But I want you too much to just walk away."

"Do you? Do you really, Michael?" Her voice was cloaked with bitter disbelief as she pulled back.

He was too stunned to answer.

"I don't know what you want in a woman and I don't think you know, either. All I'm sure of—" this time she gulped back a shuddering spate of weeping "—is that you don't want *me*."

Something broke inside Michael. He took her face in both strong hands and pulled her toward him, his lips burning hers with sorrow and desire. A sudden need leaped up inside him, a need so potent that he knew he'd never be able to keep himself away from her tonight.

Michael tugged Renata onto his lap. His tongue begged entrance to her mouth. His whole body surged and swelled with urgency.

And then he realized that she wasn't melting into him the way she had before. She was pushing him away, small hard fists against his chest, sobbing out loud in a way that made him hurt as he'd never hurt before.

He'd hoped his kiss would make the tears stop, but somehow he'd only made things worse. "Renata, I never meant to hurt you. I only—"

"Damn it, Michael, I wanted you tonight, but not this way! I won't be played with. I won't be used." Anger lapped at the edges of her heartbreak. "You want a Winnebago woman to bear your children? Fine. You go find one. I wish you a happy life. But don't expect me to be your last fling before you settle down!"

"It's you I want," he implored her. "Do you think I would have shared my soul like this with just anybody? Do you have any idea how many years I've carried these feelings all bottled up inside of me?"

Suddenly he felt her forehead slump against his chest. She was sobbing freely now, clutching at his shirtfront. Quickly he leaned over and kissed her hair, softly caressing her nape. "Renata, please—"

"Michael, I love you," she whispered, kissing the hollow of his throat. "Please understand that."

For one desperate moment her eyes met his, blue eyes full of anguish and love beyond his dearest hopes. But the anguish must have overruled the love, because after one more sob, she whispered, "Please understand that's the reason I just can't bear to see you again."

RENATA CRIED for a good long time after Michael drove away. She knew that he was upset, knew that if she'd let him in and listened to his apologies, they probably would have ended up making love. It would have been glorious…until it was all over and Michael started to pull away again. Then it would hurt even more than it did already. Assuming that was possible.

She couldn't sleep. She felt shredded inside, like a prisoner groping for a light that was just outside the window…with the shades pulled tight. She could make many adjustments for a man. She could accept his shortcomings, his background, his eccentric ways. But she could not *become* a Winnebago, no matter how much she or Michael wished she could.

It didn't matter anymore. She knew she'd been wrong to push Michael, to refuse to accept the truth he'd tried to make her see right from the start. She didn't know if she wanted to marry the man and bear his children; she only knew that she didn't want to get involved with him when she knew, going in, that that option was totally closed to her. It was like dating a married man, something she would never do. Besides, she wanted a man who wanted *her.* And Michael didn't. Not really. He'd told her outright that he had no long-term use for a white woman. Despite his conflicting desire, at bedrock he'd find no peace without a Winnebago wife.

By Sunday afternoon, Renata didn't feel any better, and the last thing she wanted to do was drive by Lydia Good Heart's before she went back to Milwaukee. But she'd promised Lydia she'd come, and Renata knew she would have welcomed Lydia's company if she could have enjoyed her without thinking of the old beadworker's tribal tie to Michael. Besides, she really did need to see what progress Lydia had made on recruiting other crafts people. She'd given Renata reason to believe that she could persuade an Oneida quillworker of statewide renown to join her at the fair. She also said she knew two Chippewa barkworkers who were interested. Renata wasn't sure how it would pan out, but at least it was a beginning.

With Michael, everything was a dead end.

"MICHAEL? MICHAEL!" A pair of fingers, with nails painted bright red, snapped before his face. "Come back to us, please."

Michael tried to clear Renata's tear-streaked face from his

mind, but it was an effort. He'd wanted to call her a thousand times since he'd left her house, but he still couldn't imagine what he could say that would be both honest and kind.

"I've worked for bosses who had a lot of trouble with Monday mornings, Michael, but you've never been one of them," Maralys chided him, in a voice that hinted of gruff concern. "You were as edgy as a cat all last week. What's going on with you, anyway?"

"Did you need something, Maralys?" he asked irritably. He was in no mood to be questioned or consoled. It was one of those days when he'd have been happy to give up his job to the first person who walked through the door. Why the hell had he chosen a career in computers, anyway?

She shook her head. "I think you ought to give it up and go home, Youngthunder. You haven't looked at me once this morning. Whatever's going on with your grandfather and that woman—"

"What woman?" He could have sworn he'd never mentioned Renata to Maralys.

"Whatever woman has got you crawling the ropes. I've seen you worried about your grandpa lots of times, Michael, but I've never seen you quite like this before." After a minute she said more gently, "Did she dump you this weekend?"

Michael wanted to tell her it was none of her business, but the truth of the matter was that he was desperate to unburden himself with a friend. There wasn't one handy at the moment, so Maralys would have to do.

"Not exactly," he admitted. "But things did come to a rather…sudden end."

"She dumped you," repeated Maralys.

Angrily he confessed, "I told her I had an obligation to marry an Indian."

"Good God, Michael!" Maralys chided him. "Forget my sympathy. You got exactly what you deserved."

"Damn it, Maralys, it's more complicated than that. There are parts of my heritage that—"

"That you think about once every other Tuesday. The rest

of the time you're white. You belong with a white woman, Youngthunder. One who lives in your world.'' She gestured around the store. ''*This* world. I don't know this woman you've been seeing, but I do know that if the only thing keeping you apart is your Indianness, you're making a big mistake.''

He shook his head, feeling hot and angry all over again. ''You don't know what you're talking about. You have no idea what it's like to be Winnebago.''

''Well, neither do you!'' Maralys snapped. ''Maybe you did when you were a kid, but that's all behind you now. I know you feel bad about your grandpa—those old folks really know how to lay on the guilt—but that's his life he's trying to hold on to, Michael. It's not yours. Give it up. Forget this Indian junk and get on with your real life.''

When Renata said she understood him and accepted him no matter what, Michael could almost believe he could abandon his obligations as a Winnebago. Put so crudely, out of another white woman's mouth, he knew there was no way he could step outside of his skin, no way he could forget the people, past and present, who lived in his heart.

Maralys had said he'd forgotten what it was like to be an Indian. Maybe she was right. But that didn't mean he could close his heart to the Winnebago world.

It meant it was time to open the door to it again.

''WE'VE ONLY GOT two more weeks until the fair, Dad,'' Alyssa pointed out over supper one evening. She'd been working her fingers to the bone for the past two weeks, and there were still a thousand last-minute things to do.

Judson Ingalls took a bite of the rump roast she'd prepared and studied her morosely. ''I don't like to see you working so hard, Alyssa. You fluttered about with this fair stuff all morning and spent the afternoon gardening in the sun, I don't think it's wise or necessary.''

Alyssa could have mentioned a lot of other things that weren't necessary, either. He didn't need to hover over her as though she were a child, and he didn't need to be silent and grumpy as he'd been most of the day. At least he was talking again, though. Last week, after Captain Keppler had shown up with questions about the gun Brick had found in Phil's belongings, Judson hadn't spoken at all for twenty-four hours.

Alyssa still didn't know what to make of it, and she didn't quite have the courage to ask. Her previous conversations with her father on the subject of her mother's death had yielded little fruit and had caused both of them a great deal of pain. What point was there in pursuing the obvious—that whoever had killed her mother had used her father's gun?

The ramifications were frightening, but still not conclusive. If Judson had used the gun, surely he would have gotten rid of it. For that matter, maybe he *had* gotten rid of it. Phil had been the family gardener in those days; he could easily have come across the ugly thing. But why had he kept it all these years? Had he simply forgotten it?

Karen had refused to divulge what Phil had said, but Alyssa knew that Brick would tell her in good time. The trouble was, she was afraid to ask.

She was afraid to ask her father for more details, either. *Dad, do you know something about Mother's death you still haven't told me?* she wondered as she watched his beloved face across the table. *Or do you guess something you'd rather not know?*

Judson brought her back with an abrupt question. "What's going on with the library? Has Elise set up an appointment with that architect?"

"Johnny got a call from the new architect, who the first one recommended. Mr. Fairmont—the new one—said he was willing to come look things over. Johnny's going to set up an appointment for him to talk to Elise."

"Well, I want to talk to Elise as soon as she meets with the man. We can't bail out the town on this one, Alyssa, as we have in the past. We just don't have the money. That's a cold, hard fact."

No, they didn't have the money, even with the sale of the lodge. Edward was the wealthy one now. Edward had Timberlake, too. The only thing he didn't have was the passion for

Alyssa that had fueled her days and nights in high school.
There were times when she found him watching her, eyes intent
as a stalking catamount, but she could no longer read his inner
feelings. There were still a great many things he wanted in
Tyler—prestige, respect, revenge for all the pain the town had
caused him.

But the sad truth, it seemed to Alyssa, was that he no longer
wanted her.

DUTIFULLY, Renata finished up the third pen-and-ink sketch
she'd done of Michael in the past six days. In this one, the
Indian brave had turned his back on the white woman, and she
in turn had turned her back on him. To the average person
looking at the work, it might appear that white society had
turned its back on the reservation Indians, and while she knew
this was the case, it wasn't the situation between herself and
Michael.

It had been a terrible, hellish two weeks since she'd seen
him last. She knew that time healed all wounds, but she didn't
think her wounds had even started healing. Every time she
managed to forget about Michael for half an hour, she'd suddenly think of his eyes or his hair or the way he'd looked the
first time he kissed her.

Or the sound of his voice as she'd run away the last time he
tried.

Renata knew, in her rational mind, that she'd done the right
thing to break things off. They'd been going nowhere in great,
painful circles. Michael had tried to be honest with her right
from the start, she had to give him that. She hadn't listened.
And worse yet, she'd tried to persuade him to go against his
own instincts, to set aside the values that seemed to be an
integral part of him. The only sensible thing she'd done since
they'd met was tell him flatly that she didn't want to keep on
seeing him.

But she couldn't tell her heart to stop loving him. The ache,
the emptiness, was getting worse each day. Renata knew that
Michael's confession at the lodge had been very painful for

him, and she wished that she could have responded in some
way that had assisted him in healing those old wounds. Instead
she'd inadvertently rubbed salt in them.

Renata had not shared her pain with Lydia Good Heart, but
she knew that the old woman had recognized her grief anyway.
Lydia had done a splendid job of recruitment and had still more
ideas for bringing in Indian artists, and Renata had tried to
sound appropriately grateful. The last time she'd gone to visit,
Lydia had given her a hug and a freshly baked loaf of bread
when she left the house, calling her some sort of endearment
in Winnebago.

Michael had used an endearment with her once—squaw. At
the time it had sounded like a joke and had felt like a break-
through. Now Renata realized that it had been no more than
an idle hope.

She had no more idle hopes where Michael was concerned.

She didn't have too many hopes about her painting career,
either. She'd done a serious assessment of her income during
one of her recent sleepless nights and had come to the conclu-
sion that nearly eighty-five percent of her income was from her
free-lance ads, and even that income was barely enough to pay
her bills. She knew she had talent, and she believed that her
recent experiments with Winnebago subjects, set against the
beautiful Tyler landscape she'd loved all her life, might be the
start of a new and wonderful phase in her work. But that didn't
change her reality.

Most of her Milwaukee friends had given up trying to make
careers as artists. They'd married, found work in some related
field and settled down. One of her closest friends had taken a
job last year with a crafts store in Madison. Another had married a Jamaican and had left the country altogether. Two had
opened a gallery in Ohio. The reasons, both personal and professional, that had first brought Renata to Milwaukee were
gradually dwindling. As were her paltry funds.

Her morose reverie was broken by the arrival of a postal
carrier, who handed her a heavy mailer. The return address was

not familiar, but she knew only one person who lived in Sugar Creek.

At once her stomach rolled and her pulse started pounding. What could Michael possibly have sent her? More to the point, what did it mean? After all this time, she had not expected to hear from him again. What was there left for him to say?

Renata couldn't think of anything she'd asked for or anything Michael had promised to send her. She'd told him she didn't want anything more to do with him, and she'd meant it at the time. But all at once she was desperately glad that he'd sent her something. Anything. How wonderful that she still lived in his thoughts!

She'd barely closed the door before she found a knife and started tearing open the package. Quickly she glanced at the books—one about Indian crafts, one an illustrated history of the Winnebago—and then tugged out the brief note on a piece of lined, yellow paper.

Dear Renata,
These are the books I once mentioned might be helpful in your planning for the crafts fair. I'd like them back someday, but no rush. Lydia tells me she's been able to help you make arrangements with some bark- and quillworkers as well as some other Winnebago friends. I hope everything goes well at the fair.

You should be glad to know that Grand Feather has finally agreed to let me buy him a small trailer. He won't leave the property, but at least I can give him a nice little place to live. The price for this is one night's dancing at a powwow on the Friday night before your crafts fair. This is a public event—mainly to sell Indian crafts to tourists—so I don't have to be afraid of botching up a sacred ceremonial, which I've lost the right to participate in anyway. I've been practicing in my apartment, feeling like a fool. Dancing used to be as easy for me as breathing, and now I'm tripping over my own feet. Or maybe my own heart.

I understand why you asked me to keep my distance,

Rennie, and I can't blame you for it. I'm not at all sure that's what you really want—and I know it's not what I want at all. But I'm going to honor your feelings until I figure out my own. I only hope that by the time I sort out this Winnebago thing, it won't be too late for you to give me another chance.

It was signed, simply, "Michael." Then there was a post-script: "Did you mean it when you said you loved me?" Renata covered her face with the letter and sobbed.

THE MORNING of the powwow, Michael felt like a Little Leaguer approaching his first time at bat. No, he decided, it was worse than that. Once he'd been so good at fancy dancing—so proud of his manhood, his Indian heritage, his flying feet. Now his feet felt like stones and he was turning into an Uncle Tomahawk. His grandfather had manipulated him into attending a public dance, but couldn't affect what was going on in his heart. Michael would go through the motions, try not to make a fool of himself, try not to look at the gawking tourists—but that was it. There was no way that a simple powwow was going to change his life.

On the other hand, he was going to prove to Maralys that he still knew how to be an Indian. He'd be damned if he'd let a white woman insinuate that he'd forgotten what it meant to be a Winnebago!

By the time he reached the campground where the powwow was to be held, Michael felt all jumbled up inside. He half hoped he'd do well dancing and half hoped he would not. What he wanted most, he realized, was to learn something monumental from the evening. He wanted to feel too white to be Indian or too Winnebago to ever forget his heritage again.

He wanted a miracle. He wanted a reprieve. He wanted Renata…which somehow seemed like the same thing.

He was, at bedrock, a Winnebago warrior, so he could not beg a woman for her love or her time. But he'd come as close as he was able by letting Renata know that he was going to dance. This terrible weight on his chest might lift if only he could see her face tonight.

It seemed like a year since he'd seen her last. Michael could still feel her hands on his face, could still feel her beautiful blond hair. It felt so right to be with her. It was here, without her, that everything felt wrong. Whom was he kidding, anyway? He had no business wearing feathers at a powwow! He was a businessman. He had a life that had room for Renata…a life that was light-years away from this cluster of Indians.

As Michael climbed out of the car and grabbed his double-bustle costume, dug out of a box in his grandfather's shack, he heard the first beat of the powwow drum. The sheer impact of it startled him. It wasn't noise; it wasn't even music. It was more like the overjoyed greeting of a dear old friend.

How long had it been? Ten years? Fifteen? The beat pulsed in Michael's ears and it pulsed in his heart. It echoed in the soul of his memory.

Suddenly his head started moving in time to the beat and his fingers tightened on the beaded lines of the buckskin in his hand. The old song came to his lips, played on them secretly, then burst forth. He sang the old words in a quiet voice, certain that no one could hear.

But he'd been certain, too, that he'd forgotten all the old ways, that none of them mattered anymore—so certain that he'd almost convinced himself he could afford to let his love for Renata eclipse the clan obligations that would dictate his choice of a wife.

Now that the drum was beating, he was no longer sure.

CHAPTER NINE

LONG BEFORE Renata reached the campground, she knew it would be a mistake to see Michael again. It would be a mistake to see him dance. It would be a mistake to come anywhere near the Winnebago part of his life from which he'd expressly excluded her.

But he had written to her, had he not? He had told her he'd be dancing. He'd shared his conflicting feelings, as he would only have done with a close friend. Was it possible that he'd really been asking her to come here today? Did he really need the assurance of a friendly face in the crowd?

Renata wasn't sure. She wasn't sure about anything. All she knew was that she was, against all logic, longing to see Michael, dying to touch his face.

There were flocks of tourists milling around, eagerly pointing to various Indian crafts for sale—she made note of all the choices—and conspicuously snapping pictures of Indians in native garb. Some of the latter looked as though they'd dressed up for the part on purpose to make the tourists happy; a few of the younger men, heavily feathered, practically preened. But there were other people, especially older folks, who wore beaded shirts over jeans as though they were part of their everyday dress. Or, Renata guessed, treasured family heirlooms that were saved for special occasions.

There was no sign of Michael. Renata wondered if she could have misunderstood him or if he had changed his mind. Indian powwows, he'd told her, were common in many parts of the country during the summer months, and Wisconsin had its fair share, too. This one was deliberately set up for tourists, who came in droves to buy some of the same Indian crafts Tyler would sell at its own fair tomorrow. Belatedly Renata wondered if they should have set up a whole powwow also. But she had difficulty imagining the Tyler townsfolk welcoming feathered, buckskinned dancers in the town square.

She drifted through the cheerful crowds toward the sound of the drumbeats, solid, forceful, strong. Rising above the drums was the eerie sound of a lone Indian singer, joined a moment later by four or five other male voices raised in song. She heard no words, just clear vocables that reminded her of the prayer for the dead that Michael and his grandfather had chanted in her yard.

I'm going to honor your feelings until I figure out my own, he'd written. *I only hope that by the time I sort out this Winnebago thing, it won't be too late for you to give me another chance.*

Had she read too much into his letter? Was she grasping at straws? Was there a chance, however hazy, that by the time this powwow was over, Michael might get this obligation to marry an Indian out of his system? Would he find some other way to make peace with his grandfather? Would he find a way to give her his heart?

Renata felt so out of place that she was certain Michael would feel dislocated, too. Surely he would feel more like a tourist than an Indian in this crowd! Yes, he had roots, but he had a present and a future. Once his grandfather died, Renata did not believe that he'd have any reason to keep clinging to the remnants of the Winnebago world.

And then she reached the dancers. They were moving in a circle around a tarp roof that protected the drummers from the sun. There were men in wolf skins and feathers and beaded moccasins. There were women in beautiful white buckskin dresses with foot-long fringe, carrying handwoven shawls that sparkled with beauty. It struck Renata, with a force that came as a shock, that there was no playacting by those who danced. Maybe the tourists were playing a game, reliving a fantasy. But the Indian people in that sacred circle, footsteps echoing those of another century, were carrying out an ancient ritual that was only slightly dulled by time.

She watched, transfixed, for maybe twenty minutes, while one group of individuals stepped aside, the drums stopped, and then the whole cycle started up again. It didn't seem to be a competition or even performance in the usual white sense of the word. It seemed that everybody who knew a specific dance, or wanted to learn it, just joined in and did it his own way. Only the entrance numbers pinned to the dancers' backs revealed that this was, in some fashion, a contest.

To Renata's surprise, the friendly voice over the microphone suddenly invited the audience to join in what he called a round dance. Apparently some of the visitors had done this before, because they quickly joined hands with the dancing Indians and began to step side to side in time with the omnipotent, heart-warming drum. Feeling a bright new sense of belonging, Renata climbed under the rope railing and joined the smiling group. An old man in a wolf skin took her left hand, and a young girl in a brilliantly beribboned native dress took her right.

For the next ten minutes, Renata felt wonderful. She felt as though she belonged. She was at the center of the world, where Indians and white people could meet and shake hands, cross lines of stress and become, quite simply, human beings. In this place, Michael could not reject her. In this place, she belonged.

And then, as the communal round dance ended and something called the Eagle Dance began, she saw the man she loved. Or rather, she belatedly recognized him. She had been watching him dance, just a few feet away, for five minutes without realizing that Michael, *her* Michael, lived inside the virile half-nude Indian whose back was covered with matching feather bustles and whose head was topped by a dramatic trailing head-dress. A native bone breastplate covered his muscled chest and a buckskin breechclout hung between his erotically masculine legs.

His face—that magnificent angular face—was painted in black-and-red stripes that made him seem like a savage stranger. His eyes were oblivious to the gawking tourists. They showed not a trace of the communal spirit that had so warmed Renata during the round dance.

His feet were thumping, whirling, pounding up and down with the same fury she heard in the drum. His body curved and jerked with a raw, unfettered passion that made Renata's blood pound the way it had each time he'd kissed her. But then he'd been a man she knew and desperately wanted to get to know better. He'd been a man who cried her name and begged her to yield to him, even as he'd forced himself to hold back.

But this Winnebago wasn't that Michael. This was Thunder Eagle, scion of his clan. He was somebody Renata didn't know…lost to the music, to the moment, to the past he wore like a proud feathered headdress. He did not see her, and if he did, Renata achingly realized, he would not know he had.

ON THE DAY of the crafts fair the sun was blistering and the humidity was ninety-two percent, but other than that Alyssa thought it was a wonderful day. The turnout was terrific—not just Tyler folks but lots of tourists and visitors from neighboring towns—and so far they'd all been generous in their purchases. The auction was scheduled for two o'clock, on the town square in the shade, and Nora Forrester had everything ready. Renata had promised to break away from the crafts tables by then to give a speech on the value of art in general and Indian artwork in particular before the bidding began. Renata herself had donated a magnificent painting of a handsome Indian in a suit, tie and traditional headdress, reading a computer printout held in one hand while the other beat on a drum. It was probably the finest thing she had ever painted, and for the first time Alyssa wondered if the young woman might have a genuine career as an artist ahead of her.

The whole town had done its best to contribute to the fair. The quilting circle ladies had donated several of their hand-sewn quilts, including a classic red-and-white hand-pieced Arrowpoint design, in keeping with the Indian theme, and another they'd designed and appliquéd with the story of Tyler's history. Marge Peterson had donated coupons for a dozen meals at the diner as raffle prizes, and Tisha Olsen had donated coupons for haircuts and manicures at the Hair Affair. Britt Hansen had set up a booth for her low-calorie cheesecake near the fresh fruit stands, and half the ladies in town had donated baked goods to sell. Alyssa was thrilled at the way everybody had chipped in.

Most of the morning she kept busy greeting the crowds, chasing pregnant Liza out of the sun and trying to buck up Judson's flagging spirits. It was almost noon when she spotted dear old Phil Wocheck hobbling along the edge of the square with Edward quietly supporting his arm. Phil's recovery from his broken hip had been slow, but at least he was out of his wheelchair now, able to navigate with a heavy cane or walker. Today he looked bright and happy, much as Alyssa remembered him from her childhood. In many ways, Edward's face was a younger version of Phil's, except that Edward was much more handsome. Recalling the last time she'd seen Edward— the night Brick found the gun—she felt awkward facing him again. Part of her wanted to talk to Phil about the gun, but she didn't want to do it in front of Edward.

Tell the truth, Alyssa, her inner voice told her. *You don't want to confront him at all.*

"Ah, *maluska!*" the old man called out, his dear old face folding into a grin.

Alyssa felt her stomach tighten as she heard her childhood nickname. As a little girl, Phil had often called her Polish endearments, including this one, but the first time he'd used the pet name after Edward had come back to town, she'd felt oddly confused and discomfited. For some reason, glancing at Edward, she felt the same way now.

Suddenly the gun loomed overlarge in her memory, and she had a frightening, ominous sensation that the word and the gun were somehow linked.

It was not a notion she wanted to pursue any further. She did not remember much about the night her mother had been killed, but she was starting to remember the gun. It bothered her terribly that she was also starting to remember things about

Phil from that time in her life—the way he'd looked, the things he'd called her, the way he'd made her feel.

And the fact remained that, forty years later, he still had her father's gun.

MICHAEL PARKED on a side street near the downtown area of Tyler and headed toward the noise. He knew there was no good reason for him to attend the town's crafts fair today and probably a number of good reasons for him not to. His last conversation with Renata had made it clear that she didn't want to see him again. She had not asked him to come. She had not responded to his subtle, aching plea for her to come to see him dance. He had desperately wanted somebody there from his other world, somebody to counterbalance his grandfather's desperate, hopeful eyes. His Winnebago relatives who were still Indian did not understand; his Winnebago friends who'd left the fold were not present. His participation had made his grandfather happy, but it had left Michael frustrated and confused.

He knew there were no easy answers. He had hoped that symbolically going back to the blanket—even for a night—would help clarify what he really wanted. But it hadn't. For a few brief hours he'd felt the old magic, the beat of his heart and the pulse of the drum. He'd joined his old friends at a nearby party, and he'd enjoyed it for a time. But here he was, less than twenty-four hours later, aching to see a white woman—*his* white woman—once again.

The bottom line was that he'd enjoyed the dancing. The drum had called him back, just as his grandfather had predicted. Amazingly, he wanted to go to a powwow again.

But the one thing the night had failed to do was wash Renata from his mind. It hadn't done a thing to ease the pain of longing or assure Michael that he was doing the right thing to honor her request. The growing ache was killing him. The simple truth was, he *had* to see her again.

When he found her hustling about between a booth of traditional Winnebago baskets and a display of very American quilts, it took Michael a moment to recognize her. Her blond hair hung in two long braids today, and both were adorned with beadwork and feathers. She was wearing a traditional Winnebago buckskin dress, magnificently beaded, one that any woman in his family would have been proud to wear. Michael didn't know if she'd bought it or had somehow learned to make it, and at the moment he didn't care. She'd chosen to dress as a Winnebago on this day when Tyler's history was being celebrated.

When she didn't even know that he'd be there.

Renata was talking to an old woman she called Martha, praising a particularly striking quilt made of dazzling red-and-white feathery-looking triangles attached to squares. She was unaware of Michael, though he stood only a foot or two behind her, until she turned to go and suddenly found him there.

He was so close she all but crashed into his chest, and she jerked herself upright like a frightened child. Her eyes grew big with shock and joy and longing. The hurt came an instant later, mixed with utter sadness and defeat. The sadness was all-pervasive. The defeat was absolute.

"Hello, Michael," she said uncertainly, as though he were an old friend she hadn't seen in years and wasn't quite sure she recognized. "I didn't expect to see you here today. Lydia's booth is down that way." She pointed toward the town square, but her eyes never left his face.

"I didn't come to see Lydia," he said quietly. "I figured that since you hadn't come to my powwow, I'd better come to yours."

There was a long, tense moment while Renata's sad eyes met his and made no effort to hide her pain and longing. Desperately he wanted to pull her into his arms, to kiss away the sadness, to tell her that all their problems had stemmed from some easily resolved misunderstanding.

But he knew it was much more complicated than that. The fabric of their relationship had a giant tear in it—a tear of his making—and it would require careful mending before either of them could trust it again.

To his surprise, Renata said, "I...I went to your powwow, Michael. I watched you dance last night."

He felt an odd lurch in his heart. Renata had been there? She'd watched him dance and hadn't even tried to say hello? Of all the things she could have said, that news was the most disheartening. If she'd found the powwow scene that unpalatable, it would have been better if she hadn't come at all.

He swallowed uncomfortably. "Should I ask why you didn't come speak to me or is it something I'd rather not know?"

She brushed a hand across her eyes. He knew she was fighting tears. "Michael, you were...magnificent," she confessed. "It was thrilling to watch you and it would have been thrilling to...to be with you afterward." He was taken off guard by the latent sensual response to his dancing that bubbled beneath those cautious words.

"So..."

Renata shook her head. "There was no place for me there, Michael. I felt like a misfit."

"There were tourists everywhere, Renata! It wasn't a sacred Winnebago ceremonial."

"I didn't go there as a tourist! I went there as...well, as whatever I am to you. But while you were dancing, in your feathers and buckskin, you were Indian, Michael. I watched you...*transform*. You weren't my Michael. You were your grandfather's *hitkunkay*—" he winced at the way she mispronounced the word "—Thunder Eagle. The kind of Winnebago who wants to marry another Indian. And when a pretty Indian woman came up to you afterward, I really understood what you'd been trying to tell me all along. Maybe she's not special to you, Michael, but she's the sort of woman you keep telling me you want. You looked delighted to be going off with her. I would have been in the way."

A terrible pain lashed at his heart. She must have been referring to Pauline Shaggy Walker, a childhood Thunderbird friend who was now happily married to a man from Buffalo Clan. "Rennie, you would never be in my way," he assured her. "I was glad to be with a friend—any friend—because I felt so out of place."

"So did I."

She tried to dry her tears again, but by now they were streaming down her face. In the background Michael could hear a voice on a microphone inviting everyone to the gazebo in the town square. When a tall blond woman called Renata's name and gestured for her to hurry in that direction, Michael knew he was running out of time.

"Michael, I can't talk about this right now," Renata said brokenly, using her fingers to dry her tear-streaked face. "I'm busy and everybody's watching and—"

"I'll go wait for you at your house, if that's okay." He hadn't planned on suggesting that, but it was the only weapon he could think of to fight the despair that rose inside him at the notion she might be sending him away.

There was a long, terrible moment while Renata simply stared at him. It hurt Michael to watch her beautiful face and see how she was falling apart inside. It was his fault—all of it—but he couldn't undo a single day. All he could do was start giving her sunshine now.

At last she whispered, "What would be the point? Has anything really changed?"

Suddenly Michael knew it had. He still had no resolution, no long-term plan that would meld the fragmented portions of his life. He knew that he could never turn his back on his people again. Not now. Not when he'd heard the drum.

But he'd also learned that he still desperately wanted Renata to be his woman.

He wanted her at any price.

Slowly Michael reached out to Renata and laid one hand on her face. His fingertips gently traced her tears.

"Yes," he said softly, feeling her creamy cheek melt into his palm. "I think something has changed."

He felt her quiver beneath his hand, watched her eyes open wide. The pain and defeat did not vanish, but there was a glimmer of hope that he hadn't seen there in a long time. When

Renata fumbled in her pocket and wordlessly tugged a house key off her key ring, Michael felt a sudden rush of desperate hope that her love for him still lingered.

He stripped one feather from her hair as he took the key, his fingers lingering against the warmth of her silken throat. Then he tucked the feather in his pocket along with the key.

''I'll be waiting for you, squaw,'' he promised. Unable to stop himself, he dropped a potent kiss on her lips before he walked away.

CHAPTER TEN

RENATA HAD LOOKED forward to the fair for weeks, but from the moment she gave Michael the key to her house, she could hardly wait for it to end. There were myriad details to attend to—money to collect, booths to close down, unsold art to pack into participants' cars and trucks and vans. Some idiot—Renata herself—had insisted that they run the fair until the dinner hour, so she was still cleaning up at seven-thirty.

It was a little after eight and the sun was sinking when she pulled into her front yard. She swallowed hard when she saw Michael's car. Part of her had been afraid he'd disappear...or that she'd imagined his promise in the first place.

Yes, I think something has changed, he'd told her. He hadn't explained. But he'd taken her key like a man who planned to spend the night, and he'd pulled off her feather like a man who planned to remove the rest of her clothing...slowly.

Her heartbeat doubled at the thought.

Renata tried not to rush inside, but she felt winded anyway when she first caught sight of him. He was still wearing his jeans, but now he was barefoot and bare-chested. His biceps rippled with sweat. Considering the heat in Renata's old, poorly ventilated house, his half-naked appearance was justified, but only a man who was very much at home would have taken off so many clothes while waiting for his hostess.

Or a man who planned to take off the rest once she arrived.

As Renata's eyes met Michael's, she felt a sudden shiver that was totally out of place for this sweltering summer night. She'd planned to start off with some prosaic question like, "Have you eaten anything?" It was a natural enough question when Michael was always hungry, and after the long day, she herself was ravenous.

But the look in Michael's eyes changed the nature of her appetite.

There was a world of feeling there—hurt, desire, apology, uncertainty, regret. And overshadowing all the other demons, something Renata had never been sure he felt for her before.

Love.

For a long moment Michael stood his ground while her gaze caressed his face. Then he whispered one word that seemed to embody everything he must have been feeling: "Please."

Renata didn't ask what he meant. She didn't ask what had caused him to change his mind or whether this time he'd crossed the line to stay. All she knew was that he'd come back to her, hat in hand, and there was no way on earth she could bring herself to turn him away.

Abruptly she bolted across the room and wrapped her arms around his neck. Instantly he clung to her, his cheek pressed urgently against her own. Renata could feel her breasts crushed by his strong pectorals; her spine tingled under his urgent hands. She loved the feel of every strong inch of him, holding her so tightly that she knew she could never get away.

When Michael's lips claimed hers, she yielded utterly, her mouth opening to his questing, conquering tongue, her body pressing back against the rigid proof of his need for her.

Her response was intuitive, her surrender absolute. She didn't ask for questions or words of sweet assurance. Michael wanted her at last—without excuses or reservations—and she wasn't going to waste a moment challenging the miracle.

Renata's hands cupped Michael's face as his hot hands slid up her ribs to explore the sides of her breasts. As his kiss deepened, her urgency grew. His fingertips traced a path toward her areolas, teasing the outer edges until she gasped and seized his wrists, pulling them up so her breasts filled his hands.

"Renata," he whispered raggedly.

"I love you," she whispered back.

"Rennie!" he breathed again, the word all but wrenched from him.

Michael's fingertips closed unerringly on her tightening buds, but the buckskin still blocked his hands from her quivering skin. Renata felt overwhelmed by the heat of the heavy garment, overwhelmed by the heat of her desire.

"Michael, take it off," she begged him. "I can hardly breathe."

A moment later the dress was lying over her living room couch, but neither her heat nor her desire had abated. Michael slipped one hand down into her bra and grasped her nipple. With the other he popped the bra snaps in back. Wearing nothing but silky black panties and tanned deerhide leggings, Renata moaned as he pulled her close again.

All the pain of wanting him, all the hurt of his rejection, seemed to vanish as his healing warmth embraced her and his hands enflamed her breasts. She buried her face against his chest and let go of one last sob.

"Rennie, don't cry now!" Michael begged her, frustration cutting off his breath. "Don't tell me you think I'm still going to hurt you. Don't tell me—"

"Michael, you're here. If you're really going to stay this time—"

"Renata—" he lifted her face with one strong hand "—wild war ponies couldn't drag me away."

He kissed her again, this time with a flaming urgency that made her rediscover every inch of her womanhood. Again she felt the proof of his own urgency as he pressed against her; her own desire unfurled as she pressed right back.

"Michael," she whispered, "you put me through hell. But I never stopped hoping. Not ever." She hadn't realized it in the midst of her despair, but suddenly she knew it was true.

He kissed her again, swallowing her words in a storm of almost frantic need. "I never stopped wanting you, either, Rennie. I never stopped trying to find a way out."

He lowered his face to her throat and kissed her deeply. Renata groaned and seized his beautiful thick hair. His mouth was hot and moist, half-open, as he kissed her throat again and again.

"Michael," she gasped, on the edge of losing all control. She clung to his broad shoulders, now slick with sweat, quivering as she tried to get even closer to him.

He kissed his way down her chest, sucking one nipple, then the other as both hands gripped her waist. Then his hands slipped lower; his thumbs slid across the front of her thighs and his palms cupped them in back. Renata felt her panties being peeled down over the buckskin leggings, felt Michael's tongue sweep over the nakedness left beneath them, felt the probing tip dart inside.

She wriggled desperately as she tried to wrap herself around him. He held her hips, fingers stroking, while his mouth performed miracles inside her.

Renata never quite figured out how she was suddenly on the floor on top of Michael, but her legs straddled his as his hands caught her breasts. Somehow the fact that he'd kissed her most private female parts while she still wore the buckskin leggings made her feel almost wanton, aroused to the core. She tried to undo his jeans and pull them off, but she was growing crazy with need and they seemed to fight her. Impatiently she cupped him through the denim, delighting in the groan of anguish that was his reply.

A moment later Michael was wrestling with his jeans, tugging something from his pocket, kicking the denim free and protecting her with a single motion both deft and urgent. A moment later he was kissing her mouth again, his sweet breath and desperate moan mingling with her own. She felt his hands caress her buttocks and pull her closer, so close she knew that any instant he would slip inside. She rolled onto her side and dragged him with her, knees hooking his as she urged him to join her. For a moment longer he teased her, his stiff body massaging her quivering core of hunger.

"Michael, please!" Renata begged him.

Only then did he roll her onto her back, filling her woman's need with his magnificent body, enveloping her with a sun shower of love. Together they rocked up and down; together they cried out and swung side to side. Michael's fingertips pressed against her upthrust nipples as Renata tugged on his hair and cried out his name. When she reached a place beyond all thinking, he rocked her hotly—oh, so hotly!—until her rising hunger crested and her desperation finally began to ease. Only then did his motion quicken, arousing her all over again. She clung to his neck and pressed frenzied kisses against his throat as he filled all light and space above her, below her, inside her. She felt his power, his need, his hunger, as his rhythmic speed grew to a rolling thunder.

When Michael moaned her name at the peak of his passion, Renata was certain he'd given up all plans for a Winnebago bride.

MICHAEL WOKE with a curious sense of disorientation. His body was relaxed and deeply satisfied. He felt as though he'd been running for a very long time and had finally come to a place of rest. Soon—tomorrow, maybe?—he might have to start running again. But for now, he was content.

He was also aroused. In the sleepy haze that surrounded his struggle for consciousness, he remembered Renata's face, eyes wet with tears of happiness. But when he reached for her, she didn't seem to be beside him.

Abruptly he sat up and took stock of his surroundings. He was in an old house—a house without air-conditioning—and he was very much alone.

Last night I made love to Renata, he realized with a start. It was everything he'd dreamed it would be. He only hoped that when he came back to his senses, he wouldn't break her heart.

At the moment she was nowhere to be found, which he doubted was a good sign. Had she awakened ahead of him and decided they'd made a mistake? Or had she never gone to sleep at all, weeping while he'd selfishly drifted off to sated slumber?

He remembered rushing to the door when he heard someone outside, only to encounter two Timberlake tourists on a hike, searching for the secret burial ground that "the crazy Indian" insisted was nearby. He remembered the way he'd greeted Renata after waiting hours for the fair to end, hopeful and frightened, eager and frustrated, afraid it would all fall apart and determined to believe that it would not. And he remembered, some time later, finding her weeping in his arms before she'd led him upstairs to her room. They had spoken tender words of desire and affection, but neither one of them had been brave enough to talk about the future. Michael didn't know if Renata was grateful or disappointed that he'd thought enough about babies to make sure that none were born as a result of their first union. It was another subject he wasn't quite ready to bring up with her.

He didn't want to risk their fledgling relationship by reminding her that he wanted to father full-blooded Indians.

Quickly he searched for his briefs and jeans, then hurried barefoot through the house calling her name. There was no answer. No note on the mantel or the kitchen table; no message in the bathroom or on the bedroom chest of drawers. But when Michael glanced outside, he saw Renata's old truck, so he figured she must be on the property.

It was a beautiful, pristine morning that promised to be a magnificent if sweltering summer day. Michael would have rejoiced in it if he hadn't been so focused on finding Renata. Desperately he needed some hint—a word, a smile—that everything between them would be okay.

"Renata!" he called out, his voice too harsh in the moist summer air.

"Over here, Michael," she called back from somewhere beyond the barn. Her voice gave nothing away.

Still barefoot, he hurried through the untended grass to the area behind the house, relieved that at least he'd found her. But he couldn't stifle a pang of dismay when he found her so engrossed at her easel that she didn't even turn to greet him.

Michael walked up behind her slowly, wondering what had inspired Renata to start the day painting while he lay in her bed. Unless she was mad at him, unless it was all going to unravel once more, it seemed to him that he should have awakened to find her lying beside him.

She was wearing bright red shorts and a paint-spattered camp shirt. A small table stood at one side of the easel, filled with jars of paint. She was holding a tiny paintbrush, dabbing at the canvas to make ocher splotches that seemed to be coming together as a tree.

There were two people in the painting. One was a white woman with long blond hair, reaching out toward an Indian man leaning against a magnificent oak. The man wore jeans and a Milwaukee Brewers jersey. He had hair down to his shoulders, braided and feathered, and dark, hopeful eyes. In an almost offhand manner, the man's fingers stretched toward the woman's hand, as though he wanted to bond with her but wasn't quite ready to admit it. Even if Renata had used some other man's face for the painting, Michael would have recognized himself.

The ends of the black hair were woven with the blond as the mingled strands lifted in the subtle hint of a breeze. He didn't need to be an artist to know what that bonding symbolized.

"Good morning, squaw," he said softly, his eyes asking far more than his words.

"Good morning." She didn't turn around until she'd placed seven more careful dabs on the painting—he counted each one—then laid down the brush. Her eyes were warm but guarded. "Did you sleep all right?" she asked, her lips curving into a cautious smile.

"Like a log. Some sleeping pill you gave me."

Renata didn't seem to get the joke, which told Michael how tense she really was. He couldn't say he blamed her, after all that had happened. Still, he'd hoped that after what they'd shared the night before, things wouldn't have been so awkward this morning.

"Am I the inspiration for this painting?" he asked. Even though it was obvious, he wasn't quite sure what else to say.

Slowly, she nodded. "I've been doing a series on you ever

since we met. I've tried to capture the traditional Winnebago crafts and clothing, but my real focus has been on the changing relationship between the white settlers and the Indians. I've sort of used our interaction as a model.''

He bathed her beautiful face with longing eyes. ''I'm not sure what we're a model of, Rennie, except the hell that modern life can put a man like me through.''

Quietly she answered, ''You're not the only one who's been hurting, Michael.''

He reached out and touched her waist, not quite sure if she'd welcome his touch. ''I tried to purge you of the poison last night. I guess I didn't do a very good job.''

An embarrassed flush tinted Renata's creamy cheeks. ''I wouldn't put it that way, Michael,'' she admitted, her expression making it clear that their lovemaking had been every bit as satisfying for her as it had been for him. ''I have no complaints about last night. None whatsoever.'' She licked her lips, gave him a cautious smile and snuggled closer. ''I guess I'm just a little apprehensive about what to expect this morning.''

Michael pulled Renata tightly against his chest and braved her eyes. The reason for her fear was obvious. ''You think I'll change my mind.''

''I'm afraid,'' she confessed. Suddenly her voice grew hoarse. ''Damn it, Michael, this isn't a game to me! I'm in love with you.''

His tone was low as he replied, ''You're not alone in this.''

Her eyes flashed open in surprise and joy, then closed when his lips found hers an instant later. It was a kiss of promise as well as passion, and it swallowed up all the uncertainties with which they'd both started out the day. When Renata touched Michael's throat with the softest stroke of tenderness, he couldn't find words to express the way she made him feel. He just put his arms around her and held her close. For a long, healing moment they simply stood that way.

Then he said, ''You said there was a series. Do all the paintings point to such a happy ending?''

"Well, not exactly. Most of them were done when I…when you…"

Michael kissed her gently. "That's over now," he promised. "From now on, we're going to be together." He waited a moment for the vow to sink in. "But I'd like to see them anyhow. I don't know much about art, I must admit, but I really think this painting is impressive."

Renata grinned at him almost shyly, trying not to wriggle with pleasure at his praise. "I sold several at the fair, Michael, but I've got two or three sketches in the cab of my truck. You want to take a look at them after breakfast?"

He smiled and pulled her closer. "Yes, after breakfast. But if you're offering to feed me—" he paused, and a heated note colored his low tone "—I've got to tell you that I'm hankering for something else right now."

"But Michael, you're always hungry!" she protested, deliberately misinterpreting his intent. "Every time you're here you eat me out of house and home!"

Michael grinned and tugged loose the top button of her blouse. "I think you'll find that my appetite changes from time to time."

"Oh?" she asked with mock innocence. "And what might you be hungry for now?"

His grin got away from him. He just plain laughed out loud. How wonderful it was to feel free to play with Renata, to tease her, to smile, to touch her whenever he wanted to. Suddenly he wanted to wrap his arms around her and tickle her until she begged him to stop. Then he wanted to explore every sweet inch of her white skin.

"I've got a yen," he said in a low, sultry tone, "for some more of whatever you were serving last night in your room."

Her smile was downright provocative. "I don't recall the recipe right offhand, Michael. Maybe if we go back upstairs and start mixing the ingredients we remember, the rest will come back to me."

They shared a laugh, then turned toward the house, arms

looped around each other's waists, as Michael said, "I don't know about you, but it's coming back to me already."

Boldly he slipped his hand down the back of Renata's shorts and fondled the firm flesh beneath her undies. She squealed in surprise, glared at him in mock rebuke, then grinned mischievously as she tweaked his bottom, too.

SEVERAL HOURS PASSED before Michael mentioned the paintings again. By then they'd had lunch—having skipped breakfast altogether on their way back to bed—and spent quite a while discussing the success of the fair and the popularity of the Winnebago work and Renata's paintings. Michael had listened attentively to Renata's concern that Lydia was limiting her market by selling most of her things in Wisconsin Dells and had suggested that what she really needed was an outlet in the southeast part of the state, where tourists were not already overwhelmed with goods from the Winnebago or Menominee. Then he started hinting that it was time to leave.

"I've been gone all weekend, Renata," he told her with obvious reluctance. "I need to attend to some basics that I don't have time to do during the week—like grocery shopping and laundry. And it's really time to vacuum."

When she grinned, he said, "What?"

"Oh, Michael, it's just hard to imagine that Winnebago brave I saw thrashing to the beat of a buffalo-skin drum vacuuming his apartment." As soon as the words were out of her mouth, Renata regretted them. The last thing she'd wanted to do was remind him of the warring parts of his life.

To her surprise, Michael chuckled. "I think you've got that backward. What I had trouble imagining was the guy who wields the vacuum wrestling with the buckskin."

"Just as long as he doesn't have trouble wrestling with me."

Michael laid one warm hand on her nape. "I don't expect to have trouble with you, squaw."

Renata laughed, loving it when he was able to tease her. "You know, Michael, I read in one of those books you sent me that Winnebago women were peacetime chiefs even though men led the warriors in battle. Is that true?'' She'd read a great deal more than that, of course, but she wasn't sure he was ready to discuss her other discoveries. She'd absorbed everything she could about the traditional duties and customs of his clan, Thunderbird, as well as Lydia's Bear Clan. She'd learned that Michael's clan was considered the most important, but that every clan had specific responsibilities for the whole tribe—one was in charge of medicine, one produced soldiers, one guarded the horses with their lives. Every aspect of life from birth to death was guided by ancient rituals. Even though Renata knew that most of the material she'd read was no longer an integral part of the modern Winnebago world, she also knew that a great deal of it still mattered, at least in theory, to twentieth-century Indians like Michael.

''Absolutely,'' he replied to her question. ''My great-grandmother was a chief. Highly respected. They still talk about her.''

''Well, it occurs to me that it might be more appropriate for you to call me 'chief' than 'squaw.' I kind of like the sound of it,'' she teased. ''How about you?''

Michael growled and crossed his arms over his bare chest in an ''inscrutable Indian'' pose. Then he laughed and tickled her. ''I'll call you Chief Squaw. How about that?''

''Make it Squaw Chief and you've got a deal.''

He kissed her, still laughing. Several kisses later, he grew more serious. ''It would really be great if you could think of some way to help Lydia make some more money. She's had a hard life, Renata.''

''She never says so, Michael. I've never heard her complain about anything.''

''No, she never does. Even when her daughter disappeared, she kept her grief inside.''

''Her daughter?'' asked Renata. ''I know she's got five children, but—''

''Only four are still alive. Her youngest girl took off to Chicago in a fit of rebellion when she was in her twenties. Nobody heard from her for four years. Lydia never even knew where she was until she got word from the cops that she had died.''

''Oh, Michael.'' Renata could only imagine the depth of the old woman's hurt. ''Did this happen a long time ago?''

He nodded. ''It's been over twenty years. But I don't think that makes any difference to Lydia. I know she still grieves.''

Renata shook her head. ''She's such a loving, generous person. The first time I was there, I told her I loved a certain dress she'd made—the one I had on yesterday—and she insisted on giving it to me at once. I'm still trying to find a way to return the favor.''

He smiled and stroked her cheek with the back of his hand. ''And when you do, she'll do you another favor, and you'll always be in each other's debt.''

He said it in a way that made Renata feel like a member of the family.

''I'm so glad I got to know her, Michael. She's such a special person. I think we'll always be friends.''

Michael leaned down to kiss her once more. ''I think the feeling's mutual. She smiles every time she mentions you. You scored a lot of points when you asked her to teach you to tan leather.''

''Oh, Michael, it's an honor to learn from her! I can't believe she's going to take the time to teach me. I'm supposed to go over there and get started next week.''

He kissed her again, lingering this time. Then he said quietly, ''I really do need to go.''

Instinctively Renata moved closer to him. She felt a bit like Cinderella after the ball. The past twenty-four hours had been so marvelous she found it hard to believe they were real. And no amount of joy could keep her from fearing that the next time she saw Michael, everything might have changed again.

''I know you need to go, and I'll try not to keep you. But do you want to see my drawings first?''

''Sure. You said they were in your truck?''

She nodded.

''Show me on the way out.''

They walked out together, holding hands. The unspoken intimacy of the gesture touched Renata even more than the weekend of lovemaking. Michael didn't need to seduce her now. He was sated. But he seemed to want to stay with her. She was sure he didn't want the weekend to end.

As Michael tossed his shirt and shoes into the back seat of his car, she pulled out the drawings from the cab of her truck—only three were left—and explained her thinking on the first two, when the white woman and the Indian man hadn't been able to find a way to communicate. Belatedly she remembered that there was a baby in a cradleboard on the white woman's back in the third picture. She was embarrassed at the thought of Michael realizing how much she really felt for him.

When she showed him the last painting, he studied it mutely for a long time. By now she knew that when Michael was silent, he was thinking...usually Winnebago thoughts that did not bode well for her. But this time things were even worse than usual. Tension knotted his bare shoulders. His fingers balled into fists.

At last Renata said, "Michael, this is just symbolic of union. I know how you feel about tribal reproduction, but—"

"What is that baby holding in his hand?" His voice was chilling.

Dread rushed through Renata's veins. *I knew it would end like this,* the voice of doom told her. *Ever since he showed up I tried to believe him, but deep inside I knew....*

Aloud she said worriedly, "Well, it's just a toy, Michael. I—"

"It is not a toy!" He whirled to face her. "How could you possibly confuse a *sacred burial baldheaded war club* with a *toy?* I thought you were starting to get the picture, Renata, at least a little bit! The books I sent you aren't perfect, but they're as close as—"

"Wait a minute," she broke in, desperate to defend herself. "I didn't get the idea for the war-club toy from your books, Michael. It's something I found in Grandpa's collection of artifacts. Remember I told you there was a box in the basement?

He found the club when he was a little boy. He always called it an Indian baby rattle and I never had any reason to question how he knew.'' She swallowed hard, hating to look into Michael's dark eyes when they were so full of tension. ''I tried to show you his collection once. It's mainly arrowheads, beaded moccasins, that sort of thing. Old stuff he just found lying on the ground.''

Michael made a choking sound. ''He found a sacred burial war club lying on the *ground? This* ground?''

''Well…'' Renata tried to remember. ''I guess. As far as I know, he never traded for any of his Indian things. They were just things he'd stumble on while he was plowing or—''

''Was it this size? A miniature? Or the size a man would use as a weapon?'' Renata had never heard so much anguish in Michael's voice before.

''Michael, please, don't be upset about my grandfather's collection. He meant no disrespect. He was curious. He was interested. He—''

''*Was the war club this size?*'' He stabbed a finger at the painting. ''Too small to be a grown man's weapon?''

Renata swallowed hard. She knew she had to answer the question honestly, and she knew that when she did, it would drive a new wedge between them. And she didn't have the faintest idea why.

''Yes, Michael,'' she whispered. ''It was the size of a baby's toy. That's why I put it in the painting. It looked like it had been carved for a child.''

Michael expelled a labored breath. ''Damn! Damn it all to hell! I'm going to have to tell him. He was probably right all along!''

Feeling sick with apprehension, Renata touched Michael's knotted arm. ''Michael, I'm so sorry. I—''

''Renata, don't you understand?'' he burst out, his eyes full of torment. ''I'm going to have to tell Grand Feather the truth. There *is* a Winnebago burial ground on your land, Rennie. And if your grandpa found a sacred burial war club here—'' he had to push out the words ''—he plowed up a Thunderbird grave!''

CHAPTER ELEVEN

MICHAEL LEFT Renata's a great deal later than he'd intended, and even then he did not drive straight to Sugar Creek. Like a homing pigeon long delayed from a return flight home, he headed straight to the Dells.

His first thought when he saw his grandfather—who was not sitting in his spanking new trailer but in his old shack instead—was not *I've got to get him out of here.* For the first time in years, it was *This is my place, my family, my people.* He felt an inexplicable need to hug the old man. He wanted to draw near to every Winnebago he'd ever known and even those he hadn't.

The mere sight of that tiny war club had accomplished more in one instant than Grand Feather had achieved in all his years of prayers and pressures. Never in his life had Michael felt more keenly Winnebago.

The past two hours had been exhausting. First he'd insisted that Renata show him her grandfather's collection of artifacts, buried in half a dozen boxes in the basement. He'd found the baldheaded war club—with distinctive marks of the Thunderbird clan—and half a dozen other "artifacts" that were clearly Winnebago. And not just generic Winnebago tools, but items that, like the war club, had surely been used in somebody's sacred burial.

At first it had been difficult for Michael to speak of Renata, harder yet to explain the wild surge of anger that had left him shaking. He felt—how could he put it?—guilty that he worked in the white man's world, wore white man's clothes, was even considering joining a white woman for life. It was not rational, he knew, but neither was it a feeling he could deny. He'd tried to share his feelings, tried to assure Renata that he was not mad at her. But their parting had been awkward, if tender, and he knew that neither of them parted as happy as they'd been the night before.

He found his grandfather slumped in the twilight, calmly watching some fireflies dance just outside the taped-together window. A quiet smile warmed his features when he saw Michael hurrying toward him. It was the third time Michael had caught him in the shack instead of the trailer, but this time the old one did not apologize.

"I did not expect to see you for a while, grandson," he said softly. "I thought you would hide from me while you let the demons have their way with you."

Grand Feather didn't know about the new demons; he was talking about the ones that had trailed Michael to the powwow. Michael had had the distinct impression that Grand Feather had been pleased by his grandson's frustration and misery that momentous night, certain that his anguish would bring him back to the blanket. Michael couldn't bear to tell him what had happened with Renata since then.

He squatted beside the old man and laid one hand on his thin, frail arm. It was a tender gesture, almost beseeching, and it caused Grand Feather's eyes to widen with alarm.

"*Hitkunkay,* what is wrong?" he whispered in Winnebago, his quavery voice breaking on the last word. "You are not ill?"

Michael shook his head. "I am angry, but not with you. I am…angry with the whole white world."

Grand Feather looked shocked, then angry in his own right. "What have they done to the son of my son? What have the beasts done to you?" He sat up straight in his creaking carved pine chair. "Is it that white woman? I'll cut out her heart if she's—"

"No, it's not like that. She has not…she has been good to me." Michael knew it wasn't going to be easy to explain what he'd discovered without making Renata's people—and therefore Renata—look bad. "But she has found something very important, Grand Feather. Something I know you must have."

He reached into the pocket of his cutoffs and produced the sacred war club, suddenly wishing that he had a buckskin pouch in which to carry it. There had been a time when he'd carried all of his things in the old way; Lydia had even taught him how to tan his own deer hide. But that was long ago, before the VCR and the CD player. Before the answering machine.

He bowed his head before his lifelong leader, then placed the precious war club in the old man's gnarled hand.

Grand Feather's jaw went slack; his eyes narrowed with a fierce, impassioned light. "Where did you find this, Thunder Eagle? What grave has been desecrated by white men?"

Helplessly, Michael said, "It has been in a box in Renata Meyer's basement for the better part of fifty years. Her grandfather found it while working the land."

"The land her family claims? The land by the lodge?"

Michael nodded. "They used to have a hundred acres, so there's no way to be certain how close the grave might have been to the house. We looked for an hour for any clue, no matter how tiny…" How hard he'd searched for a red stick or a broken branch, planted at the foot of the grave the way pioneer Christians placed a cross. "But we never found anything else."

Grand Feather took the tiny club and pressed it to his chest. His old eyes grew misty. "Do you feel the spirits calling us, Michael? Do you feel them begging us to help them rest?"

For the first time in years, Michael fully understood the powerful sense of the ancestors tugging on his grandfather's soul. "Yes, I feel them," he confessed.

The old man gripped Michael's neck and pulled his head against his chest as though Michael were a small boy. Tears ran down his wrinkled face. "How I have prayed for this moment! I have found my people! I have found my place to rest! And my last child has started his long journey back to his home."

Michael hugged the old man, so full of love for him he felt like crying himself. How could he tell Grand Feather that the proof he'd uncovered, worth gold to an ancient Winnebago, would mean nothing to a white court? How could he tell him that he'd really come no closer to helping the old one be buried with his own people when he died? And how on earth could he admit that he'd given himself to Renata?

He loved her. He should marry one of his own, but he loved her too much to give her up. He knew it, and he thought Renata finally knew it, too. In time, he'd have to tell his grandfather.

But this was not the time.

RENATA WAITED tensely for Michael to arrive in Tyler the next Friday night. She'd spent another week in Milwaukee doing some free-lance advertisements to help pay the rent, but she'd found herself wondering why she bothered. Her professional career was, well, faltering. She knew she did good work, and she did sell a painting now and then. But when push came to shove, she knew she was kidding herself; she wasn't making her living as an artist. Her true income came from drawing pictures of rich gentlemen's golf clubs and rich ladies' shoes. And for what? So she could pretend she was a successful artist living in a big city?

Renata had spent more time in Tyler this summer than she had in years, and she was finding it harder and harder to leave her family home. Now that she'd made her peace with Michael—and, she desperately hoped, had not broken it—her interest in Milwaukee had dwindled further. Commuting for work or play was a thousand times easier between Sugar Creek and Tyler than between Milwaukee and anywhere. It took half an hour just to crawl through crowded streets to her apartment once she left the freeway.

If she moved back to Tyler permanently, Renata knew she'd still have to supplement her painting income doing something, but with Sugar Creek, the county seat, within commuting distance, there might be something she could do on a small scale. She wouldn't need nearly as much money to live in Tyler—

she had to pay property tax each year anyway, and the farm mortgage had long since been paid off—and there was a chance, she profoundly hoped, that sooner or later she'd be sharing her living expenses with Michael.

It was, Renata knew, a foolish dream that she shouldn't put much stock in so soon. Michael had made no long-term promises; he'd simply told her things would be different now. She'd confessed her love for him several times over the weekend. At the time, she'd been sure he'd said the same thing. In hindsight, she realized that while he'd muttered some sort of affirmation, he'd never come right out and said what he was feeling.

Until the end, of course, when he'd found the war club and had turned back into an Indian. He'd calmed down before he left and told her he knew it wasn't her fault that her grandfather had "desecrated" his ancestors' graves. He'd even kissed her goodbye and promised to return after work on Friday, sometime before nine. But some of the weekend's passion had faded from his eyes.

Renata hadn't heard from him since then, and she wasn't at all sure what to expect when he finally arrived.

If he arrived.

The fear that he wouldn't always lurked in her mind.

It was almost nine o'clock when she heard the buzz of a car radio and the sound of wheels slowly crunching over her private gravel road. Unable to stop herself, Renata hurried to the window and watched the BMW slowly slide into her driveway. Without haste, Michael—oh, how good it was to see him!—pulled out a small overnight case and moved slowly toward the front door. He looked like a reluctant visitor.

Or maybe a very tired man who'd had a hard week and was just relieved to be home.

Renata tried to fix a smile on her face as she opened the door, but she could already feel herself trembling.

Michael looked exhausted. His eyes showed his strain. Still, his lips curved into the tiniest bit of a lover's grin. "Got room in your lodge for a weary warrior, squaw?"

"Squaw Chief," she corrected him, certain that if he was

calling her "squaw" again, everything must be all right. She slipped one hand into his thick hair and gently tugged him toward her. "And the only place I've got room is under my own blanket."

He dropped the overnight bag and wrapped both hands around her waist. His tired smile grew mischievous now. "Not my first choice, Chief Squaw, but I guess it'll have to do."

Renata slapped him lightly on the chest. "Not your first choice!" she teased. "Maybe you'd rather sleep in the barn."

Suddenly his grip tightened, and he pulled her very close. His eyes swept over her with poorly concealed desire. "Not unless you plan to spend the night in the hay."

Then Michael kissed her, kissed her hard and kissed her long. It was the sort of kiss they'd shared a week ago, the sort of kiss that told her everything was going to be all right.

Until that moment, Renata hadn't truly faced the depth of her fears that she might still lose this magnificent man. She wanted to believe in his love for her, but there was a part of her that had waited all week for the phone call or letter that would say he'd changed his mind.

Now joy mingled with relief as she pressed herself against him almost too urgently, craving assurance far more than sexual release.

Michael saw into her heart at once. "You were scared again, Rennie? After last weekend?" he asked in some surprise.

She hugged him tightly and relaxed when he kissed the nape of her neck and hugged her just as tightly back.

"Only after you left with the war club," she confessed. "I thought you'd go straight to your grandfather."

"I did."

She pulled back and met his eyes. "What did he say?"

"He said he was sure his people were buried here, and he refused to die until I found a way to bury him in sacred ground."

Renata really didn't have an answer to that. Even if they found the burial ground, there were probably a thousand restrictions against burying somebody there. The only reason her own ancestors had been buried in the family plot was because it had been designated a graveyard before the state laws were enacted.

"Maybe we can think of something, Michael," she said gently.

His eyes were bleak and haunted. "I told him I'd find a way."

Renata kissed him on the cheek. How like Michael! He disagreed with his grandfather on almost everything, but he couldn't refuse the old man's dying wishes. She loved him for his loyalty, but she hated it when that loyalty drove a wedge between them.

Now, cautiously, she asked the question that had been burning inside her all week. "Did you tell him about us, Michael?" She knew she shouldn't have pressed, but she couldn't help herself.

He ran one strong finger across her lower lip. It was a gesture so full of tenderness, so full of promise, that Renata closed her eyes.

"You mean, did I tell him that I love you, Rennie?"

It was the first time he'd ever uttered those words, and they filled Renata with a joy that washed away the last dregs of her fear. When he kissed her then, in a new and potent fashion that did not encourage mundane discussion, she completely forgot her question.

It was not until he slept beside her later, replete with her love, that she realized he'd never answered it.

MICHAEL SPENT Saturday morning cutting some poplar roots that were growing under the concrete porch while Renata cleaned out the barn. It was not really a game plan that they discussed, but rather a natural set of activities that somehow evolved. Last weekend had been inevitable and glorious. This weekend things were different. The passion was still flaming, but they both wanted something more. It was too scary yet to talk about the future, but in their own quiet way, they were starting to prepare for it. Michael knew that Renata wanted her

old home to be more than an abandoned cabin to hide out in
once a month. He'd felt the change in her since they'd met.
She'd never explicitly said how she felt about living in Tyler,
but he was almost certain she was thinking of moving back
home soon…preferably with him.

Michael could guess why she'd stayed in Milwaukee so
long. As a child, Renata had felt sheltered by the love in this
old house. Now that it was filled with friendly specters, she
didn't want to live here alone. She needed to share it with
somebody who loved her and would make it a home again.

Michael wanted to share it with her, but he wasn't sure he
could. Oddly enough, despite his endless clan connections, he
felt somewhat like an orphan, too…at least he would once his
grandfather died. In his fierce, emotional moments, he denied
that the end was near. But he was a rational man, and he knew
that the old one had seen more than a century. He could not
possibly live forever.

After he was gone, what would Michael's life be like?
Would he keep on running in place, playing the role of the
successful businessman? He liked his job and did it well, but
it was only a job, after all, and when he came home at night,
his plush apartment was only a rented set of rooms. He'd
known for years he was ready to get married, but since his
aborted engagement, he'd never met a woman he could imagine
growing old with…until he'd met Renata.

Unfortunately, he couldn't imagine bringing her home to
meet his clan. She couldn't have been kinder to his grandfather,
but the old man still viewed her with nothing but disdain.

They spent the afternoon watching a Brewers game on TV,
indulging in a sensual seventh-inning stretch all their own. Renata, wearing only a T-shirt and an enticing hint of silky un-
derwear, was just beginning to fix some hamburgers for dinner
an hour later when Michael heard a car pull up outside.

"Expecting company?" he teased her. "Get your dates
mixed up on your calender?" He waited for her to come up
with a tart remark, but as he watched her face, he realized that
she couldn't seem to think of anything sarcastic to say to him.

To his surprise she said gently, "Michael, since the day we met, you've been the only man on my calender."

He felt oddly touched by her proclamation, so touched that he forgot that he, too, was not dressed for company. To be precise, he was not dressed at all.

He was halfway across the kitchen, suddenly in need of a potent kiss, when the doorbell rang and reminded him of their situation.

"Rennie—"

"Go upstairs and get something on, Michael! I think I left my shorts in the living room."

Grinning at her discomfiture, he did as she asked. It took him only a minute to pull on his cutoffs and a T-shirt, the most he wanted to bother with in the stifling heat. If Renata's company got the impression he felt at home here, well…so be it. He had a hunch he was going to be spending a great deal of his free time in Tyler, and the locals had better get used to it.

By the time Michael went back downstairs, Renata and her visitor had moved to the living room. He could hear their voices, hushed and uncomfortable, as he sauntered in.

"…And she said she remembered a whole bunch of oak trees," said a familiar voice. Lieutenant Brick Bauer's voice. "She's not sure of the shape, but she remembers seeing them in a picture."

"You mean a painting?"

"No, a photo. In the newspaper. Some social event—wedding, deer hunt, I don't know. It's only a sliver of a memory, Renata, but I thought you should know."

Michael's throat was dry as he entered the room. The policeman looked up with a smile, but Michael was too overwhelmed with the news to smile back.

"Michael!" said Brick, doing a bit of a double take. He glanced uncertainly from Michael to Renata and back again, then smothered a knowing grin. He made no comment, however. He just greeted Michael with a cheery handshake and said, "You're just the man I wanted to see."

As Michael took Brick's offered hand, he remembered how

he'd felt about policemen in his other life and marveled at how many things had changed. He'd once believed that all law-enforcement authorities were his enemies. Now he genuinely considered this white cop a friend. "I caught the end of it, Lieutenant," he told Brick.

"I think it's time for you to start calling me Brick," he said, winking at Renata.

Michael was mindful of the honor, but his focus was on something else right now. The ghosts of a thousand Thunder-bird warriors were suddenly dancing around in Renata's living room. Each and every one was reminding him of his clan ob-ligations. "Did I hear you right…Brick?" he asked again. "Did somebody find the horseshoe of oaks?"

As Michael sat down, Brick answered, "Not exactly. But the old folks at Worthington House, where my grandmother lives, were chatting about the ground-breaking ceremony one night—" he said the words straightforwardly, as though the ceremony hadn't been one of the most mortifying experiences of Michael's life "—and Grandmother mentioned the first time you came out here to look for the trees."

When Michael's eyebrows lifted, Brick said quickly, "I don't normally share police business with her, but things were really terrible with Karen when you showed up that first time—you remember?—and Grandmother could see I was upset and…well, you know grandparents. She got the whole day's story out of me."

Michael slowly nodded. He remembered the strange tension between Brick and the lady who'd later become his wife. At the time he'd been sympathetic and had even offered his ad-vice. He liked Captain Keppler and he was glad she'd ended up with Brick. But their problems were solved. At the moment he had his own to cope with.

"So your grandmother…" he prompted.

"My grandmother says that one of the old ladies at Wor-thington House remembers something about the oak trees. In the newspaper, she says. Not at the lodge, but somewhere near it. Actually, she remembers whatever it was from her girlhood.

so it could have been the land the lodge is on now, since it wasn't built then.''

Renata touched Michael's leg with the quiet intimacy of a wife. ''Michael, if anybody still has copies of old local newspapers, it's Elise Ferguson. The library might be closed by now—''

Brick shook his head. ''Not till five o'clock.''

Michael turned to Renata to ask her to hurry, but she was already reaching for her shoes.

''So you have found proof of our ancestral burial ground,'' said Lydia Good Heart when Renata returned for her first buckskin-tanning lesson. They had worked together for more than an hour, scraping flesh and hair from the soaking hides. Renata's hands were already feeling raw, and her respect for Lydia's painstaking skill was growing monumentally. It made her more ashamed than ever of how blithely she'd accepted the old lady's gift of the beautiful beaded dress. She was even more determined to find a way to repay all the kindness this wonderful old woman had shown to her.

Renata had been asking around to see if there were galleries or shops in Milwaukee that wanted Winnebago beadwork, and had discovered that many shop owners would be more than happy to sell Lydia's things if they could take the lion's share of her profits. While Renata was glad to learn that she'd been right about the potential interest in Lydia's creations, she was not about to suggest that her friend virtually give away her work. She needed a middleman who wouldn't gouge her.

''We found an old newspaper photograph at the library on Saturday,'' Renata explained, turning her mind back to the burial ground. Elise Ferguson had kept the library open an hour late for Renata and Michael, tugging out old newspapers from her precious Tyler collection on the second floor and finding old books of Tyler history for them to take home and study later. It turned out that Martha Bauer's quilting pal was right. There *was* a photo of the Meyer homestead on the front page of a 1909 issue of the local paper. The occasion was the burial of Renata's great-grandmother. The tiny family burial ground was where the shot was taken, but in the background was, unmistakably, a half circle of oak trees.

They'd rushed right home with a photocopy of the picture, comparing angles and distances. Michael had mapped out roughly where he thought the oak trees ought to have been and had found one stump that might or might not have been close to the others. It wasn't particularly close to Renata's lone oak. He'd spent most of Sunday dragging a steel rake around, trying to bump into some promising clue beneath the topsoil, but he found no further indication of oak stumps or a graveyard.

Renata knew, by Lydia's comment, that she'd already heard the story; Michael had left Tyler Sunday night with plans to go straight to his grandfather's, and surely the word had spread from neighbor to neighbor and clan to clan. There was no point in going over everything again. Instead Renata confessed, "I've known about it all my life, Lydia. I feel so foolish that I was too blind to see how important it was."

Lydia smiled. "Sometimes we are all blind. When I first saw you, I thought you were a stranger. A white one at that. It was not until much later that I saw that you had the eyes of my little girl."

Renata glanced up, startled. It was not an idle comment, and the tone of Lydia's voice left Renata profoundly touched. Right from the beginning she'd felt a special kinship with this old woman, but she'd felt awkward about putting it into words.

Now she said honestly, "When I listen to you talk about your beadwork, I sometimes feel like I'm hearing my own grandmother's voice, from when she taught me to sew." She wanted to add, *I feel like I'm part of the family of women, handing down the old ways from mother to daughter, generation to generation, old to young.* But it sounded sappy and sentimental, so she held back the words. It was hard enough to say, "I'm just so glad that you're willing to teach me what you know."

Lydia rewarded her with another sweet smile. "I'm glad you want to learn. Nowadays the young girls are not always interested. Especially the ones who go away. The longer they live in the city, the harder it is for them to come back.''

Renata wondered if she was talking about Michael. It was too late, far too late, for him to ever move back to the Dells and feel like a true member of the Winnebago community. But she knew he still longed for some sort of Indian connection in Sugar Creek. Now she wondered how many other Indians felt the same way.

As Lydia loosened the fat of the hide with an old bone scraper, she began to speak with quiet nostalgia. ''There was a time Michael's grandfather remembers when we clung together, a time when all the people still knew the old ways. Now we have to find new ways of staying together.'' She stopped to flip the hide over and started scraping against the hair. ''It is hard for us sometimes to see past the old hurts and worries. But every now and then we meet someone like you, and we learn again that we all are people.'' She gave Renata a healing smile. ''I am grateful that Thunder Eagle got to know you.''

Renata smiled back, feeling magnificently warm inside. ''So am I.''

After a moment, Lydia said, ''Michael...he is very special.''

''Yes.''

''He is special to you.''

''Oh, yes.'' Renata didn't know if Michael had mentioned to Lydia yet how things were between them, but he'd never told her to keep it a secret.

''Do you want to marry him?''

''He hasn't asked.''

Lydia's keen gaze impaled her. ''That was not my question, daughter.''

Touched by the endearment, Renata told Lydia the truth. ''When I look at Michael, I can't imagine ever turning away from him.''

There was a long, thoughtful silence as Lydia absorbed her words. Then she said, ''It does not trouble you that he is an Indian?''

Renata's eyes met the old woman's. She didn't try to hide her love for Michael…or her fear that his awakening Winnebago roots might someday strangle his love for her. "It only troubles me that his background troubles him. He does not know how to love me and still be the Winnebago his grandfather begs him to be. I wish I could find a way to ease his hurting, but I don't know how."

"If you left him, do you think it would help?"

Renata fought back a sudden lump in her throat. Surely Lydia wasn't suggesting that she give up Michael! "I tried it once, Lydia. It nearly broke us both."

Lydia nodded, but didn't answer.

For several minutes they worked in silence as Renata tried to think of how she could help Michael juggle his future and his past. But, as always, she could think of no solution. The only thing she was sure of was how very much she loved him.

She wasn't nearly as sure of how much he loved her.

"He's going to that Indian center in Milwaukee again to ask what to do about the graveyard now that we've found some proof that it exists. I think it's great that there's a place like that to help solve problems. It's too bad there isn't something like it closer."

Lydia shrugged. "We help each other solve our problems. It is not like the old days, when Bear Clan policed the village and Buffalo announced everything and Thunderbird led all of us, but we are still one family here."

"Here in the Dells?"

She nodded. "There are many other parts to the family, but we come together. The young ones wander, but they always come home." She grew sober for a moment, then added "They almost always come home."

Renata wondered if Lydia was thinking about her youngest daughter, the one who'd died in Chicago. She could imagine how lost and frightened the girl must have been. The only succor Renata had found when she first moved to Milwaukee was from her cluster of artist friends. She didn't think she would have made it through the first month without some sort of group to enfold her.

"When they are away from home, especially for a long time, don't they need a place to feel welcome?"

Lydia pondered that a moment. "No true Winnebago is at ease away from the People. But to have a tiny island of goodwill and hot food and a blanket…this would be good for folks far from home."

With no visible show of emotion on her face, Lydia reached out and squeezed her shoulder. Suddenly Renata felt as though the tiny house had been flooded with sunlight. She'd first come to this dear old woman because of Michael, but now, curiously enough, Renata knew that even if Michael turned her away someday—a fear that still lurked deep within her—she would always be welcome here.

IT CAME TO ALYSSA slowly in a dream. She was a little girl, a tiny moppet with blond hair and blue eyes, clutching a raggedy stuffed animal to her side. She was climbing down stairs that threatened to squeak, listening to something she shouldn't have heard, looking at something she shouldn't have seen.

The gun was suddenly thrust out in front of her, as though a camera had moved in for a close-up. It was black and ugly, ominous as a glint of light reflected from it in the dark.

Behind the gun was a familiar scene with familiar faces. Her mother's face. Her mother's bed.

Another person. A man's back, then a man's face. A face she knew.

Then, with the force of a cannon, the gun went off, shattering her dream with terror. As the smoke cleared, the loving male face changed, distorted by shock and anger. His rage made Alyssa quake.

She woke up abruptly, her mind as clear as a bell. She had an eerie feeling that she'd just heard the gun in real life. But the house was absolutely still.

Then she remembered. The gun at Anna's. Her father's gun in Brick's hand.

And Brick had found it buried in Phil's belongings. Was it the gun that had killed her mother? Why on earth did the old dear have it in the first place? Why had he kept it all these years?

Alyssa had no answer to any of her questions, no way to see whether this latest discovery would make things easier or harder for her father. But she did know, with a certain sinking queasiness, that she was not at all satisfied with the explanation Phil had given to Brick Bauer.

There were many reasons the old man might have hedged the truth with Brick, but he wouldn't lie to Edward point-blank if he asked him outright what had happened. Yet Alyssa couldn't bring herself to talk to Edward about her dreams and vague suspicions, and she couldn't bring herself to press Phil for explanations, either. What he'd told Brick would have to do. She'd loved the old man all her life, and she knew he'd tell *her* the truth, too, if she pleaded.

And the truth just might be something she didn't want to know.

"I HAVE FOUND a way to give you your wish, Grand Feather," Michael said quietly, trying to decide how to put the past two weeks of struggle into words. He cast a sad eye on the nearby trailer as he joined his grandfather on the old couch in his shack, making a mental note to arrange to take the trailer back. It was obvious to Michael that he'd wasted his money, just as he'd always wasted his breath trying to get his grandfather to move out of this pathetic shack. "It is not exactly as you wanted it, but...it is more than I had hoped."

It hadn't been easy. He'd talked to people in Milwaukee, in Tyler, in Sugar Creek. Brick Bauer and his wife had made calls for him. Renata had filled out forms. It had been her idea, a good one, the nearest thing to a miracle he could have hoped for. If his grandfather agreed to her plan, he could die in peace. And Michael could *live* in peace.

With Renata.

The old one met his eyes. "What have you learned, *hitkun-kay?*"

Michael took a deep breath. "I know the burial ground is not too far from Renata's house and the fenced place where her ancestors are buried. I have the war club and the picture, and I know where the spirits spoke to you." It was important to mention the last fact, the one his grandfather put the most store in. Michael was more impressed by the war club and the photo, but he didn't see any reason to mention that. "But I cannot prove the location of the burial ground according to the white man's law. Even if I could, all I could do would be lead a Winnebago fight to protect it. I could not legally bury you there."

When his grandfather's eyes narrowed, Michael knew he was swimming upstream.

"But we do not need to protect it as long as it is on Renata's land, because she believes me. She believes *you.* She will honor the burial site. No one will ever touch it as long as she owns the land."

There was a great deal more he could have said about Renata, about their quiet weekend afternoons and potent summer nights. He could have mentioned that he'd timed the distance from Tyler to his store and knew it was a reasonable commute. He could have mentioned that Renata had been making noises about leaving Milwaukee and finding a more practical way to earn a living close to home. He could have mentioned that, as he searched for remnants of his people on Renata's land, he had found his own place, a place where a white woman lived now and his own people had lived before. He did not understand the combination, but he knew that he was never more at peace than when he was strolling through Renata's fields holding her hand. It was a kind of peace he'd spent years hunting for.

Grand Feather did not reply for some time, and when he did, his tone was dark. "I do not want to be buried anywhere but with my people, Thunder Eagle. You promised you would do this for me."

Michael couldn't even look at him. He'd promised to try, and he had. He'd done every legal thing he could possibly do. But even if he'd been willing to bury the old man illegally—and even if Renata had agreed—he couldn't get away with it. Brick Bauer knew every step they'd taken right from the beginning; he'd cashed in favors for them, done legwork, bent a few rules. Michael knew he couldn't con the man—and wouldn't if he could. His personal integrity superceded any conflicting notions of tribal honor.

"There is another way for you to be buried near sacred ground," he suggested now. "Maybe even in it."

A guarded light touched the old man's eyes. "I am listening, Grandson."

Michael cleared his throat and sat down opposite the old man. "You remember the tiny burial ground we saw near Renata's barn? Where her grandparents and great-grandparents are buried?"

Grand Feather nodded, looking a bit suspicious now.

"At the time, this kind of burial was legal. Even now, the graveyard is authorized and held sacred in that tiny area inside the fence, even though nobody's been buried there for decades." He leaned forward and took Grand Feather's trembling hand. "Renata has given permission for you to be buried there. It will take a while to cut through the red tape, but Lieutenant Bauer is—"

"You want to bury me in a white man's grave?" The old man's voice crackled in disbelief.

Michael squeezed his hand but could not meet his disillusioned gaze. "There are white people everywhere, Grand Feather. You must be buried with some of them. In this place you would be near the ghosts of our own people. You would be on sacred land."

For a long moment, the old one was quiet. Then he demanded in an irritated voice, "Why would a white woman give her permission for an old Indian to be buried on her property?"

Michael still did not look at him. "You met her. She is different from many people. She is kind."

"She is white," the old man said bluntly. "Do not marry her."

Michael struggled for words. He'd never mentioned a word of his feelings for Renata to his grandfather, but he had not denied them, either. The old man knew him too well, knew by what he hadn't said just what she meant to him. Michael had avoided bringing the subject up precisely because he didn't want to hear those words, *Do not marry her.* He didn't want to feel torn between what he owed to his grandfather and what he owed to Renata.

But he'd been torn between them right from the start. He loved this old man. He would never do anything to hurt him. Yet Grand Feather was his past, and he wanted Renata to be his future. He knew that if he had not been Winnebago, if he had not carried the guilt of his past and the burden of his obligations to his people, he'd be making plans to move in with her full-time instead of just driving back and forth to Tyler on the weekends.

To speak against his grandfather's wishes violated everything Michael believed in, but to repudiate his love for Renata would surely be a sin.

"We have not talked of marriage," he finally replied, hedging between the literal truth and the truth that lived in his heart. "But Renata now walks at my side."

The old shoulders slumped. The ancient eyes grew dark with anger and despair. "Do not marry her, Thunder Eagle!" he repeated. "Marry one of your own kind."

"If I married her and you were buried on her land, you would be with family." Michael tried again, fighting the sick sense of hopelessness rising within him. "I could live near you for the rest of my life."

"And would you offer the sacred prayers I taught you? Would you sing the four Thunderbird songs for me when I die?"

"If this is what you wish, Grand Feather."

"It is my wish," the old one answered tartly, "that you do not marry her."

CHAPTER TWELVE

IT WAS A THURSDAY afternoon, around three o'clock, when Maralys appeared at Michael's shoulder and said, "There's a woman over there who says she wants to see the manager. She won't tell me what it's about."

Michael rolled his eyes. He was not in the mood to deal with a recalcitrant customer. It had been a long, difficult week, full of headaches at work and phone calls from his uncle about Grand Feather, and he didn't think he was going to be able to be as tactful as his position dictated. It was three hours before closing, and he was counting every hour until tomorrow night when he could lock up and head for Tyler. Ever since Michael had told his grandfather that he loved Renata, he'd felt confused and guilty—as though he'd somehow betrayed them both. He needed to see her, to hold her in his arms, to explain the quandary he was in. She already knew how badly he was torn, but somehow he felt that just sharing his frustration with her would lessen it.

"How nasty did she sound?" he asked Maralys.

"Not nasty at all, actually. Just firm about who she wanted. She's about thirty and awfully pretty. It it were a man, I'd handle it, Michael. But women are not my forte."

Michael found a grin. "I'm not sure they're mine, either."

"Don't be ridiculous. Give her that tomahawk smile and she'll fall at your feet," she teased him.

Michael shook his head. "I'm not taking any scalps this week, Maralys. I told you, I've already got a squaw."

Maralys shook her head. "I don't know, Youngthunder. This one's awfully pretty."

"She could look like a goddess and it wouldn't sway me."

Maralys laughed. "That's what they all say, Michael. Five minutes from now you'll probably be giving her a key to your apartment."

Michael was feeling a bit more cheerful when he crossed the store, hopeful that the woman had a complaint he could deal with diplomatically. But the minute he saw that long blond hair and the riot of colors on the full-skirted dress, he knew that Renata hadn't come to complain…and that Maralys had probably known who she was all along.

"Hi," Renata said, tightly gripping her knapsack as though to keep from touching him. Her eyes shone with love, but, as always, he could read the tiniest hint of a question lurking in the back of them. He knew she believed that he loved her. She just wasn't sure that he loved her enough.

"I hope you don't mind my dropping in like this, Michael. I was discreet with your staff. That woman thinks I'm just a customer."

Michael's heart began to hammer. Quickly he reached for Renata's hand. Longing made him squeeze it hard, then prudence forced him to release her.

"I'm delighted to see you. It's been a hell of a week, and I can't think of anything I'd like better than to have a good squaw waiting for me when I get home."

"How about a good supper?"

He laughed. "That, too."

"Lydia's been teaching me how to cook Winnebago style."

Michael shook his head. "I'm not picky, Ren. I don't even have a fireplace, and I'm not all that fond of Native food anyway. Anything that doesn't come out of the microwave will do." He studied her face, then asked with fresh concern, "Is anything wrong? I mean, is there some reason why you didn't wait to go home tomorrow?" His first thought was that something had happened to his grandfather, but then he realized that Renata wouldn't be the one to bring him that news…unless the old one had done something crazy again in Tyler.

She shook her head. "I just finished up everything in Milwaukee and decided I wanted to go home. Halfway to Tyler I realized that going home meant—'' she swallowed hard and dropped her voice ''—going straight to you.''

Deeply touched, Michael reached out to cup her face. Then he turned over his hand so his knuckles could caress her jaw. He wanted to pull her into his arms and tell her he felt the same way, but he was the boss and there were customers on the far side of the store. ''I know just what you mean,'' he said in a low tone. ''My apartment feels like a big empty shell these days. I like my job, but lately I've found myself counting every day till the weekend.''

He glanced around, then kissed her quickly. A moment later he pressed his key into her hand. Then he turned around to find Maralys laughing at him.

''What did I tell you, Youngthunder? You men are all alike.''

With sudden glowing pride, Michael laid one hand on Renata's back and ushered her toward his sharp-tongued assistant.

''Stop looking daggers at me, Maralys. This is Renata. My Chief Squaw.''

''Squaw Chief,'' Renata corrected him smartly, holding out her hand.

Maralys laughed as she shook it. ''Whatever he calls you, there's a feather in his hair with your name on it, Renata. I sure hope you're crazy about this guy.''

Michael felt a burst of pride that almost smothered his guilt when Renata answered gravely, ''He's my sunrise and my sunset.''

Her eyes met his with such tenderness that he knew she wasn't kidding.

RENATA FOUND her way to Michael's place without much difficulty, even though she'd never been to that particular part of Sugar Creek before. It was a nice two-bedroom apartment, reasonably neat and definitely clean. Only the empty refrigerator and the overfull freezer—stocked with microwaveable dinners—made it clear that a man lived here alone.

The rest of the place reminded Renata of a cookie-cutter motel. It was classy and respectable, but it reflected none of Michael's character. There were no photographs or knick-knacks or symbols of his heritage. The only personal sign of Michael was the bookcase, full to bursting with books about Wisconsin and Winnebago history, mainstream fiction and a smattering of mysteries. One shelf was devoted to CDs and old LPs. Neatly tucked on a nearby table was an extensive cassette tape collection of jazz, classical and rock oldies. When Renata turned on the machine, she was surprised by the tape he'd left in it: the deep double-beat of a powwow drum.

It was nearly a month since Michael had danced in Wisconsin Dells. Had he not bothered to turn on the tape machine since then, Renata wondered, or was he still finding solace in his people's music?

She eyed the music collection—nearly two hundred recordings—and decided that this was a man who loved music. It was more than likely that he'd chosen to listen to Winnebago music recently.

Renata listened for several minutes to the driving beat and the high-pitched warrior cries. It reminded her of Michael's magnificent body, his strong legs pumping, his feet pounding the earth. She felt a sudden rush of longing to make love to him with this drum pounding in the background.

But she had a dark feeling that he would never play this music while she was in the room. He was still trying to keep his Indian self separate from the part of him that loved her. He'd introduced her to his white co-worker with pride, but she knew that he was somewhat ashamed to reveal his feelings for her to his grandfather. Sooner or later she'd have to press him. It was ironic that he'd broken things off with his white fiancée because she'd refused to take his grandfather home to meet her family, when to some extent he was doing the same thing to Renata. Oh, she'd met his family—the only one who remained—but she hadn't been "taken home" in any meaningful sense. Lydia was the only member of Michael's world who made her feel welcome. How she wished that Lydia had been his mother, or even one of his aunts! Then she might have had a fighting chance of winning favor in Grand Feather's eyes. As it was, he refused to even come face-to-face with her again.

She knew that if she married Michael, his grandfather would shroud him in guilt for the rest of his life.

MICHAEL CAME home at six o'clock, sniffing the rich aroma of spaghetti sauce as he came through the door. Renata, in the kitchen, was barefoot and naked except for his old barbecue apron, which covered part of her chest and most of her thighs, somewhat like a breechclout. Her shapely backside was totally exposed except for the waist tie, and the sides of her breasts peeked out, full and inviting.

"I didn't want to get spaghetti sauce on my dress, so I borrowed your apron." Renata's grin was positively wicked. "I hope you don't mind."

Michael grinned back, his fatigue quickly evaporating. Like a kid in a candy store, he longed to touch everything he could see. "Hey, you're cooking my dinner. How can I complain?"

She took a few steps toward him and pressed a welcoming kiss onto his mouth. It was long, warm kiss that promised a lot more than a homecooked meal. "Hi, honey, how was your day?" she asked in a parody of a television wife.

He glanced down and noticed that one of Renata's breasts had completely slipped out from the bib of the apron. Instinctively he reached out and tapped the brown center with his fingertips.

"Not as good as my night is going to be."

Renata chuckled and slipped her arms around his neck. The motion caused her whole breast to fill his hand. "Meyer Catering aims to please. Is there anything special you want that's not on the menu?"

His fingertips closed over the stiffening nipple until Renata gasped. Delighted with the effect of his touch on her, Michael bent over and took the nipple into his mouth. He sucked until she pressed against him and whimpered softly. "I think I've decided what I want for an hors d'oeuvre," he murmured.

Renata's grip on his shoulders tightened. Then she let go and clutched at his hair. "Michael," she whispered, "if you keep that up much longer I'm not going to remember how to cook."

He reached behind her and turned off the stove. Then he untied the apron and let it fall to the floor. "Dinner can wait," he told her.

"MICHAEL, I've been thinking," Renata said the next morning while they were still in bed. It had been a gloriously sleepless night, and she was still glowing too much to feel tired. "Every time you have a problem with the graveyard, you have to go to Milwaukee. Every time Lydia tries to find new buyers for her beadwork, she's told she'll have to yield most of her profits. There are thousand of Indians in Wisconsin, lots of them near Tyler and Sugar Creek. Why isn't there any sort of Indian center or shop closer to them?"

Michael wrapped a long arm around her waist and pulled her nearer. "Because it takes a huge amount of commitment and experience to run a center like that. Most Indians don't have the administrative experience and most white folks don't have the commitment. Besides, it also takes some start-up cash."

"I've got a beaded dress worth a thousand dollars," she pointed out.

Michael eyed her warily. "That's a gift from Lydia. Surely you wouldn't sell it!"

"No, of course not," she assured him. "But when I think of all the white storeowners selling dresses like this in tourist areas, I think, why not here? And why not make sure that the artists who do all the work get more of the cash?"

She knew she had his attention now. He was still lying close to her, but he'd stopped trying to sneak a fingertip up to the edge of her breast.

"There are a lot of places that sell Indian art, Renata."

"Not in Sugar Creek. And there's only so much the official Winnebago outlet can handle over in Wisconsin Dells. Besides, from what Lydia said, there are several different tribes here. They need a place to bring their things. They need a place to gather. I know just how they feel.''

''No, you don't,'' he said softly.

''Well, maybe not exactly,'' she conceded, bristling at the implied rebuke. Would he ever forget that she wasn't an Indian? ''But I do know how it feels to be alone in a new city. And I know how it feels to have artwork you're proud of and can't sell. Judy Hall says I really found my niche since I starting painting Winnebago scenes with a Tyler landscape, Michael. I think that an Indian arts outlet would be just the place to find my clientele.'' When he didn't answer, she plunged on, liking the idea more and more as she expanded on it. ''I think a lot of people would prefer to make their purchases from an Indian support center. A simple place with low overhead shouldn't be too hard to maintain.''

Michael shook his head. ''Rennie, you're an artist. You know your craft. But I'm a businessman, and I'm telling you, every business operation is loaded with sand traps. You haven't the slightest idea what you'd be getting into.''

She smiled at him as the perfect solution—to everything!—suddenly struck her. ''That's why I need a business partner who knows the financial end of things, Thunder Eagle. Somebody who's used to dealing with Indians.''

Suddenly Michael's hand grew very still. His eyes had a grave, warning look in them that quickly stole her zeal. ''Rennie, are you just…exercising your mind, or do you have a real idea?''

Until he asked the question, Renata wasn't sure how seriously she'd been pursuing the notion. Tiny seeds planted in her mind over the past few weeks, were finally starting to germinate.

''Well, Michael,'' she answered truthfully, ''I really don't know. I hardly make enough on my paintings to justify paying rent in Milwaukee when I could live for free in Tyler. I don't mind drawing ads, but I don't get any great joy out of it, either. If I ran an art outlet, or support center, or whatever it turned out to be, I could still paint, collect my own commissions and explore some new Native arts forms with Lydia. She knows so many Native crafts people with wonderful skills that need to be celebrated and preserved, Michael! Absolute magicians in quillwork or beads or bark.''

Despite Michael's silence, Renata was starting to feel buoyant as the idea took shape in her mind. ''The tourists and townsfolk in Tyler loved their stuff. They bought it like crazy! There's got to be a big market in this area if we can just find a way to tap it—and a way to make sure that the Native workers get all the profits for what they sell.'' She was picking up speed now, glowing with enthusiasm. ''Aside from the tourists, I could use some of my art connections to move things out and around…especially the paintings and sculptures with Native themes. I've already sent out some feelers for Lydia. I haven't worked out all the details yet, I'll grant you, but…Michael, don't you think it's got possibilities?''

For a long moment Michael's eyes were dark and pensive. His hand lingered on her body, but it lay still.

Renata began to feel queasy. Michael never rushed into commenting, but this time he was taking far too long to ponder her proposition.

At last he said, ''Renata, you're a wonderful artist and you've got a good heart, but you don't know the first thing about running a business.''

''No, I don't,'' she answered, glad he hadn't added what she was sure he was thinking: *And you don't know the first thing about Indians.* She met his eyes and bravely said the obvious. ''But you do.''

He looked away. ''I have a job. I have a promising *career.*''

''You have an obligation to your people that you feel sick about not fulfilling. This might be a way to do it and still use what you've learned.''

''It's also a way to tie me to you.''

His voice was low, but his words whipped Renata in the face. She was not prone to displays of rage, but suddenly she couldn't bring herself to lie beside him. Her fledgling idea had been heartfelt, an outgrowth of her own professional needs, her deep affection for Lydia and her increasing concern for Michael's people. Setting a marriage trap had never entered her mind.

"Rennie, come back here," Michael ordered as she bolted out of bed. Anger and regret battled in his terse tone.

She ignored him and began dressing, fiercely jabbing arms and legs into the wrong holes in her clothing while silent tears raged down her face.

"Renata, I'm sorry." His regret was palpable. "That was out of line. Will you come back here so we can talk about it?"

"I don't want to talk to you, Michael Youngthunder," she snapped. "You haven't a clue who I am or what I want if you think I want to run an Indian arts center to trap you. I don't want a man I have to trap! I want one who loves me more than anything in the world." Her eyes blazed at him. "Until this morning, that's how I thought I felt about you."

He bounded out of bed then, stark naked, and seized her shoulders. He looked desperate now. Almost afraid.

"Squaw Chief, you know you still do."

It was the first time Michael had ever gotten her playful title right, and Renata didn't know whether it was an accident or a turning point. She only knew she couldn't keep living like this, never knowing when the other shoe would drop. How many times had he told her he could love her regardless of her race, only to prove it wasn't true?

For a moment they stood perfectly still. The only sound in the room was Renata's tearful breathing. She couldn't seem to march out of there, but she was too angry to forgive him right away. She wasn't even sure she wanted to.

But Michael was determined. Despite her defiance, he slowly eased his hands up to her stiff neck and started a soothing massage. Some of Renata's anger began to melt away, resettling in her heart as hurt and loss. When he tenderly cupped her face with both strong hands, she couldn't stop her tears.

"Renata, I do love you," he said quietly, his eyes utterly sincere. "I won't give you up without a fight."

She swallowed hard. "I'm not the one who's fighting you, Michael."

The guilt on his face made it clear that he knew what she meant. His grandfather might as well have been right there in the room.

"I told Grand Feather about us," he revealed.

Bitterly, Renata said, "I'm surprised. I thought you were too ashamed to own up to it."

"Rennie, please don't be like this."

Despite her yearning to make peace with him, Renata pulled away and started to dress again. She felt as though she'd gotten trapped on a Ferris wheel in this relationship. It was exciting at the top, but she was getting tired of dragging on the ground each time the wheel went around.

"Sometimes I don't think anything has changed from the day I met you," she confessed, her voice thick with anguished frustration. "The only thing that's different is that I love you more, so it hurts even worse."

He put his arms around her and pulled her close, but Renata forced herself to remain stiff and unyielding. Too many times he'd sweet-talked her into forgiving him, clouding the issues, giving her the illusion that something fundamental had changed.

The reality of the situation was that she was still white and he was still Winnebago, and he'd made precious little progress toward resolving his dilemma.

"Rennie, please!" Michael pleaded, soothing her back with his warm hands. "Would you rather I lie to you? Tell you everything's okay when I still haven't a clue as to how I'm going to work all this out?"

"No." Reluctantly she shook her head, her long blond tresses brushing his wrists. Her hands balled into fists of frustration as she told him the truth. "I just wish you could see that you've got more in common with me than with your romantic fantasy of a traditional Winnebago."

Tenderly he rubbed her neck again. "I know that, Rennie. But Grand Feather doesn't."

"I don't want to marry your grandfather."

It was the most direct reference to marriage Renata had made to Michael so far, and she knew it was a mistake. But he'd been the one to force the issue, though he hadn't given it a name. And the truth was that she *did* want to marry him, and she thought he wanted to marry her. If neither of them had been interested in marriage, they wouldn't have had any dating problems at all.

"Our children would be half-breeds, Renata," Michael sadly pointed out. "They wouldn't fit into either world."

"They'd be just like *you,* Michael," she countered bluntly. "You're the one who told me that your cousins don't treat you like one of them. You told me once, it's not a matter of blood, it's what's going on inside your skin."

"I am still Winnebago," he said stiffly, dropping his hands. "And that's what I want my children to be."

He took a step back and met her eyes with great sorrow. "Can you really look at me and say that if you had your druthers, you wouldn't prefer for your children to be white?"

Renata thought about it. She truly did. She examined every corner of her heart before she told him the absolute truth. "I want my children to know their father cherishes them as much as he loves me."

"That's all?" he asked, astonished.

"My dad was honest and loving and loyal to a fault. That's what I loved about him. That's how I want my kids' daddy to be. Are you going to tell me that only a white man fits that description, Michael?"

He looked away. He couldn't answer her. Instead he whispered, "I have a duty to my people, Renata."

"You also have a duty to yourself! Whether or not you marry a Winnebago isn't that big a deal to the tribe, Michael. You said yourself that most of them don't even consider you one of them anymore. Are you sure they'll even know who you marry or even care?"

"My grandfather will know! My grandfather will care!"

"Your grandfather isn't going to live very long, Michael. Maybe if we just wait—"

"He told me not to marry you. He told me to marry a Winnebago woman! He gave me a long speech on the proper clans I should choose from, as though I'd forgotten everything! He wants me to go through the traditional marriage ceremony, just as he wants a traditional burial when he dies."

Renata was so frustrated she couldn't begin to fight the flood of fresh tears. Was there no way to get through to him?

"Michael, I would be more than happy to marry you in the Winnebago way before or after we make our marriage legal in Wisconsin. And I'm doing everything in my power to arrange for your grandfather to be buried on my land. I just don't know what else I can do!"

He gazed at her solemnly. "You can't do anything else, Renata."

His voice was kind, but the look in his eyes told her that it was not enough.

WHEN RENATA LEFT an hour later, Michael tried to tell himself that they'd healed the breach caused by his thoughtless words, but it was obvious that her mood was too subdued. He had assured her that he loved her, that he would find some way to work everything out. She had told him she'd cook something special tonight, but there had been no joy in her eyes when she said goodbye.

Michael drove to work thinking about the Native arts center she'd mentioned. He knew it would be a reasonable union of their respective skills, and he knew that if anybody but Renata had suggested it, he might have given it serious thought. But the moment she mentioned her idea, he'd seen a vision of his grandfather's face. "White man's tricks," the old one would have said. "Look at the way they always cheated us at the trading post."

Michael didn't want to argue with the old one, who looked more frail every day. He didn't want to think about the possibility that he was deliberately trying to keep his future with

Renata in abeyance until his grandfather passed away. If he was, he was being unfair to both of them…and dishonest with himself. Besides, would Grand Feather's death really change anything about his feelings for Renata? Family obligations didn't die with the dead. If he couldn't make peace between Renata and Grand Feather now, the old one would still haunt their union from the grave.

It occurred to Michael that, once before, his grandfather had offered him a trade, one Winnebago favor for another. It had resulted in his performance at the powwow, in exchange for his grandfather accepting a decent place to live. Michael had kept his end of the bargain, but when his grandfather hadn't, he'd taken the trailer back and resigned himself to Grand Feather living out the rest of his life in that old shack. Didn't that switch the scales of balance? Didn't Grand Feather owe him one?

If he gave up his job to work for his people, maybe Grand Feather would realize how much he wanted to be a true warrior. Maybe he would forgive him for loving a white woman. After all, he wasn't the first Winnebago to have done such a thing. Even a hundred years ago there had been, from time to time, women who had married into the clan under special circumstances or even been adopted by somebody who'd lost a daughter. The bloodlines of these women had been forgotten in time. Their hearts had become Winnebago, and they'd been completely assimilated into the tribe.

As he opened the door to Katayama Computers, Michael realized anew that his allegiance to the place was purely professional. He liked his career, but he did not live for it. He couldn't go back to the blanket, but there wasn't any reason that he couldn't use his professional skills in some other productive fashion. Had he discarded Renata's idea too quickly? Could it possibly solve more problems that it created? Could it tie up the threads of his life and give him a way to feel *right* about marrying Renata?

There were a zillion details to work out, but maybe…maybe it was worth some more thought. Michael knew that Maralys would be only too happy to step into his shoes here at Kata-yama; he wouldn't be leaving his company in the lurch if he gave sufficient notice. The real question, he realized darkly, was how the idea would strike his grandfather. Oh, he'd love the idea of Michael opening an intertribal support center. But he'd hate the idea of his grandson forming any sort of part-nership with a white woman.

Michael's mind was still toying with the possibilities when he reached for the phone to order flowers for Renata. It was a very white thing to do, almost a cliché, but he'd hurt her badly this morning and he couldn't think of any other way to soothe her feelings until he could join her tonight.

An hour later the phone rang. When Maralys told him it was Renata, Michael said with some relief, "Boy, that was quick. I'm surprised the flowers arrived so soon."

Then he noticed that Maralys's face was grim. "I don't think she's calling to thank you for the flowers, Michael. She sounds really upset."

With a fresh wave of concern, he snatched up the phone, wondering if it had been a mistake to send the roses. Maybe he'd overreacted to their squabble this morning. Maybe he'd just reminded her of it and made things worse. Maybe she'd decided that she couldn't forgive him after all.

"Rennie?" he said cautiously.

She didn't answer, but that was because she was sobbing.

"Rennie, what's wrong?" he asked with a rising sense of alarm. "I love you, Squaw. I'm sorry I was such a cretin this morning. I just sent the flowers to apologize again."

By this time she was struggling to frame words, words that didn't relate to his apologetic speech in any way.

"He was here when I drove up," she burst out as she wept. "There was nothing I could do. I'm so sorry, Michael. When I got home…when I found him—"

He knew exactly what she was going to say before she said it.

"Your grandfather was already dead."

AFTER SHE HUNG UP the phone, Renata forced herself to return to the front yard, forced herself to approach the body lying there. She tried to tell herself that Grand Feather couldn't hurt her—he was just a human being with no more breath. But the eerie sight of death left her shaking. She had not loved this old man—he had caused her a great deal of pain—but she'd never wished him ill. Michael had loved him, almost worshiped him, and she knew that he'd failed utterly in his practical attempts to prepare for his grandfather's death. Grand Feather was the one person in the world who had unfailingly loved Michael since his birth, and now he was gone. Nothing would ever be quite the same for Michael again. Her grief was for him.

Renata had arrived entirely too late to call an ambulance and she knew that the last thing Grand Feather would have wanted was to die in the midst of bright lights and the other trappings of modern medicine anyway. He had come back to her home—his land—to die, and she was certain he was exactly where he wanted to be. It was possible his return was even his way of telling Michael that it was all right for him to marry Renata.

Or at least that it was all right to be buried in the Meyer family plot.

She didn't want to leave him out on the lawn, but she didn't think she was strong enough to bring him inside. Except for Brick Bauer, she couldn't think of anybody to call who would understand her situation, and if she called Brick, Michael's hands would be tied. Once the death was officially reported, all sorts of legal procedures might interfere with Michael's tribal obligations. She didn't remember all the details of the traditional Winnebago burial she'd read about in the book he had loaned her, but she knew Michael intended to follow them to the letter. It was the last thing Grand Feather had begged him to do.

Abruptly Renata remembered that Michael's book showed pictures of the face paint used by each clan. Hadn't there been a page of the proper markings for burial? If she could start painting Grand Feather's face, he would not look so lifeless so abandoned, when Michael arrived. He would look like somebody loved him. He would look like a proud member of the Thunderbird Clan when he was dead, just as he had when he was living.

It would be her very special gift to Michael.

IT USUALLY TOOK Michael up to three-quarters of an hour to reach Tyler, but this time he made the drive in thirty minutes. There was a burning, jagged hole in his chest that made it hard to think clearly; emotionally, he kept trying to stanch the wound. He had known for years that his grandfather was terribly old and losing strength day by day. For months now Grand Feather had been preparing for the end, trying to get Michael to do the same. But at the moment, none of it mattered. Michael's closest relative in the whole world had left him, and the woman he loved the most was alone with the fear of death and the knowledge that the old one had rejected her for all time. Michael did not know how he could take care of Grand Feather and comfort Renata simultaneously.

He found her sitting on the lawn when he got there, wearing the same parrot-colored dress as when he'd kissed her goodbye a few short hours ago. Grand Feather was wearing traditional buckskins, clutching the tiny war club in his fist. Michael knew at once that his grandfather had come back here to die.

As he approached the still form that had once housed the soul of the man who had selflessly reared him, Renata's gaze lifted to meet Michael's. She sat perfectly still. She did not speak. She waited.

Michael felt a fresh wave of shock as he stared at Grand Feather's face, so dear and familiar, yet so foreign. At first he thought the shock was only because he was greeting him in death. Then he realized it was because the old one was already wearing Thunderbird burial face paint: two horizontal stripes, black and red, above the red spots on his forehead; the traditional red stripes across his mouth and throat; a half circle covering his chin.

Did you really think you had to do that for yourself? he

mutely asked his grandfather. *Did you have no faith that I would carry out my obligations—as a man, as your grandson, as a Winnebago?*

Suddenly Renata rose, rushed across the lawn and crushed herself against Michael's chest. He tried to hold her, vaguely patting her back in a comforting manner, but he couldn't think about her right now. He could neither give her comfort nor receive it from her. He was in another place, a place where drumbeats echoed, and he needed another Winnebago beside him.

"He did his face," he whispered aloud, unable to get over that stark proof of his grandfather's final assessment of him. "He didn't trust me to do it right. He thought I'd betray him at the end."

Renata was shaking her head. The long blond hair flashed against his hands.

"No, Michael, I did it. I copied the pattern from one of your books. I didn't want him to lie there looking as though he had no clan, no Thunderbird people to bury him."

Michael felt a great wave of sadness well up within him, oddly tinged with anger, relief and regret. Renata had tried— how hard she had tried!—to find a place in the Winnebago world. But she didn't belong and she never really would. A book could show her how to paint a dead man's face, but how could it reveal that she'd usurped Michael's familial duties and clan obligations? He barely knew how to be a Winnebago anymore, but he'd paid careful attention to learning this sacred task because he'd known that the last thing he would ever be able to do for his grandfather was to bury him in the traditional way.

All the guilt Michael had ever felt about loving Renata welled up inside him. He could see Grand Feather shaking his head. *Is this what it's come to, Thunder Eagle?* the old one's spirit seemed to say. *A white woman painting me like a picture for somebody's living room?*

He knew Renata had tried to help him. He knew that painting Grand Feather's face had been an act of love. But he also knew that, for him, preparing the old one's face for a Thunderbird burial was a gift of contrition and love he badly needed to give to his grandfather. It was a gift his grandfather had needed to receive from him.

In her heartfelt ignorance, Renata had stolen it from both of them.

THE NEXT FEW DAYS were horrible—there was no other word for them. Michael stayed at Renata's while Brick Bauer helped them rush through the red tape getting permission to bury Grand Feather in Renata's family plot. And three days later, they gently laid the old one in his finally resting place on sacred ground.

They had discussed the details thoroughly. Grand Feather's friends and extended family had been invited to gather at the old shack afterward, with Michael serving as host in the time-honored Winnebago way. The traditional treatment of the body at the beginning and end of the four-day wake would have to be modified. In the old days, the body would lie near the wake site—always the deceased's home—so the mandatory prayers were incorporated into the activities of the gathered clan. Since Grand Feather's body would have already been interred in Tyler, Michael would say the traditional prayers over the body before he and Renata left for the Dells. He'd come back and say the last part at the end of the four dark days.

During the weekend, Michael said little. He rarely touched Renata, and he usually did not respond when she touched him. He slept in her bed and let her hold him, but a quiet good-night kiss was as close as they came to their normal tumultuous lovemaking. Renata knew how much he was hurting; she knew that the old guilt had risen to the fore. She'd done everything in her power to be supportive, to make no demands, to give him the space he needed to come to terms with his conflicting feelings and unresolved last words with the old man.

But she was frightened. There was a chance that Michael's distance and discomfort stemmed only from the pain and stress he was going through, but she feared it was far more than that.

The fact that she couldn't share her hurt with him—couldn't do anything that might make things harder for him—made her feel the emotional distance between them even more keenly.

She had done everything she possibly could do to be a loyal partner during the burial in Tyler. She would do everything she could to fulfill the proper role of a Winnebago wife during the traditional wake. She would take Lydia aside as soon as she arrived—surely Lydia would be there—and ask her for advice. Renata knew how crucial this ritual send-off would be to Michael, and she wanted to be sure she did nothing whatsoever to embarrass him in front of his fellow Winnebagos.

She asked Michael what he wanted her to do when he prepared for the first set of traditional prayers after Grand Feather was laid in the family plot, but he told her that he'd have enough trouble recalling the proper burial chant without an audience. Trying not to take the rebuke personally, she had waited inside, watching him through the kitchen window, hoping that during this difficult time for him, no more gawking tourists would hike by. She'd never seen him look more lost and frightened, and it took all of her willpower not to stroll out there and stand mutely by his side.

When he came back in, she tried to hug him, but he patted her head and pulled away. For the rest of the evening he didn't talk, but stared wordlessly at a televised baseball game.

The next morning, when they were scheduled to drive to Wisconsin Dells to begin the wake, Michael got out of bed, dressed in silence, then turned to Renata and said in a voice that was deadly calm, "Rennie, I don't want you to go."

Renata, still a bit drowsy and half under the covers, sat up and studied him shakily. "I can be ready in half an hour. We're not expected till ten o'clock. I—"

"I don't want you to go." Michael didn't meet her eyes.

She battled a sudden surge of sheer panic as she stared at him. Surely she'd misunderstood him! "If you want to spare me something, Michael, it's not necessary. I can roll with the punches. What's important right now is that I stand beside you. Whatever—"

"I don't want you to go." His voice was low but impassioned now, full of regret and sorrow. "I'm sorry, Squaw. I've been going round and round with this in my head for days. You're my woman. I love you. When this is all over, I'll be back to sing the four sacred clan songs. I'll be back *to stay.*" This time his eyes did meet hers, and his eyes promised the same thing as his words. "But I cannot—" he swallowed hard and seemed to choke "—I *cannot* walk into my grandfather's wake with a white woman at my side. It would be like spitting on his grave."

Renata felt the air rush out of her lungs, felt all her strength slide to the floor. He'd kicked her in the shins, cut out her heart, stomped her body black and blue. The worst of it was, she couldn't holler at him, because he was already hurting so badly. He wasn't angry. He was not trying to be cruel. He knew exactly what he was doing to her, and she knew that he sorely regretted causing her such pain. But he'd taken a careful measure of his priorities, and when push came to shove, Michael had abandoned Renata in favor of his people...some of whom he barely knew.

He looked terrible. His eyes were dark and full of torment. His bronze complexion looked tinged with gray. "I'm sorry, Rennie," he repeated helplessly. "I wish there was some other way."

She couldn't answer. What was there to say? For days she'd been the perfect, loving spouse, ignoring his silence, alternately offering comfort and getting out of the way. She'd given herself to him selflessly, bundling up her own fears and concerns and storing them for another day. She could have waited until his hurt abated, but she could not ignore the fact that he had calmly chosen to lock her out of the most vital experience of his life. She loved all of Michael. She could not marry just the half that pretended he was not Winnebago.

"I'll be back on Friday morning," he promised.

"Make yourself at home." Renata couldn't bear to tell him outright that it was over, but neither could she pretend that when this was finished, they could just pick up where they'd left off. She'd done everything any white woman could do to accept Michael's heritage, and it still was not enough. It would *never* be enough. It was time to accept the fact that Michael had been right all along. There was no future for the two of them.

His eyebrows lifted. Every line of his face revealed that his grief was killing him. "You won't be here?"

"Why should I be?" She couldn't mask her bitterness. "You've made it crystal clear I'd just be in the way."

CHAPTER THIRTEEN

ALYSSA WAS WEEDING the roses when she heard the car pull up to the front of the house on Wednesday evening. She was hot, dirty and disheveled after an hour in the sun and was ready to go in and fix a glass of lemonade. An unexpected caller would be the perfect excuse to knock off for a while.

As she poked her head around the side of the house and called, "I'm back here!" she was surprised to see the dark hair and vigorous stride of Edward Wocheck.

It was a long, long time—about thirty years—since he'd shown up at this house unexpectedly, and it wounded Alyssa that the sight of him now filled her with a swarm of feelings that were half melancholy, half joyous. Alyssa knew it was far too late for her to repair the damage she'd done to Edward's love for her a thousand years ago; it would be foolish beyond imagination to give her feelings free rein with him again. But she also knew that sometimes old lovers make the best friends. It wasn't much comfort, but after the troubling nightmares about Phil and her mother she'd been having recently, she was willing to take whatever crumbs of comfort a small lie to herself might offer.

"Good morning, Edward," she said as cheerily as she was able. "This is a nice surprise."

He swallowed uncomfortably as his gaze slowly drifted to the soil on her hands, then back to her face. "I never thought I'd see Alyssa Ingalls dirty her regal fingers." He never called her by her married name, never really acknowledged that she'd been married. "Can't your father afford a gardener anymore?"

The bitterness in his voice was restrained, but Alyssa heard it nonetheless. After all this time, why were Edward and her father still at war?

"I love to work in the garden, Edward," she said softly. "When I was a little girl, a kind man taught me to love flowers."

Edward quickly glanced away. Alyssa was surprised that she'd found a way to hurt him; surprised that she'd wanted to. But she'd long outgrown apologizing for her family's wealth. They'd been lucky to have it. Now, with the economy putting a strain on everyone, they'd be lucky to hold on to what they had.

"He taught me the same thing," Edward finally answered, offering a hand to help Alyssa to her feet. "He also taught me lots of other things."

Alyssa rose uncomfortably, trying to ignore the feel of Edward's hand on hers. Unbidden, she recalled the kiss under the mistletoe they'd shared at the lodge last Christmas. How hard she'd tried to avoid that kiss…how hard she'd tried to forget it! But it was hopeless. When she looked at him now—a grown man who still wore that old-time bad-boy smile—she knew that it wouldn't take a great deal of effort for Edward to melt her reserve. She told herself she was lucky that so far he hadn't shown any interest in doing so.

"How can I help you, Edward?" Alyssa suddenly asked, deciding that since he had undoubtedly come by on business she would be wise to act businesslike with him. "My father is down at the plant if—"

"I…came to see you." For the first time he looked awkward and unsure of himself.

It reminded Alyssa of the old days, the old Eddie, a constantly changing mixture of adolescent arrogance, insecurity and sheer sensual magic. She found the glimpse of uncertainty quietly endearing now.

"Would you like to come in and have some lemonade?" Alyssa asked, her brief pique with him evaporating.

"No, I…I only have a few minutes. I wanted to talk to you about what happened the other night."

At first Alyssa wasn't sure what he meant. She couldn't think of anything odd that had happened between them lately. The last time she'd seen him was at the fair, in broad daylight. And the night she'd bumped into him at the Kelseys', they'd hardly spoken. She didn't think she'd even remembered to say goodbye. She'd been too upset about the gun.

Since then she'd vowed to speak to Phil about the reasons he'd still had her father's gun, but she just hadn't had the courage to do it. She knew that Phil had never liked her mother, but she'd always assumed it was because he'd been so fond of Alyssa herself. Margaret Ingalls had not been the best mother in the world. It was natural that anyone who loved her daughter would resent her. But surely Phil couldn't have hated her that much! Unless there was some other reason…something that had happened between them that Alyssa didn't know.

Something she might be better off not knowing.

She stepped under the welcoming shade of a massive oak and peered up at Edward's face. He looked tense, frustrated…almost frightened. It was years since she'd seen him wear that expression. The last time was the night she'd given him back his rhinestone engagement ring thirty years ago.

"Edward—"

"I know you're wondering why my dad had that gun," he said bluntly. "So am I."

Alyssa's eyes met his. She felt a sudden chill that not even the summer's sun could ward off.

"You know he told Brick he couldn't remember. I asked him privately, Alyssa, and he told me the same thing."

"Maybe he really can't remember," she ventured, afraid to ask if Phil had made that pronouncement while looking his son in the eye. She couldn't remember much from that time period either. If Phil had ever known anything, maybe he'd decided it was better to let sleeping dogs lie.

"Brick doesn't want to push him, but that hard-nosed captain-wife of his has grilled Dad pretty roughly," Edward continued. "Twice. I don't want him upset, Alyssa. He's an old man. He's tired. And he's loved you all his life."

Alyssa's lips tightened in dismay. "What are you saying, Edward? What are you asking me to do?"

"I'm saying that your family still says what goes in this town. If you tell Karen Keppler you believe Dad just got that gun accidentally when he packed up his things from the lodge, she'll back off and let him be."

Alyssa wasn't sure that was true. Karen Keppler Bauer had impressed her as a strong-willed woman whom not even Brick could always control. In the brief months she'd been in Tyler, she'd shaken up half the town and made it clear that she thought Judson had had something to do with his own wife's death. Oh, she hadn't said so outright, but it wasn't hard to tell she was suspicious. It wasn't likely that she'd leave old Phil alone on Alyssa's say-so.

As a thought occurred to Alyssa, she said, "Edward, you know Karen as well as I do. Better, in fact. She used to live at the boardinghouse with you."

He shook his head. "I get along fine with Karen, but Phil's my father. She's not going to think I have any objectivity around him."

"Well, you don't. And I'm not sure you should. But I don't really, either. You know how much I've always loved him."

Suddenly Edward took her hand and squeezed it hard. But it wasn't a lover's touch. It was the desperate plea of an old friend. She couldn't believe how much it hurt to see him beg.

"And he'd do anything for you, Alyssa. Anything at all. I'm begging you to do this one thing for him."

That was when she knew. The truth ripped at her insides, shook her down to her toes. Edward believed that his dad had had something to do with her mother's death! Was it possible that Phil knew who'd killed her or—*God, no!*—that he'd done it himself?

Until that moment, Alyssa had never been able to admit to herself that she half believed it, too.

BY SIX O'CLOCK the next morning, Renata had come to a decision. She couldn't stay in Tyler for another minute. She could not stay in this house alone. Every wall, every room, every window reminded her of Michael.

Going outdoors was even worse. Rising the instant there was a ghost of sunlight to chase away the night's tears, she got no solace from her lengthy walk at dawn. Another damned tourist picked this morning to come searching for the burial ground that "the crazy old Indian" claimed was nearby, and Renata was afraid she'd encounter more early-morning hikers from the lodge. Besides, no matter where she turned, she couldn't keep her eyes away from the family plot. Grand Feather seemed to be mocking her.

I won in the end. Blood will tell. Even dead, I still have power over him, she could almost hear him crowing. *He will never marry you.*

Renata had given up arguing with Grand Feather. Everything he'd said had turned out to be true.

How was Michael feeling this morning, she wondered, surrounded by people who meant more to him than she did, some of whom he barely knew? She ached for him, hated him, loved him. Her whole body felt numb and battered. Her very soul grieved.

Not long ago Renata had told Michael that she had nothing left to keep her in Milwaukee, and she knew that very little drew her there now. She'd hoped to give her landlord notice within the next couple of months, but now she was glad she'd never mentioned that dream to anyone. In desperation she packed her things and grabbed the books she'd borrowed from Elise's prized Tyler collection. Elise would worry about them—she treated all of her books like children—if Renata didn't return them before she left town.

She did not plan to come back to Tyler for a long, long while.

Blindly Renata drove into town, oblivious of her speedometer and of the stares of the drivers she blitzed past on the road. Valiantly she tried to drive Michael from her mind, but he seemed to follow her from the family homestead. Achingly she wondered, *Will he always follow me everywhere I go?*

She had not believed that it was possible for Michael to hurt her all over again. She had forced herself to believe that they had finally laid all the old troubles aside, passed on to a new place of love and unity that had no color. With five simple words, "I don't want you to come," Michael had destroyed that illusion.

He'd tried to tell her it was just this one time, this one place, this one moment, before he severed the last of his Winnebago ties. But Renata knew he didn't want to sever them, and she didn't want him to. She didn't want him to sever ties with her, either—she just wanted him to find a way to bring all the loose ends of his life together. But it turned out that she was one of the loose ends he'd chosen to cut off and discard.

The instant Renata pulled up in front of the stately old library, she knew that something was wrong. The front door was wide open and a pile of soggy books was perched haphazardly on the porch a few feet from the steps. As she parked her truck and hurried inside, Renata followed wet footprints back to the small Biography room, where she found Elise clutching five dripping books to her chest.

And sobbing.

Not once, not ever, had Renata seen Elise cry. She would have sworn it was not an activity in the librarian's repertoire. Of all the strong and stoic women she had ever known, Elise Ferguson was the most composed, the most capable, the most in charge of her life. But at the moment she looked like a lost child—despite her no-nonsense shoes and attractive shirtwaist dress, which were soaking wet.

"Elise…" Renata croaked, unable to assimilate the sight before her. "Whatever has—"

"Look!" Elise cried out, gesturing toward the ceiling. "I told you. I told the whole town that something like this would happen! A pipe has broken. The water soaked through the plaster and a piece of the ceiling fell down!"

Renata's eyes widened as she followed Elise's gaze to the nearest bookcase, to the wall, to the ceiling. A large section of plaster had indeed fallen, exposing the water-darkened lath be neath. And more threatened to crumble at any second. A steady spray of water spewed against the wall and the two or three hundred books beneath it. Sprinkles fell like raindrops on Elise's glasses.

"Did you call somebody, Elise?" Renata burst out. "We've got to get the water stopped!"

"We've got to save the books!" she wailed, as though they were children drowning in a river.

Renata suspected that the books were ruined—or at least so fully saturated that another five minutes wouldn't make much difference to their future. But this wasn't a good time to say so. She just started pulling books off the shelves and dumping them on the table in the middle of the room.

In five minutes the bookshelf was cleared, but the floor was still awash with water. It was obvious to Renata that at the moment Elise, normally the most clearheaded of people, wasn't able to think at all. She needed a friend to do her thinking for her.

They needed help—help to stop the leak, help to dry the books, help to make sure this didn't happen again. And when anybody in town needed help on that grand a scale, they called one family—the Ingallses.

Renata made the call while Elise cleared still-dry books from the shelves near the leak, then she joined her with the good news. "Alyssa's sending her son-in-law, Cliff, right over here. She says he's a great handyman and will know what to do to stop the water. She said she'll have a book-drying crew over here as soon as she can. Elise, she's going to mobilize the whole town for you."

Elise seized Renata's hands in a sudden gesture of gratitude. After that she seemed to get a grip on herself. "Thank you, Renata. Thank you for being here."

Renata gave her a hug, then asked, "What else do you want me to do?"

Elise was just beginning to explain how wet books needed to be laid out with fans blowing, and to have their pages turned on a regular basis, when Cliff Forrester rushed in with a tool-box in his hand. Alyssa was right behind him.

While Elise showed Cliff the source of the flood, Renata gave Alyssa a recap of Elise's directions as she started gathering wet books to bring to the porch. She was too busy to think about Michael or his grandfather or any of the reasons she'd been so anxious to get out of Tyler. She was needed here. She *belonged*. In a crisis, the needs of her old community outweighed anything else she might be feeling.

It was amazing how quickly the tired old library came to life. Patrick Kelsey showed up with two electric fans. His wife, Pam, arrived with five members of the high school football team, who started carting in tables gathered from all over town. The Hansen kids showed up to lay out books, and ten minutes later, two of Nora Forrester's employees joined them. In a matter of minutes the library had become a book-drying factory.

Everybody pitched in all morning. Elise seemed to calm down, until she suddenly noticed the clock around noon.

"Oh, Renata, I forgot!" she declared, slapping her cheeks with both hands. "After lunch I have an appointment with that man!"

"What man?"

"The architect who's coming to see if we can still build the new library! Robert Fairmont! I can't let him see me like this!"

Renata wanted to tell her how pretty she looked, but she knew that between the soggy plaster, the bookshelf dust and the water, neither Elise's dress nor her hairdo could be easily salvaged.

"Elise, you go home and change and I'll hold down the fort here," Renata urged her. "I'll tell Alyssa what you said and I'll make Mr. Fairmont welcome if he gets here before you come back."

"Oh, Renata, would you?" Elise looked like a child who'd just been let out of school. "It's so important that he decide to help us. You understand now why we've just *got* to have a new library, don't you?"

"Yes, Elise, I understand."

"If that pipe had broken over the Tyler collection upstairs…" She shivered.

"But it didn't," Renata pointed out gently.

Elise gave her a sad but grateful smile, then hurried off to
change.

Less than half an hour later, Renata turned to see a tall, well-
muscled man standing in the doorway. He was about Elise's
age, but he looked like the sort of man who'd be able to charm
the socks off any woman from nine to ninety. His thick wavy
hair, raven-black except where it was sprinkled with silver,
made him look distinguished and debonair. His golden eyes
were striking—radiant and thoughtful—as he instantly assessed
the enormity of the crisis. Renata hadn't even had time to say
hello before he asked in a deep, commanding voice, "What do
you want me to do?"

Recalling Elise's directions, Renata greeted him as professionally as her own damp and streaked countenance would allow. "Mr. Fairmont? Elise Ferguson will be with you in a few
minutes. She's looking forward to meeting with you this afternoon, but she had to go home and change due to this…disaster.
Apparently a pipe broke upstairs during the night."

Robert Fairmont didn't seem to hear her. He was already
whipping off his well-cut blazer and hanging it over the nearest
chair. Quickly he strode toward a pile of dripping books and
hauled them outside.

He didn't seem to notice that his arms and chest were soon
soaking wet.

BY THE SECOND DAY of the wake, Michael knew he'd made a
terrible mistake. He had believed that he couldn't endure this
additional gathering with Renata beside him.

Now he wondered if he could endure it *without* her.

The way his grandfather had described the four-day gathering had sounded so esoteric, so Winnebago, that he hadn't been
able to imagine bringing an outsider to it. But this wasn't the
'90s, it was a century later, and most of his grandfather's

neighbors and extended clan did not recall a great deal mor
about the old ways than Michael did.

They didn't bring fresh-killed game to cook over an ope
fire; they plugged in crock-pots of chili they'd been keeping i
the freezer. They didn't sleep in deerskin blankets around
central lodge fire; they slept in sleeping bags, vans and overca
campers. The older ones went home at night, and the younge
ones looked more uncomfortable than Michael.

He did not regret holding the wake. It had been his gran
father's wish that he do so. But now, as he gazed around th
tiny shack that had been his refuge as well as his nemesis f
so many years, he realized that his grandfather had had no rig
to tell him not to marry Renata. He'd had no right to make h
feel unwelcome here. *This is your place. It will always be yo
home,* his grandfather had told him. And if it was his plac
why wasn't his woman welcome here?

The problem was, Michael wasn't sure Renata was still h
woman. Her eyes had been those of a stranger when she'd sa
goodbye. He'd kissed her lips, but they'd been stiff and co
She always stood on the porch until he drove out of sight, b
when he left on Monday, she'd stayed inside.

Michael desperately wanted to call her, but Grand Feathe
shack didn't have a phone. Even if it had, what was he su
posed to say? "Gee, I changed my mind, Renata. Would y
hop right over here?"

He did not know how to make things right between the
He couldn't tell her again that everything had changed, becau
it hadn't. Not really. He was still Michael Youngthunder
Winnebago by blood, white by life's battles, torn between t
worlds. He couldn't promise that he would never hurt h
again.

Michael had been sitting silently in Grand Feather's favor
old chair when Lydia joined him, one gnarled hand resti
softly on his shoulder.

"Thunder Eagle, I am disappointed in my daughter," s
said straightforwardly. "I cannot imagine why she did
come."

His eyes lifted quickly. Was Lydia growing senile? Two of her daughters had been with them for the past three days. The third had died in Chicago when she was young.

"She told me that she loved you. This is the time when you need her most. How could she stay away?"

It took Michael a moment to realize that Lydia was speaking of Renata. But why had she called her "daughter"?

"It's my fault, Lydia," he admitted. "I asked her not to come."

The old lady's brows rose in dismay. "You do not return her feelings?"

He lifted his hands helplessly. "I love her. I want her to be my wife. But I—" he glanced around the tiny crowded room and shrugged "—I couldn't see bringing a white woman here during Grand Feather's last days."

For a long moment, Lydia said nothing. Then she asked, "Your Grandfather, he said you must marry a Winnebago?"

He nodded.

"He told you what clan?"

Actually, there were several acceptable clans, but Michael hadn't given any thought to tracking down a woman from any of them. He wanted to marry Renata, plain and simple. He had no intention of reaching out for some other woman just to fulfill Grand Feather's grand plan.

But he didn't think he could ever give Renata what she deserved, either. Now with Grand Feather's decree hanging over him for the rest of his life.

Then Lydia said quietly, "You are Thunderbird. You should marry Bear Clan."

He didn't know what to say. Lydia was Bear Clan, and she was right that her clan was an appropriate traditional choice for a Thunderbird man's bride. But under the circumstances, her comment made no sense. Still, he didn't want to offend her.

"Lydia," he reminded her softly, "I want to marry Renata."

She squeezed his shoulder one more time and repeated in a new and urgent tone, "I know this, Thunder Eagle. I want you to marry her, too.''. After a meaningful pause she inexplicably repeated, ''I want you to marry Bear Clan.''

AFTER THREE miserable days in Milwaukee, Renata buried the last dregs of her pride and went to see Judy Hall. She didn't really think Judy could help her, but there wasn't anybody else to turn to. Lydia Good Heart was the only other Indian besides Michael whom she knew well, and Lydia was probably still with Michael. Besides, it wouldn't be fair to ask the old woman to get tangled up in their problems. Renata felt a keen, unspoken sense of kinship with the elderly Winnebago lady, and she knew that learning about Renata's problems with Michael would cause Lydia great distress.

Unfortunately, if she couldn't find some other way to open an Indian center in Sugar Creek, she would hurt Lydia anyway. Renata's enthusiasm for the idea hadn't vanished because of Michael's rejection, but she didn't really know where to go from here. She couldn't run a Native crafts center without him, or someone like him. And what business partner, Indian or otherwise, could possibly be a substitute for Michael?

The instant Judy saw Renata's face, she excused the art student standing near her desk and led Renata swiftly out into the hallway, which was empty at the moment. ''Renata, for heaven's sake—'' Judy's eyes radiated compassion ''—you look like your world has come to an end.''

Holding back another rush of tears, Renata whispered, ''It's Michael. Again.''

In a way, that said it all, but eventually Judy got the whole story out of her. She listened patiently while Renata cried, choked out her feelings, then cried again. At last she laid a quiet hand on Renata's back and counseled gently, ''Rennie. Rennie, listen to yourself. You don't need to listen to me.''

''What do you mean?''

''You want this man. You want him enough to forgive him for hurting you.''

It was true, but Renata wasn't sure that made any difference. The question wasn't whether she could forgive Michael. The question was whether she could endure being pushed and pulled back and forth between Michael, who wanted her, and Thunder Eagle, who didn't, for the rest of her life.

"You need to go back to Tyler before Michael gets there," Judy advised. "Do you really want to make him say his last goodbye to his grandfather all alone?"

Just thinking about Michael's pain hurt Renata, but that didn't change her situation. "He didn't want me with him when he started the burial prayers," she replied. "Why would he want me now? He told me to go into the house and leave him alone."

"But he *knew* you were there, Renata. Grieving right beside him. And he'll be devastated if he comes back and finds you gone. No matter what you said to him when you saw him last, he'll be expecting you."

Renata shook her head. "I won't lie to you, Judy. I'm not too mad to make up. I gave up my anger several days ago. The problem is much deeper than that. I can't spend the rest of my life waiting for the other shoe to drop." She told herself she wasn't going to cry again, but somehow there were fresh tears on her cheeks once more. "He's told me right from the start that he wants to marry an Indian. And that's one thing I can never be."

Judy studied her carefully. After a long, thoughtful moment, she said with a gentle note of optimism, "You know, Renata, that's not entirely true."

"What do you mean?"

"It's not unheard of for white people to be adopted into a tribe."

"Judy, this isn't the nineteenth century! It's not like I'm going to move into a tepee after my family has been massacred by outlaws!"

Judy shook her head. "I'm not talking about moving into a tepee. There are times when somebody, usually somebody who's very old, just feels a special kinship with a younger person and wants to make that feeling known. It's not a legal adoption in the white man's way, but it carries a great deal of weight among the adoptive parents' people. At least, it does with the Sioux. I can't speak for the Winnebago.''

Renata had read of such things in the books Michael had lent her, but that didn't give her any hope. The only person she could imagine adopting her was Lydia Good Heart. While the notion filled her with a sudden rush of warmth, she knew she could never ask Lydia to ''adopt'' her just so she could marry Michael. The very thought made her feel presumptuous and incredibly humble. It made her wonder how she could ever go visit Lydia again.

But she had to go see her. Lydia had become her precious friend. No matter how awkward things might prove to be because of Michael, there was no way she was going to cut Lydia out of her life. Not unless it was a choice that Lydia herself made someday.

The very notion made her shiver. Was there no end to this Indian heartbreak? Would the wounds inflicted by past generations keep hurting their descendants for another hundred years? Wasn't there some way to heal the scars and stop the cycle?

''When's he due back?'' asked Judy.

''Tomorrow morning.'' A thousand times Renata had replayed the mental tape of their last conversation, when Michael had told her he'd come back to her and she'd told him, in essence, that it would be too late.

''And you told him you wouldn't be there?''

''Not in so many words. It wasn't…well, it wasn't like we had a fight, Judy. He'd just buried his grandfather. I couldn' bear to tell him it was all over. But he's not stupid.'' She fel sick inside, empty with the enormity of her loss. ''He knev the price he'd pay for telling me I wasn't wanted at the wake He won't expect me to be waiting for him.''

''In other words, he'll expect you to abandon him at the firs hint of trouble, just as whites traditionally have abandoned thei Indian 'friends.'''

Renata straightened. Her tears fled. ''Judy, that's not fair!'

she protested. "He's the one who kicked me in the teeth, not the other way around!"

"Renata, Michael is a Winnebago. He's performing a sacred rite to send his beloved grandfather on his final journey. If it were *your* grandfather, and you knew it meant everything to him to be buried a certain way, wouldn't you expect Michael to understand?"

"Yes, but that's different."

"Different how? You're only looking at this as an Indian-white thing, but it's also a family matter. When push comes to shove, you stand by the people who are close to you. You don't rub salt into their wounds if you can help it."

Renata had a sudden image of Elise Ferguson, looking overwhelmed and afraid. How beautiful it had been to see the whole town rally to her aid! Renata hadn't had to make any great sacrifice to do her part in the disaster. But suddenly she realized how terrible it would have been if Michael had arrived at just that moment and said, "Choose between us, Renata. I want you to turn your back on your obligations to Tyler Clan, or you'll never see me again."

She felt a flood of shame that washed away the righteous indignation that had buoyed her when he first told her he didn't want her at the wake. Was it possible that she should have looked at the big picture right from the start and made the offer not to go? She'd told herself that she wanted to stand by Michael because he needed her. But in hindsight, she realized that she'd also had a second, less noble motive.

She'd wanted to claim her own place.

Renata swallowed hard. No matter what Judy had to say, she knew that until Michael could stand up before his clan certain of their approbation, he could never marry Renata with pride. And she would not, could not, marry him knowing she caused him shame.

Still, the thought of Michael saying his last Winnebago prayers for his grandfather all alone was more than she could bear. One more time—and one time only—she would set aside her grief and answer the call of her love for him.

WHEN MICHAEL reached Renata's farm on Friday morning, he was surprised to find her driveway empty. Despite her angry words as they'd parted, he hadn't really allowed himself to believe that she'd leave town knowing he'd promised to come back to her to stay.

Now he felt more than the painful grief and uncertainty of the past few days. He felt a rising sense of panic that maybe it really was too late to forge a life with Renata. Too late to tell her what Lydia planned to do for them, too late to tell her what he'd learned about himself during the past few days. She might not love him enough to endure any more heartache. She might not be willing to give him one last chance. She might not want to risk having him break her heart again. He couldn't really blame her.

Michael could not go to her in Milwaukee until he finished singing, and until he planted the sacred broken branch with the red stick at the end of his grandfather's grave. That much Renata surely knew.

When this last rite was over, he would go. It was not so far to drive. It was not so hard to apologize…to plead, to urge, to coddle.

But he was still a Thunderbird warrior. He could not beg.

Besides, he could not pretend that there would never again be moments of stress between them. He desperately hoped he would never hurt Renata, but it was not a promise he could make. He was just now starting to find his way back to his people. There would be times he might stumble and fall. He needed to know that a brave-hearted woman walked beside him, one strong enough to deal with whatever the winds of life blew her way.

"I am back, Grand Feather," he said in Winnebago when he reached the burial plot and stood respectfully before the grave. "I have performed the wake and all the sacred traditions just as you asked of me. I am ready to send you on your journey now. I have brought food for you to eat on your way."

He sat down quietly in his ceremonial garb beneath the solitary oak that sheltered Renata's house and the family plot readied his heart and began the first of the four sacred songs. His voice held more confidence than it had the first time he'd prayed with Grand Feather on Renata's lawn. Then he had been following his grandfather's directions. Now he had no one to teach him. He had no one to teach.

He had not been chanting more than fifteen minutes before he first noticed a white couple gawking at him through rose-bushes. Abruptly, the woman squealed and ran off toward Timberlake Lodge. Minutes later, she returned with some other people. One man started snapping photos with a telephoto lens. Two teenagers scampered up and started imitating Michael in high, irritating voices. An older woman started to giggle.

There had been a time, in his youth, when Michael would have reveled in all the attention, used it to prove the shallowness of white people. There had been another time, not so long ago, when his embarrassment would have been overpowering because he longed to be one of them. Today he wobbled on new ground, but he was beginning to find his footing. He was doing what was right for him, for his grandfather, for his people, and he did not care so very much what anyone else thought of him. He was secure in the knowledge that he was being true to himself. Yes, he was Michael Youngthunder, successful businessman. But he was also Thunder Eagle. He was a proud American. He was a proud member of Thunderbird Clan.

Above all, he was a man.

As he gave himself to the second sacred Thunderbird song, he felt an almost primeval need to share his voice with someone. Despite the cluster of strangers gathered all around him, he had never felt more isolated. Michael felt like the first Thunderbird who'd descended from the heavens. He felt like Adam without Eve.

Never had he ached so much for Renata.

When Michael first heard the rumble of heavy wheels over gravel, his whole body tensed with fresh hope. Could it be Renata's truck? Or did the sound herald the arrival of yet another stranger?

As he heard soft footsteps hurrying toward him, his heart

began to pound. The rustle of leather sounded like a person wearing Winnebago moccasins. A moment later he saw his woman in her white buckskin dress, fringe swinging gracefully from both elbows. Her long blond hair was wrapped in feathered braids. Beaded moccasins covered those beautiful legs from toe to knee.

Renata's lips were tight with fear, but she proudly threw her shoulders back as she headed straight toward Michael. He could see that she was trembling, but she did not flinch as her brave eyes met his.

Blue eyes. White woman's eyes. Eyes shining with untarnished love.

I am here for you, Michael, whether you want me or not, her determined face promised him. *I will not abandon you when you need me most. I will be as loyal as any Winnebago.*

At first the crowd ignored her. Then somebody cried out, "Look, it's another Indian!" and a few people stepped back in surprise. One or two looked respectful now.

Heart hammering, Michael watched Renata sit, cross-legged, at his side. As her knee brushed his, her devotion brushed his heart, and for the first time in four days, the terrible knot in his stomach began to uncurl.

He started to chant in a voice twice as loud and reverent, proudly lifting up the words that meant so much to his grandfather. He was more certain than ever that they also meant something to him.

And then he heard it, very close by. Another voice. A white voice, sharing the ancient Thunderbird song, struggling to share the ritual of prayer that Thunder Eagle had promised his grandfather he would send up in honor of the dead.

Renata didn't know the words or vocables, but she did not parody them, either. She followed Michael's voice as closely as she could, breaking off when she lost the flow, but joining back in whenever she was able. Her participation was a change from the traditional ceremony, but to Michael this change felt absolutely right.

The minute he heard her voice, the great emptiness within

him vanished. He no longer saw the crowd or heard their comments…some ignorant, some awed. He no longer worried about the prayers for his grandfather's spirit; he *knew* he was doing them correctly. He saw nothing but the parts of his life coming together, felt the fragments of his two worlds meld into one solid whole.

Because he'd finally found what it took to be complete again.

He had found Renata.

By the time they started the last sacred song, Brick Bauer had arrived in his police cruiser and started to shoo the strangers off. The front lawn was quiet and they were alone again when Michael finally rose and placed the broken branch and red stick at the foot of his grandfather's grave. Respectfully he said goodbye, and felt fresh peace within him as the old one's spirit started on its way.

Then he turned to Renata and helped her to her feet. She rose in silence, her eyes full of love for him, but laced once more with pain.

"He has started on his journey," Michael said softly, brushing the back of one hand across her face. "And it's time for me to start on mine."

When her lips tightened in a sudden wrench of fear, Michael knew she'd misunderstood him.

"I was referring to a journey of the spirit, Ren. The kind a man makes when he knows he's going to walk forever with a woman by his side."

He cupped her cheek and waited until her eyes sought his again. Slowly they pooled with disbelief, then fresh hope, then joyful understanding. She didn't ask again if anything had changed. This time he knew she read the answer on his face.

"A warrior on a new journey needs a new name," he continued, his voice soft and low. "There is no one left to call me *hitkunkay*."

Renata slipped her arms around his shoulders and snuggled closer. Her lips slowly curved into a smile as she kissed his cheek. "Is there something special you want Squaw Chief to call you?" she asked, following his lead.

He grinned. Renata grinned back. He kissed her lips—his motion slow and full of promise—before he whispered, "You can call me *hiko'no*."

"*Hiko'no*," she repeated provocatively.

Once Michael had been appalled at the way she mangled Winnebago, but now he found her mispronunciation utterly endearing. He kissed her again, a little more urgently this time, before she asked, "What does it mean? Is it one of those special nicknames that have to do with relatives and friends, or can anybody call you that?"

He pulled her close, oblivious to anything but the magical sunshine on her face. "Only one person can call me *hiko'no*, Squaw," he teased her. "She's got to have a long, complicated list of qualifications." He ticked them off. "She's got to be my business partner. She's got to be my wife. She's got to be adopted daughter of a beloved Bear Clan lady who's known me all my life."

A fresh wave of tears filled Renata's eyes, but this time Michael knew that they were tears of breathless joy. She pressed her hands against his cheeks and whispered, "Oh, Michael, darling—"

"*Hiko'no*," he corrected. While she clung to him fiercely, he whispered against her hair, "It's the Winnebago word for 'husband,' Renata. You don't know how long I've wanted to hear you call me that."

But neither of them was in the mood for talking now. They were too busy sharing kisses of healing and hugs of love, touches of promise and looks of pure forgiveness. Michael clung to Renata and Renata clenched him back. She wept new tears and he soaked them up with broad, gentle fingertips. She promised him love and he promised her children. They vowed to stand together against each and every challenge they ever faced in their partnered lives.

Filled with a joy that extirpated every last root of his lifetime sorrow, Michael tossed aside the crippling rule book he'd carried so long in his mind. He had done his duty. He had made his peace with the past. Now it was time to enjoy the future with the white-skinned Bear Clan woman he so proudly cradled in his arms.

"Let's go inside, *hiko'no*," Renata whispered.

No matter how she said the word, to Michael it sounded just right.

And now,
an exciting preview of

BACHELOR'S PUZZLE

by Ginger Chambers
the eighth installment
of the Tyler series

Elise Ferguson is considered a paragon of virtue for her unselfish devotion to her disabled older sister, Bea, and for her thirty years of service to the town of Tyler as its librarian. But paragons don't secretly yearn to be free—or respond in such an unseemly way to the curious interest shown by visiting architectural professor Robert Fairmont. Meanwhile, Alyssa realizes she cares for Edward, and the coroner's office announces more news about Margaret.

Watch for it next month, where Harlequin books are sold.

CHAPTER ONE

ELISE FERGUSON BRUSHED her fingertips through her short pale hair, smoothing it at the same time as she tried to fluff it. The perm she had gotten a few months ago was already loosening and she knew that soon she would have to get another. But right now she just didn't have time to think about it.

She leaned forward, peering closely into the mirror at the fine lines that seemed to have appeared from nowhere over the past few years. Then she moved back, checking whether the hurried makeup job had been sufficient. From a distance, it worked. She didn't look substantially worse for wear than any other fifty-three-year-old who had just spent a morning in hell. And with the donning of her dress-for-success, reserved-for-meetings suit, she gave the illusion of complete competency. No one would believe that a scant half hour before, dampened through and through, she had raced into the bathroom, streaked with dirt from head to toe, her baby-fine hair sticking out at odd angles and her dress a shambles.

Elise's stomach gave a nervous rumble. She knew she probably should eat something, but there wasn't time for that, either. She had to be back at the library in—she checked her watch—five minutes. *Five minutes!* Impossible!

She reached for a bottle of her favorite scent and misted a light bouquet of spring flowers over herself. Then, grabbing a pair of tiny gold studs, she slipped them into her ears as she hurried down the stairs.

"Elise!" Her sister's voice held a petulant edge. "*Elise!* I need you to do something for me!"

Elise veered into the living room, where her older sister, Bea, sat before the television set, their fat yellow cat, Buttercup, in her lap.

Bea's gaze revealed her disapproval. "I asked before you went upstairs, but you didn't hear me, I suppose. I'd like my wrap! It's cool in the house today. You left too many windows open."

It was summer; the temperature outside was in the mid-eighties. Still, Elise didn't protest. "Would you like me to close them?" she asked.

Bea frowned grumpily. "No, just get my wrap. And the mail. I heard the postman come about an hour ago."

Elise hurried onto the porch, checked the mailbox and withdrew some bills and a magazine. Bea's doll collectors' magazine. That would make her happy. She hurried back inside and delivered the magazine before moving into the kitchen. "I'm just going to warm up leftovers today, Bea," she called into the next room. "I have a meeting I'm already late for."

Her sister mumbled something that Elise didn't understand, but she didn't ask her to repeat it. Elise popped a bowl of yesterday's shepherd's pie into the microwave, arranged a small salad, buttered a piece of wheat bread and sweetened a glass of iced tea. All this she balanced on a serving tray and brought to her sister.

Bea shifted the cat from her lap, all the while grumbling beneath her breath. Finally, she said clearly, "I'm *still* cool!"

Elise groaned and glanced at her watch. Then she hurried into the bedroom just off the living room to find the wrap. "Here," she said, spreading the soft material over her sister's shoulders. "Is there anything else?"

At one time Bea had been beautiful, with silver-blond hair flowing softly to the middle of her back, bright blue eyes that flashed with anticipation and a delicacy of features and build that the two sisters still shared. Now, Bea pulled her hair into an unbecoming knot at the base of her neck, discontent had faded the color of her eyes and bitterness contorted the fragility of her features.

Adjusting her wheelchair to a more comfortable position at

the side table, Bea said dismissingly, "No, I wouldn't dream of asking for anything else. I wouldn't want to keep you from your meeting."

Elise suffered a pang of guilt. "It's with the architect, Bea. The professor who's going to see if he can help us build the new library. I'd forgotten all about it what with the water leak and everything. Remember when I first came in, I told you that a number of books had gotten wet and that people from all over Tyler had come to help?"

Her sister fixed her with a cool gaze. "You said something, but I didn't understand. I thought you'd fallen into a mud puddle."

Elise sighed and rubbed a hand across her brow, a telling gesture that she was unaware of using. "I'll explain everything this evening, all right? Right now I really have to…"

"Go. I know. You *always* have to go."

Elise wanted to scream. She wanted to yell at her sister that she couldn't help it if she had to hurry off to her job. That if she hadn't done so for these past thirty years they wouldn't have eaten very well. There would be no house, no television, no leisurely outings, no subscriptions to doll collectors' magazines, no vast collection of dolls…. But she kept her tongue, just as she had for all these years, knowing that Bea had reason to be bitter. "Yes, I do," she agreed. "I'll try to be home by six-thirty, but if I can't, I'll get Josephine to come make your dinner. I'll let you know."

Bea picked at the shepherd's pie with her fork and didn't say anything, a point Elise didn't regret as she finally left the house. She was already nervous enough about her meeting with the architectural professor. The stakes were high—as in whether Tyler would continue to have a library and she herself a job!

Elise dashed for her car, a moderately old, tan Ford Escort, and quickly backed out of the drive. In her mind she rehearsed an apology for being late, one she hoped she would be able to deliver with a modicum of dignity.

THE ALBERTA INGALLS Memorial Library was housed in a spacious home built around the turn of the century. A series of narrow, vertical windows showcased the second-floor exterior, while a large wraparound porch with strong white columns gave character to the first. Over the years, Elise had planned the landscaping herself, encouraging the growth of rich evergreen shrubs along the base of the porch and seasonal flowers in the accompanying wide beds. The grass had a lush green cast, with shade provided by both oak and maple trees.

Normally the scene was placid, inviting patrons to come inside for a leisurely browse, but that was not the image presented today. Elise was forced to bypass the jammed parking spaces in front of the building and add her car to the numerous others crowded end to end along both sides of the street.

The library was a hive of activity. People moved busily inside and out. The front porch, usually reserved for quiet reading, was congested with folding tables. They in turn bore the weight of numerous books that were being set on end and fanned open so that they could begin to dry, even as more books continued to be removed from the water-damaged room within.

Elise gathered her purse from the passenger seat and hurried toward the scene. She was grateful to all the people who had turned out. It seemed as if everyone in town who could help had come when told about the emergency.

As Elise stepped onto the porch, Delia Mayhew, one of the library's two part-time aids, rushed to greet her. "We've gotten almost all the books out now, Elise. We're down to the V's on the last shelf!" Delia's dusky cheeks were flushed a becoming shade of pink and her dark eyes were shining. She had just turned twenty-one and had seldom, if ever, traveled farther than a two-hundred-mile radius from her home. For her, the accident that morning was a cause for genuine excitement.

Alyssa Baron looked up from her work with the wettest books. Elegant, blond and regal of bearing, Alyssa could always be counted on in times of trouble. As the only daughter of the town's most influential man, she seemed to feel service to the people of Tyler was her duty. She and her very pregnant daughter, Liza Forrester, were carefully placing sections of paper toweling between individual pages to act as blotting agents. "It's a good thing the accident happened in the Biography Room," Alyssa murmured after hearing Delia's somewhat oddly worded description. "Otherwise we'd have a hard time telling exactly where we were."

Grinning at her mother's wry jest, Liza agreed, "Oh, definitely. The Dewey Decimal classification 973.629A just doesn't have the same ring to it as a V, does it?"

Cliff Forrester, Liza's husband, came up beside them. "What's this about V?" he asked, watching as his wife tore off another section of paper towel and placed it between two pages. "You're not planning names for the baby, are you? What starts with a V? Let's see: Virgil, Venus…"

Liza tilted her head and gave a devilish smile. "What would you do if I wanted to name our child Venus?"

Cliff smiled slowly and surprised Elise by winking at her. Normally, he was so quiet and self-contained. "Why, I'd agreed," he said. "What else?"

Johnny Kelsey dropped an armload of books onto a table behind Elise. "I've talked with Pastor Schoff," he announced, causing Elise to turn toward him. "We can have the church hall any time we want it. When I get off work this evening, I'll bring some of the men from the F and M and we can shift all this again." He motioned to the tables and books scattered along the porch. "That's still what you want, isn't it? To get this lot moved inside somewhere?"

Elise met the deep-set gray eyes of the man she'd known since childhood. "If you could do that, Johnny, it would be wonderful. Do I need to speak with Pastor Schoff myself?"

Anna Kelsey arrived just in time to hear Elise's question. She, too, was delivering an armload of damp books. "Probably should," she said. "I'm sure he could arrange fresh volunteers for tonight if you ask him."

"I'll call right away. *Oh!*" Elise suddenly looked stricken. Once again she had gotten carried away by the immediate problem and forgotten the more looming threat. "Has anyone seen Professor Fairmont?"

There was a series of shrugs and head shakes. "Not since earlier," Alyssa said.

"What about Renata?" Elise asked. "She said she'd watch out for him."

Again Alyssa shook her head.

Elise's stomach tightened. Robert Fairmont's reputation was impressive. As a practicing architect, he had won numerous design awards, and his track record as a teacher was impressive, too. A growing number of his former students were beginning to make names for themselves, with many attributing much of their success to him. Had he been insulted that she was late for their appointment, and so had decided to leave?

"Where's Pauline?" she tried yet again, starting to feel more than a little desperate. Delia pointed to a group of people at the far end of the porch. With a soft murmur, Elise excused herself.

Pauline Martin, the library's only full-time aid, was a plump woman in her early forties with short, light brown hair and a perpetual expression of amused good cheer. An earth-mother type, she loved working with the children who came to the library, and along with Elise had developed a program that several libraries in other small towns now emulated.

When she saw Elise, Pauline broke into a beaming smile. "You look perfect! Don't touch a thing! Otherwise you'll get all dirty again. Have you heard? We can use the hall at Fellowship Lutheran. Pastor Schoff didn't understand at first why we couldn't just put the books in another part of the library, but when Johnny told him about the dampness spreading to the rest of the collection, he agreed right away. Just like Johnny understood when you told him earlier. He—"

Elise broke into the ongoing stream. If Pauline were turned loose, they could be standing there for hours. "Pauline, Professor Fairmont—have you seen him?"

Pauline frowned. "Why, yes. Just a little while ago. He

was…somewhere.'' She scanned the people on the porch. ''The last time I saw him, he was by the front steps.''

''Was he leaving?'' Elise questioned urgently. She couldn't help the note of alarm in her voice.

Pauline frowned in puzzlement. ''Why would he leave when he's come all this way from Milwaukee?''

''I'll check inside.'' Elise turned and hurried through the open double doors that led into the library proper.

A steady stream of people was moving up and down the hall that led to a room at the rear of the library. There, a buildup of water from a leaking pipe had caused a portion of the ceiling to give way. Some people exiting from the hall were heading to the porch with damp volumes. Others had been assigned the task of stacking the numerous books that had managed to remain dry in an area off to one side of the circulation desk.

Elise shivered, remembering the horror of the moment when water had first sprayed everywhere. For a short space of time, her emotions had given way as well as she tried frantically to rescue the books nearest the disaster.

At the Biography Room's door, the tall young man next in line stood aside to let Elise enter. He was Ricky Travis, a recent graduate of Tyler High School. ''Miss Ferguson,'' Ricky said respectfully.

A glimmer of a smile touched Elise's lips. Ricky was a person it was sometimes hard to like. A typical teenager, he'd had his share of ups and downs over the past year. In particular, he'd had difficulties on the high school football team. Some in town thought him cocky, but Elise knew another side of him. She remembered the little boy who had devoured books on dinosaurs the way other little boys eat cake. The fiercer the dinosaur, the better. Ricky had been able to rattle even the most complicated scientific names off his tongue. Next, he had progressed to adventure tales and finally to science fiction—his current favorite. ''Ricky,'' she acknowledged softly. She included a couple of Ricky's friends in her smile and stepped into the chaos of the room.

Even though they had finally managed to cut off the water

supply to the library, occasional drops still fell from the raw open wound on the ceiling. Bits of soggy plaster clung to the gaping edges of the hole, while other pieces cluttered the wet floor, mixing with dirt that had collected in the lath for nearly a hundred years. Elise had tried to clear away the worst of the muck before she went home, sweeping it to one side, but numerous feet trampling through to rescue books hadn't helped the situation. Several thick cotton towels had been spread as doormats into the hall, in an attempt to keep tracking to a minimum, but their success was debatable.

Josephine Mackie, principal at Tyler High School, waved to Elise from across the room. Elise lifted a hand and started to make her way toward her, all the while murmuring encouragement to those in the process of removing the last of the books as well as those taking down the free-standing shelves.

Several people in the rescue force Elise didn't recognize, but she was grateful for their willingness to help even if she didn't know them personally. One man in particular seemed to be enjoying himself. With his sleeves rolled up to his elbows and smudges of dirt on what once had been a pristine white shirt, he braced one of the metal shelf units so that Patrick Kelsey, Johnny and Anna's oldest, could loosen the bolts that held it to the next section. Grinning, he said something that made Patrick laugh.

He was an attractive man, probably somewhere in his mid to late fifties, with wavy black hair sprinkled lightly with silver, an olive complexion that made him look as if he had a year-round tan, a capable, active-looking body and a rather rugged set to his features. He glanced up as Elise continued to watch him, and she was struck by the fact that his eyes were a curious shade of yellow and brown, rimmed with thick dark lashes. But it was not so much their unusual color as their expression that unsettled her. Confident, vital and knowingly amused, they lent him the air of a man who could all too easily see the foibles and fantasies of the people around him.

Illogically, Elise averted her gaze, afraid that he might see inside of her, too. A moment later, after castigating herself for being fanciful, she looked back, only to find that his attention had returned to Patrick Kelsey.

Continuing on to Josephine's side, Elise was angry that her heart rate had quickened. It was this horrible day, she told herself firmly. Nothing more than too much stress. She had passed her recent physical exam with flying colors; the only caveat the doctor had given her was to lighten up and not work so hard. *Her? Lighten up?* With one library literally falling down around her head and a new one whose construction, because of fiscal problems, had ground to a halt with only the foundation work complete? And to top it off, she had now lost the visiting professor, the only person who could help them solve their problem!

Josephine Mackie was almost seven years Elise's senior, closer to Bea's age than her own. But that illusionary difference had evaporated over time, and they'd been best friends for more years than either of them cared to think about.

A slender, gray-haired woman with a long thin nose, and pale gray eyes that hid behind round, rimless glasses, Josephine had presided over the high school with an iron hand for almost as many years as Elise had been Tyler's chief librarian. She demanded that students and teachers alike do their best, holding them to strict guidelines. But she also ruled with fairness and maintained an open-door policy to anyone who had troubles. She had seen a lot and helped a lot, and the sharpness of her expression concealed a tender heart. As head of Tyler's Friends of the Library organization, she frequently worked with Elise on various projects.

"Don't look so panicked," Josephine rebuked her fondly, taking a guess at the cause of Elise's worried expression. "Everything is under control. The plumber's on his way, the pipe will be fixed in no time, and then we can get the water turned back on and begin the cleanup."

"It's not that," Elise replied, looking around anxiously. Her gaze skimmed over the man at the shelves before moving on to the other strangers in the room. None of them fit her idea of how a professor of architecture should look. "I've really messed things up, Josephine. He's not here. I think he's gone home...gone back to Milwaukee. He'll probably never agree to meet with me again. I'll have to go to the town council and tell them that I—''

"Elise," Josephine interrupted her pleasantly. "He's over there."

"What? Where?" Elise's head swung round, trying to follow the direction her friend pointed.

"At the shelves, with Patrick Kelsey. I saw you looking at him just now. I thought you knew."

Elise closed her eyes. That man was Professor Fairmont, and he had been roped into helping. A man of his stature. "No," she said weakly. "I didn't know."

Josephine rubbed her grimy hands on the rag she had been using to wipe down the shelves. "He's really quite nice," she said mildly. "He impressed me. He arrived early for your appointment, saw the mess and didn't hesitate. He just took off his jacket and dug right in."

"Oh, God," Elise breathed.

Josephine looked at her. "What's the matter? Should I have stopped him?"

Elise shrugged guiltily. "Oh, no. I didn't mean that. It's just..."

"Elise." Josephine gave her one of the patented principal looks she had been honing on recalcitrant students for years. "Go talk to the man. Apologize. Thank him for helping. It's all you can do."

Patrick had succeeded in releasing the final bolt that held the first shelving unit to the next, and as a result, the unit swung free. Immediately, a strong pair of hands compensated for the release of tension, balancing the unit until Ricky and his friends could come forward to relieve the holder of its weight. Then the unit itself was spirited out of the room.

Elise's nerves fluttered. She'd known what she was going to have to do even before Josephine told her. She drew a deep breath and, after a quick, heartening glance at her friend, closed the distance between herself and the professor.

Robert Fairmont concentrated on his work, watching as Patrick bent to release the initial bolts holding the next unit. Elise stopped just in front of him. The neat crispness of her reserved-for-meetings suit seemed so out of place in the circumstances, her makeup too carefully applied. She was the only person in the library who wasn't working, who wasn't sullied.

"Professor Fairmont?" she asked, her voice strained. He looked up and again she was struck by the uniqueness of his eyes. She smiled to cover her nervousness and thrust out a welcoming hand. "I'm Elise Ferguson, the chief librarian here. I'm sorry I wasn't available to greet you earlier, but as you can see, we've had a little accident."

"This whole place is an accident, if you ask me," Patrick Kelsey declared, straightening. "When Mom called to tell Pam and me what had happened, we thought it was the roof. Another bad storm and the whole thing could blow off. I'd hate to think of the cleanup then!"

"So would I," Elise murmured.

Robert Fairmont started to take her hand but paused first to wipe his own along the side of his dark slacks. His touch, when it came, was warm, sure. "This is enough of a calamity, I should think," he said.

His voice set off a series of alarms along Elise's already disturbed nerve endings. It was low and soft, the voice of a man who didn't have to shout to be heard because people automatically listened.

Patrick motioned for someone else to assist him, then said to Elise, "We can take care of this if you two need to talk. I was just telling Robert here how badly we need the new library, then I found out who he was. Sure hope you two can work something out."

Robert Fairmont's smile was assured. "We'll do our best."

Elise was conscious that he followed closely behind her as she walked out of the room. At a quiet corner in the hall, she turned to face him. "I'm sorry about all of this," she said. "It couldn't have come at a worse time. Would you like to talk in my office? It's just down the hall. It's dry," she added as an extra incentive.

An array of lines crinkled the corners of his eyes and the creases in his cheeks deepened when he smiled. His was a strong face, weathered by life and tempered by experience. "Dry has a definite appeal today," he agreed.

Elise turned away, unsure if he was laughing at her. She decided to take his reply at face value.

"Are the books salvageable?" he asked as he fell into step at her side.

"Hopefully most will be. Even the wettest. Our worst enemy is mold, not water. That's why we had to get them into circulating air so quickly, so they could start the process of drying. We couldn't afford to wait. Only the books with coated pages will have to be sent away to a vacuum chamber to be dried—they'll fuse into hard blocks otherwise. Again, hopefully, there won't be many of those, because the procedure can be expensive...something we just don't need right now."

She unlocked the door to her office and ushered him inside. The room was cramped, as were most of the other rooms in the library, both in the public and staff areas. Boxes were stacked on the floor; books and catalogs rested on every available flat surface. Notes fluttered from her small bulletin board. The town had outgrown the facility a number of years ago, far longer than the past two or so years that they had spent planning the new building. Not even continued weeding of books and materials could create enough space for everything and everyone.

Elise made no apology for the condition of the room. It was something she just couldn't help. She took a seat behind her work station and nodded toward the empty chair. "Our ability to make coffee is hampered, of course," she said. "But if you'd care to have some, I'm sure we can find someone who wouldn't mind..."

"No need," he said, folding his length into the proffered chair. His gaze once again searched the room before alighting on Elise. "Actually, I have a proposition to put to you. Why don't we postpone this meeting for a day or two? Possibly even longer than that. You have your hands full now and I'm in no great hurry. I can wait."

Elise had managed to school her face of all emotion, but at his suggestion, she jerked forward, her expression intent. "But we can't do that!" she cried. "The new library can't wait! You've seen how bad the situation is here. You've heard about the roof…and that's not all! I love this old house. I've loved it all the years I've worked here and even before, when I came as a child to use it. But we've reached the point where we just can't stay any longer—not with everything like it is. We *have* to build the new library. Either that or we make the necessary repairs, and I'm afraid that after all the money the town's already spent on plans and contracts and fees, there won't be enough money left to… Then we'll lose everything—buildings, books…"

She stopped, her throat tightening. He didn't need to know all that. She didn't need to tell him.

After a moment he said, "A day or two won't matter at this stage. Relax a bit. You can't build a new library all on your own. That's why I'm here. To see if I can help."

"But…"

Robert Fairmont, professor of architecture at the University of Wisconsin, Milwaukee, leaned forward to still the fingers that worked against each other on top of her desk. His smile flashed reassurance. "Relax," he repeated softly. "In a few days we can talk. Say, on Friday. In the meantime, you can get things under control here and I'll go over the plans I have from the firm in greater detail. The time won't be wasted."

As she listened to him speak, Elise felt the tension she had been carrying all day melt away, as if his certainty could protect her. It was a nice feeling; her burdens had somehow been lifted. But the magic didn't last. The difficulties both she and the town faced could not be ignored for long. She pulled her hands away, severing their connection. Still, what he said about delaying the consultation made sense. With all the people working nearby, she would be divided in her allegiance. She would want to be in both places at once. "All right," she agreed tightly. "We'll meet again on Friday."

"Good," he said, smiling. Then he stood up.

Elise remained in her chair. She continued to stare at him, completely unaware, for the moment, of what she was doing. Then she, too, got quickly to her feet, her cheeks flushing with embarrassment. She was a competent woman. People trusted her to do the right thing. They trusted her with the growing minds of their children. She was responsible for every program and every book that came into or went out of the library. She was responsible for budget planning, for equipment purchases, for not indulging in gossip when she was in the perfect job for it. She knew everyone's tastes, everyone's interests, and sometimes, it seemed, everyone's problems. Yet at this moment she felt like a little girl again, off center, off balance. It *had* to be the day, she told herself. It had to be.

She led him back to the Biography Room, but just outside the door, she paused to say stiltedly, "Don't feel you have to help any longer. You shouldn't have been pressed into service in the first place. We have enough people now. There's no need for you to stay."

He met her look levelly. "I helped because I wanted to. I love books and old houses. I think I'll stay a little longer…that is, if it's all right with you."

Elise shrugged, trying to maintain some kind of cool facade. "As you wish, Mr.… Professor…"

"Robert," he suggested. "Just call me Robert. And I'll call you Elise."

Elise's heart jumped when he said her name, a fact that startled her. What was *wrong* with her? Maybe she should go see Dr. Baron again and have another checkup.

"All right," she murmured, and walking into the damaged room, she headed directly for the safe harbor that was Josephine.

She tried not to notice Robert Fairmont as he worked—that after checking to see if Patrick had further need of him, he started to shift the fallen debris, carrying out the larger pieces of plaster Elise had pushed to one side and disposing of the rest with a dustpan, broom and mop.

Then she tried desperately not to notice that she *had* noticed.

LARGER-PRINT BOOKS!

GET 2 FREE LARGER-PRINT NOVELS PLUS
2 FREE GIFTS!

◆ HARLEQUIN®
Romance®

From the Heart, For the Heart

ReaderService.com

You can now manage your account online!

- Review your order history
- Manage your payments
- Update your address

> *We've redesigned the Reader Service website just for you.*

Now you can:

- Read excerpts
- Respond to mailings and special monthly offers
- Learn about new series available to you

Visit us today:

www.ReaderService.com

LARGER-PRINT BOOKS!

GET 2 FREE LARGER-PRINT NOVELS

HARLEQUIN®

INTRIGUE®

PLUS 2 FREE GIFTS!

Breathtaking Romantic Suspense

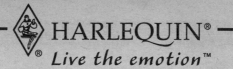

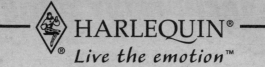

LARGER-PRINT BOOKS!

GET 2 FREE LARGER-PRINT NOVELS PLUS
2 FREE GIFTS!

HARLEQUIN®

Super Romance®

Exciting, emotional, unexpected!

YES! Please send me 2 FREE LARGER-PRINT Harlequin® Superromance® novels and my 2 FREE gifts (gifts are worth about $10). After receiving them, if I don't wish to receive any more books, I can return the shipping statement marked "cancel." If I don't cancel, I will receive 6 brand-new novels every month and be billed just $5.44 per book in the U.S. or $5.99 per book in Canada. That's a saving of over 15% off the cover price! It's quite a bargain! Shipping and handling is just 50¢ per book.* I understand that accepting the 2 free books and gifts places me under no obligation to buy anything. I can always return a shipment and cancel at any time. Even if I never buy another book from Harlequin, the two free books and gifts are mine to keep forever.

139 HDN E5SR   339 HDN E5S3

Name _____ (PLEASE PRINT)

Address _____ Apt. #

City _____ State/Prov. _____ Zip/Postal Code

Signature (if under 18, a parent or guardian must sign)

Mail to the Harlequin Reader Service:
IN U.S.A.: P.O. Box 1867, Buffalo, NY 14240-1867
IN CANADA: P.O. Box 609, Fort Erie, Ontario L2A 5X3
Not valid for current subscribers to Harlequin Superromance Larger-Print books.

**Are you a current subscriber to Harlequin Superromance books
and want to receive the larger-print edition?
Call 1-800-873-8635 today!**

* Terms and prices subject to change without notice. Prices do not include applicable taxes. N.Y. residents add applicable sales tax. Canadian residents will be charged applicable provincial taxes and GST. Offer not valid in Quebec. This offer is limited to one order per household. All orders subject to approval. Credit or debit balances in a customer's account(s) may be offset by any other outstanding balance owed by or to the customer. Please allow 4 to 6 weeks for delivery. Offer available while quantities last.

Your Privacy: Harlequin Books is committed to protecting your privacy. Our Privacy Policy is available online at www.eHarlequin.com or upon request from the Reader Service. From time to time we make our lists of customers available to reputable third parties who may have a product or service of interest to you. If you would prefer we not share your name and address, please check here. ☐

Help us get it right—We strive for accurate, respectful and relevant communications. To clarify or modify your communication preferences, visit us at www.ReaderService.com/consumerschoice.

TYHSRLP10